THE BLACK SHEPHERD

THE BLACK
SHEPHERD

Steven Savile

This first world edition published 2019
in Great Britain and the USA by
SEVERN HOUSE PUBLISHERS LTD of
Eardley House, 4 Uxbridge Street, London W8 7SY.
Trade paperback edition first published
in Great Britain and the USA 2019 by
SEVERN HOUSE PUBLISHERS LTD.

British Library Cataloguing in Publication Data
A CIP catalogue record for this title is available from the British Library.

ISBN-13: 978-0-7278-8887-7 (cased)
ISBN-13: 978-1-78029-608-1 (trade paper)
ISBN-13: 978-1-4483-0225-3 (e-book)

All Severn House titles are printed on acid-free paper.

Severn House Publishers support the Forest Stewardship Council™ [FSC™],
the leading international forest certification organisation.
All our titles that are printed on FSC certified paper carry the FSC logo.

Typeset by Palimpsest Book Production Ltd.,
Falkirk, Stirlingshire, Scotland.
Printed and bound in Great Britain by
TJ International, Padstow, Cornwall.

WHAT WENT BEFORE

SIX MONTHS AGO

In the dark of the night there is no god.

In the dark of the night there is no hope.

For six girls – they weren't women no matter how desperately they pretended they were – the dark of the night hid the promised land.

They tumbled out of the back of the beat-up VW Camper Van into the anti-climax of heaven.

She tried to mask her disappointment but saw the same look on the faces of the other girls. The eldest of them couldn't have been more than eighteen, the youngest maybe thirteen. She looked around at the snow-covered huts dominating the forest clearing, struck by how much they resembled an army barracks. The compound did not look like a place of peace and happiness. *Welcome to the Broken Promise Land.* The words echoed through her mind as one of the doorways opened and two men emerged – one overweight, bald, and bearded, the other stick-insect thin, with hollowed-out sockets for eyes.

She didn't like the way they looked at her: like she was meat.

'Will we get to see him tonight?' one of the others asked.

'Soon,' the driver promised.

The men nodded, walking in a slow circle around the newcomers.

'So, what happens now?'

What indeed?

The details had been vague, focused on the temptations they knew six broken souls couldn't hope to resist.

She looked at the girls with her, standing in a circle now, so far from the bright lights of the city, lured here with the promise that he had the answers, that they would find that elusive *something* that was missing in their lives. They were so different, from such different walks of life, and yet, in that one essential way, they were exactly the same. They lacked a reason for being.

'Follow me,' the driver said. The only baggage any of them had was inside their heads. This was their new start. In the moonlight it didn't look like much, but how much did it really need to look like, she wondered. What mattered was that it was a chance to leave the past behind, not the place's Trip Advisor rating.

She followed him, enjoying the feel of the fresh falling snow against her cheeks.

It was cold without being unbearable, but the promise of much worse was in the sky.

'In here,' the man said, pushing open the door to the largest building. It was some kind of meeting hall. There were chairs laid out in rows facing the front, six more looking back at them. 'Come on, inside. Seats up front.' He ushered them in, then left, locking the door behind him.

'Are you excited?' one of the girls asked, her voice too loud in the churchlike quiet of the hall.

Another nodded.

There were candles along one wall that threw flickering light across the chairs.

'We should sit,' another said. 'He told us to sit.'

But she didn't move.

'I can't wait to see him again,' the same excited girl said. She knew it was the silence, it made you want to fill it.

She didn't feel like feeding it.

A key rattled in the lock and the door opened.

The man they knew as The Shepherd stood in the doorway. He had long dark hair that cascaded halfway down his back and a smudge of black beneath his eyes that made him look like a fading rock star. It was his eyes that had attracted her first. They had made her think that, for the first time in a very long time, everything was going to be all right.

He offered them a brilliant white smile, and just like that five of the six girls were his. Their expressions were nothing short of rapturous.

It made her skin crawl.

'Welcome home,' The Shepherd said, knowing that more than anything these lost souls craved somewhere to belong. It was a simple manipulation, but all the more effective for it. He stepped aside to let several more men follow him inside. They came bearing food and drink. 'Now, dear hearts, I have a special blessing for you. Are you excited?' There were nods from the girls around him. 'Good. I am, too. I've been waiting so long for this moment, to join your souls.'

'What do you mean? I don't understand,' she said before she could stop herself. The interruption drew a sharp look from The Shepherd, which was quickly consumed by that unwavering smile of his.

'It is no accident you found me, or I found you. You are half of a whole. I want to make you whole. That is the key to happiness. And for you to be happy is what I want more than anything.'

But for the first time she didn't believe him.

She felt the chill underlying his words, and it was far more hostile than the gathering snowstorm outside.

'These are good men,' The Shepherd promised. 'Their work is vital to the well-being of our flock. Every day they are out there, trying to make a difference. These are my faithful. They are worthy of your adoration. You will give it to them, won't you?'

She nodded. Anything else would have made her stand out from the others. In her case, it was self-preservation, but the others were so eager to please him. She couldn't explain it. It was stronger than gratitude or infatuation. It was as though he had a vice-like grip on their souls.

'Tonight, my only wish is that you take the time to get to know each other, to learn your mate, before the dawn bonding.'

She bit the inside of her bottom lip so hard that she tasted blood. This was a mistake. Being here was wrong. She didn't belong with these girls. She looked at the youngest of them, who in turn looked at The Shepherd like he was some messiah, and felt sick to the core. She was a child.

But what could she do? Things were racing away from her. She couldn't stand up against the six men who had followed The Shepherd inside. Right now, the only thing she could do was try to survive. Two of the six men looked as lost as she felt, one of them as horrified as she was at the possibility of being paired with a thirteen-year-old bride, but the others had a brutal arrogance about them that was purely animalistic.

The Shepherd walked the line, appraising the girls. He leaned in, cupping one of them, the red-head, Christiana, by the chin and tilting her head up as though he intended to kiss her lips. Christiana gazed into his eyes and she heard the wistful sigh as he let go, his fingertips lingering on her cheek before breaking contact. The loss of his touch physically hurt the girl. She seemed to shrink, as though she'd failed him somehow. He moved down the line, placing a finger on the lips of the youngest, who parted them at his touch. He smiled lovingly down at her and nodded.

Had they already been paired up, or would it be like gym where the men got to pick their partner, the most virile and important of The Shepherd's followers given first choice as a reward? Or would it be some kind of lottery? Drawing lots?

Did it matter?

Sometimes dead was better, she thought, remembering the brutality she'd been subjected to during those first few nights on the streets; the things that they had done to her – and believed they had a right to do to her – purely because they were paying for the pleasure.

It was dehumanizing.

She got lucky with her mate. One of the more timid souls came to kneel before her, offering her an apple like it was the greatest gift he had to give.

She shook her head, and started to say, 'I'm not hungry,' when The Shepherd said, 'You need to eat. You need to keep your strength up. It is going to be a long night,' and she realized that she did need to eat. Hunger weakened you. So, she took the apple from him and bit into it. Her man smiled like she'd just accepted his proposal and came back with more plain food. The more she ate, the hungrier she realized she was.

The girls were led off one at a time by the men, all of them stepping out into the snow willingly, until it was only her, the man she was promised to, and The Shepherd and there was no putting it off any more. He reached out a hand to her, desperate for her approval.

The Shepherd nodded his encouragement.

She took his hand.

She rose slowly.

'Walk with me,' he said, kindness in his voice.

Maybe it wouldn't be so bad?

He led her across the snowy compound to one of the last huts.

It was warm inside, a log fire had been slowly burning down while they ate in the main hall. There was little in the way of furniture; a narrow cot with a hardwood base, a table and two chairs that looked like they'd been rescued from a dumpster and repurposed. There was a rug that looked like it had been rescued from the same dumpster, and a threadbare couch that had seen better days.

'Welcome to your new home,' he said.

'You don't even know my name,' she said, but what she really meant was she didn't know his name. The words were confused on her tongue.

'The Shepherd has told me all about you. I chose you. I want to fill your life here with joy,' he said, and for a heartbeat it sounded pure and innocent, until she began feeling woozy. She held up a hand to steady herself, and saw her fingers losing their shape as her vision blurred.

The light trailed diamonds and sapphires around her hand as she moved it through the air. The colours were hypnotic and hallucinogenic.

She was losing herself to the trip.

And that made her vulnerable.

There was something in the food.

Ketamine?

He took her by the hand and led her over to the bed. She didn't think she would make it. Her knees buckled on the third step, and on the fifth she stumbled and fell forward onto her knees, reaching out to catch herself from falling but missing the bed. She tried to stand, but her legs were having none of it.

Then she was looking up at the ceiling and he was undressing her.

There was nothing timid or gentle about his hands.

She tried to fight him off, but her body wouldn't obey her. She tried to say no but the word wouldn't come.

She was outside of herself, looking down at the girl with the tracks of tears drying on her cheeks, and it broke her heart. She was meant to be safe here. This was supposed to be her happy place. Her sanctuary.

He whispered sweet things, like he thought she might enjoy her rapist's touch.

He planted butterfly kisses on her neck and she wished fervently that he would bite down and tear a chunk out of her throat, ripping the artery in the process.

But it was never going to be that easy.

She disconnected.

She was meat.

She let her soul go, flee, fly.

She took refuge in the emptiness.

She curled up into a foetal ball after he climbed off her.

She still didn't know his name.

It wasn't meant to be like this.

How had this become her life?

The Shepherd had lied to her, that was how.

She didn't look at her abuser as he dressed again.

She barely had the strength to roll over to face the wall. Her world narrowed down to the shapes moving within the grain of the wood and the ragged in and out of her breathing. She felt the erratic flutter of the blood pulsing through her veins and wondered if she was going to get the way out she wanted. She couldn't keep her eyes open.

She heard the soft sound of the door closing and knew that she was alone but couldn't move. It was all she could do to fight the darkness off, but eventually she succumbed.

The candles had burned down to stubs when she came around. A surge of nausea clawed up her throat as she tried to sit up in the bed. She couldn't see him. She barely remembered the van and the girls. Everything else was lost in fog.

Her clothes were on the floor.

There was dried semen on the sheets.

Two edges of a fragmented nightmare stitched together.

She forced herself to get out of the bed. She needed the support of the chair to stop her from falling. Through the window she saw the moon through the snow. It was still night. But night in winter lasted for ever here.

Without a watch she had no way of knowing how close sunrise was. It could just as easily have been two in the morning as four or six. The snow only served to make things worse.

She struggled to get dressed. Wishing she had warmer clothes as she tried the door handle, but it wouldn't open.

She was locked in, but she had a chair and a window. She broke the glass, and scrambled through, cutting herself in the process – a long deep gash on the arm, and a hole in her palm where she put all of her weight on a jagged piece of glass still wedged in the frame. She fell forward, hitting the ground hard, and scrambled to her feet. She left blood in her tracks.

Presented with too many choices, none immediately more attractive than the others, she had no idea where to run, only that she had to.

There was a dirt track that had led them here, she remembered, though there was no sign of it beneath the thickening snowfall. Did it matter which way she ran when she had no concept of distance or geography? The nearest town could be a hundred miles away, or more. The windows of the van had been blacked out and offered no clues.

She ran, head down, into the churning snow as it battered her.

Lights lit the central compound. The hum of the generator was muffled by the snowstorm. She couldn't see anyone. She stayed away from the light, moving across the outskirts of the compound.

Then she saw the light.

It burned in the windows of a cabin.

There were three vehicles parked up outside.

The Camper Van was gone.

She thought about stealing one, but without keys she was going nowhere. Which, she tried to convince herself, was for the best. Steal a car, they come looking for it. All she wanted to do was slip away and disappear, find a different street in a different city to call her home. She wasn't going to bind her life to a man who would drug and rape her. That was fucked in a very different way. No. They could do their binding rituals and pretend marrying a thirteen-year-old kid off to a grown man was natural, but she wasn't going to be a part of it. Part of her wanted to try to save the girls, but they didn't want saving, and it wasn't like she could even save herself. And what if she did? What if by some miracle she found a way to get them all out of here? The Shepherd would find more and replace them easily enough. There were thousands of lost souls out there looking for the light he offered.

So, she slipped away, running into the night and the darkness of the forest.

She moved slowly at first, conscious of every sound.

Moonlight barely filtered through the skeletal limbs of the trees, casting silver and shadows across the virgin snow. Every few yards she stumbled and reached out for the support of the nearest trunk to stop herself from falling face-first to the ground. Every time she reached out she left blood on the bark. Fear had her heart beating faster, her breathing coming shorter. The drug was still in her blood, diluted by the adrenaline, but still potent.

She didn't look back, because if she did there was every chance she'd still see the lights from the compound.

She ran with no sign of the trees thinning out, and no lights up ahead.

She ran towards the dawn, knowing they were going to wake up, knowing they were going to miss her, knowing that they were going to hunt her.

She had never been so afraid of sunlight.

She ran on, praying to the night.

Stay dark.

But she couldn't run forever.

She needed to find somewhere to rest.

Somewhere to hide.

She saw the torches, their lights waving around in the darkness. She heard feet crunching through the snow. She should have known they'd find her. She'd left scuffed tracks and blood. All she could think was run, outrun them, keep running, and never look back.

She looked for a path through the trees, torn between sneaking and plunging headlong into the forest. She had no idea how the sound would travel. Every footstep sounded so loud in her ears. She needed to believe she could make it. That there was a way out.

The hope lasted a matter of seconds.

She heard a voice cry, 'There she is!'

She threw herself forward, overhanging branches clawing at her face as she plunged through them. She ran until she thought her lungs were about to burst. And then she ran some more, stumbling and slipping in the snow and on the roots that grew up out of the soil. And still she ran, lungs heaving, as the voices behind her grew relentlessly closer.

She leaned against a tree, struggling to breathe.

The ice-cold air burned her lungs.

She turned around with her hands held up in surrender.

'I'm sorry, I'm sorry,' she said, though the words came out wrong, anything beyond the placatory sound lost in the gasps between them. She shielded her eyes against the torches that shone painfully brightly in her face, seeing only black shadows where there were men behind them. 'I woke up in a strange place and I panicked . . .'

'You disappoint me,' The Shepherd said. There was such sadness in his voice.

She held out her hand for him to take, a little girl lost, wanting to be brought back to the light. She was thinking fast, desperate thoughts, trying to save her herself by becoming what she thought he wanted.

'I don't like this feeling. I had such high hopes for you. I thought you were ready. I was wrong.'

She heard the shot after the bullet had slammed her up against the tree trunk, punching the air out of her lungs. She wanted to say something; to say sorry. It didn't hurt. She couldn't feel anything.

She still held out her hand as she slid down into the dirt.

He didn't take it.

ONE

t felt strange to walk into the bright, shiny new glass-and-steel monstrosity they now called home. He wasn't going to get used to it in a hurry. It wasn't him. Peter Ash was more the grim broom-cupboard dweller, at home in the cramped darkness of River House. Whoever had decided that Bonn should become the centre of their universe needed to take a long hard look at themselves. The Eurocrimes Division's purpose-built headquarters stood on the outskirts of a massive industrial park. It was the height of fiscal responsibility, and the depths of soulless architecture. Every time he set foot in the place he was reminded of the line about cities not being concrete jungles but rather human zoos.

That's exactly what this place was, a zoo.

They were on display like animals.

It wasn't like they'd had a choice and thought, *Hey, let's up sticks and move to Germany.* He was quite happy back in London. He even missed the crowded insanity of the walk along the river to the small coffee shop where Laura fed her addiction. The same went for Frankie Varg. That was the thing, she'd worked alone long enough that she'd grown used to taking risks that she'd never take with someone else's life on the line. They were similar like that. Not exactly broken, but incapable of giving enough of yourself to be a proper partner. Still, it wasn't as though this was for ever – at least not if the bods in Westminster got their way, sleepwalking the country off a cliff into the splendid isolation of Brexit. It didn't matter whether you were a Remainer or a Leaver, the schism this thing had wrought was deep and felt irreparable. The number of viral videos with nasty little thugs being given permission to let loose their prejudices on the world was disgusting. The spike in hate crimes and racial intolerance was staggering, but it shouldn't have been surprising.

But it wasn't just a British thing, was it?

This whole isolationist kick seemed to have gripped the world. You only had to turn on the television to see capitalism running wild, stealing pension-fund surpluses and giving trillion-dollar tax breaks to the one-per-centers while separating kids from their parents at the border and putting them in concentration camps in everything but name, all in the cause of making America great again, fancy red hat made in China and all.

The world was going to hell in a handcart.

It was obvious they were locked in psychological warfare with the Russian machine playing them like puppets.

Someone was going to have to fix the world.

All Pete could think was thank fuck it wasn't his job.

Still, it wasn't as though he or Frankie could complain about being seconded to Bonn. It was part of the job description. They were field agents for a cross-border joint policing initiative. He joked he worked for Cops without Borders. All twenty-eight member states were represented, sharing their expertise and local knowledge as they investigated crimes that crossed national jurisdictions. But Laura was different. She was a homebody, settled and loving life in London, with family and friends that she wouldn't want to leave behind. Sure, she'd talked about having an adventure, but she was happy where she was. London was a great city. Not just a vibrant one. It was the centre of the world. But it turned out that Laura was the same as him. She had work. The nearest thing she had to friends were in a choir she sang with on a Friday night on the rare occasions she managed to get away from the office in time. She didn't even have a cat. So quite literally there was nothing keeping her in London when the call came.

'Who knows, maybe I'll get one now,' she said, looking at one of the endless cat memes scrolling across her screen. She sipped at the foam of her cappuccino, which, as she'd told him twice a day for the last six months, just wasn't as good as the one from the cart down on the River. 'It's that or a man, and cats eat less.'

He tried not to laugh because his ribs still hurt.

It had been six months since he'd been discharged from the hospital to begin his recovery.

He still woke in the middle of the night sometimes, damp sheets sticking to his skin, the taste of the smoke still acrid in his mouth and the crackle of the flames from the burning church fever-bright in his mind. The physio had warned him that it could take at least a year for him to regain full mobility, that he needed to keep pushing himself through the exercise regime, but that patience was more important than determination. The problem was that neither was easy. He wasn't by nature a patient soul, when it came to his own physical well-being he'd never exactly been the stubborn type.

'Look, you know I love you, right?'

'I don't like where this is going,' Pete said with a wry smile.

'You think you're so clever, Peter Ash, but I know you better than you know yourself,' Laura said. 'And I know when you're pretending. So, I'm going to ask you again, friend to friend, are you *really* sure you're ready to be back out there?' She leaned closer so that no one else in the room could overhear. 'There's plenty of stuff you could help me with.'

She meant well, but he was fast going out of his mind.

'You mean paperwork? I think I'd rather suffer a second crucifixion. Now, what have you got for me?'

'Nothing exciting's come across the transom.'

'Where's Frankie?'

'Why don't you read the ongoing case log.'

'I was kinda hoping you'd save me the effort. You're Google, after all.'

'You should read the case log.'

She was being cagey, and he didn't like it.

'What aren't you telling me, Law?'

'Read it.'

'I want you to tell me.'

'I'm serious, Pete. Read the log. If I tell you, I'm going to miss a detail, you'll go off half-cocked, and I'll be for the chop. We've got a lot more eyes on us here. Just do me a favour, read the log. Then you can yell at me. I'll get a fresh coffee while you play catch-up.' He knew full well her cup was still half full, and comfortably warm, meaning she was making herself scarce. She smiled and patted his shoulder as she got to her feet. 'It's good to have you back.'

'It's good to be back.'

'Let's see if you still think that after you've read the log.'

TWO

The ferry journey was a rival for Odysseus's black ship on the long journey home. Sixteen hours between Scylla and Charybdis – meaning, literally, two evils.

Frankie had managed little sleep.

The decision to travel via Stockholm meant she'd been able to tie up a few loose ends renting out her apartment. She'd been tempted to sell it, but it was prime real estate, and right now the property market was spiralling in the city, meaning what might cost four million kroner now could be selling for six or seven by the time she was ready to return home – and at those prices her own home was going to be well out of reach, so better to sit on it. She'd needed to get permission from the condo board to rent the place out, and legally wasn't allowed to make a cent profit on the deal. The letting laws were weird – very much a throwback to the country's socialist roots – and meant she wasn't allowed to charge anything beyond the interest levels on the mortgage, and nothing in regards to the amortization of the loan, so it was still costing her a couple of thousand a month to keep it, but it was a solid long-term investment. Plus, she liked the place.

The journey across the Baltic to Tallinn gave her plenty of time to think about the job, the changes that had been thrust upon her from Division, and what she wanted out of life. The problem, as far as she was concerned, was that they amounted to the same thing.

She stood on the deck as the ferry approached the terminal. Thick black cloud in the distance marked the forest fire that had been burning for over a week now. It stretched across the horizon, towering over the city. Reports put it at little more than a hundred kilometres from the city, which sounded like a lot, but out of control, wildfires could spread at ten kilometres an hour, meaning it was not much more than ten hours away from the medieval city. All it would take was a change in wind direction.

These raging fires were becoming far too common in the long

overly hot summers of climate change. Twice in the last few years Sweden had been ravaged by them, needing the Italians to fly in their water-bombing planes and a convoy of engines and firefighters from all over Europe to quite literally put all hands to the pump to bring them under control. The most recent one, last summer, had covered an area the equivalent of ninety-six thousand football pitches, and burned right up to the outskirts of her parents' home in Sala.

Without make up, her blonde hair cropped short, she could pass for a young woman – if young meant maybe twenty-five. In the right clothes, even younger. The ripped jeans, scuffed boots, and battered leather jacket would do the job. The slightly grubby sleeping bag she had strapped to a rucksack enhanced the illusion.

No one was going to mistake Francesca Varg for a cop and that was all that mattered.

She could have flown, but no self-respecting backpacker would take the plane, and there was nothing to say the people she was hunting weren't watching the docks for people like her, travelling alone, vulnerable. It was all about playing the part.

She watched the faces down on the terminal hardstand and through the glass windows as the ferry docked, but no one stood out.

By the time she was walking away from the ferry terminal, eyes on the signs into the city, Frankie was already feeling grubby.

There were plenty of people back in Division who weren't happy with her wasting her time on this case. The prevailing wisdom was that any sort of investigation was going to take far too long, and the chances of any sort of meaningful results were negligible. Nikola Akardi, their ODA – Officer of Divisional Affairs – was adamant they had more than enough work on their plate and took her aside to tell her just that. But Frankie was a field agent, which gave her a certain amount of leeway with investigations. They were still getting used to the chain of command. She had to admit it was a bit weird taking orders from a guy seconded to Division from the Greek offices where before she'd been autonomous. Akardi oversaw the entire Eastern European operation. He'd only been in the post for three months and was growing into it. It wasn't like he had a choice. They were all learning on the job.

Akardi's primary concern was that even if she hit pay dirt it was going to be virtually impossible for her to do anything about it.

But that was only because he didn't know the truth, the whole truth, and nothing but. Only Law did: no agent was permitted to work a case where they had a personal connection, no matter how distant. She'd weighed up the ethics of the situation, but how was she supposed to ignore her cousin's cry for help when it was exactly the kind of hell she could help with? She could have passed it across to someone else, let Akardi assign another team; it wasn't as though she didn't trust her colleagues, but it was personal and there was no way she wasn't going to do everything in her power to bring Irma Lutz home.

She hadn't seen her cousin since she was three, but that didn't make her any less family, and Frankie's extended family stretched like a spider's web across northern Europe. She'd only met a fraction of them but had heard all sorts of stories from her mother, who was very much at the centre of the web.

Irma was nineteen, a student at the University of Technology in Tallinn. By all accounts she was a bright girl, destined for great things. But something had derailed her, and she'd lost interest in her studies. It happened more often than people realized; someone with the world at their feet would fall in love, or just not cope with those first few months out of the nest and they'd lose themselves in the social side of university. As far as she'd been able to tell, there wasn't much that was actually remarkable about Irma's circumstances right up until the day she disappeared.

Frankie had liaised with the local police, who weren't interested, and spoken to her tutor, her housemates, and the staff of the coffee shop where she worked part-time. Every conversation circled back to the same thing: she'd had some sort of spiritual awakening and had found religion. Her housemates said she'd paid up her term's rent and gone to join some kind of commune out in the middle of nowhere. And that wasn't illegal. As police, their hands were tied. As family, hers weren't.

The officer in Tallinn had been more than happy to forward a copy of her file, not that there was much to read.

Irma's tutor had gushed a little too much about just how talented she was and gave her the names of a couple of other students she seemed close to. All but one was already on the list of police interviews in the file.

Her first thought was, why hadn't they spoken to the last girl?
That was the way her mind worked.

So, she'd written the name Annja Rosen on the pad in front of
her and drawn a circle around it.

It didn't take Laura long to track down a mobile number for the
girl, and within half an hour of hanging up on the Estonian police
Frankie was listening to the girl tell her a story that had the fine hairs
on the nape of her neck bristling.

'I warned her. I told her not to get involved with them,' Annja
said. 'But she wouldn't listen.'

'Them?' Frankie said.

'One World. They suck you in, they tell you what you want to
hear, but they're fucking evil. When they've got you, they won't let
go. They're a cult. They're not a religion. They're scum. They've
all drunk the Kool-Aid,' she said, meaning the one lasting legacy
of Jim Jones and Jonestown, where the entire cult downed the
grape-flavoured Kool-Aid in a mass suicide rite. 'I told the police
all about it.'

That stopped her cold.

'You told the police?'

She leafed through the pages of the file. Not only wasn't Annja
Rosen's statement on file, there wasn't a single mention of One
World anywhere in the printout, which threw a massive shadow
across the veracity of the investigation as a whole.

'An officer came out when she first went missing. I told him
about her obsession with One World.'

'Do you remember his name?'

There was silence on the line for a moment then, 'No. Sorry. I
didn't think it was important.'

'Don't worry. I don't suppose you have any idea how she got
involved with One World in the first place? Did she see someone
preaching or . . .?' Frankie shrugged her shoulders, meaning 'or
any of the many possible ways young girls might fall in with a
cult', not that Annja could see the gesture.

'They run a soup kitchen down by the docks. She volunteered
there for a while. I went to help out, once, but it was all a bit creepy.'

'Creepy?'

'It was like they were clones, you know? They all looked the
same. Tall, stick-thin, blonde, blue eyes, you know the sort.'

She did. It was all very *Stepford Wives*.

But that wasn't what had Frankie's sixth sense bristling.

Statements being buried? A cult like One World tied up in it?

There was something rotten in the state of Tallinn.

THREE

'One World? That's . . . not ideal,' Peter Ash said as Laura put a mug down in front of him. The EU flag on the chipped china was beginning to fade from the dishwasher's abuse. He was sure there was some sort of metaphor in that.

'Ah, so you've made it onto page two without getting a nosebleed?'

'Nope,' Pete said, with a grin. 'Halfway down the first page in Frankie's summary.'

'Smart woman. She knew you'd never get to the end.'

'But One World? One *fucking* World. Of all the bat-shit crazy cults in this bat-shit crazy world, she had to walk into theirs?'

There was a snort from the other side of the cubicle's not-so soundproof barrier.

'Half of the law-enforcement agencies around the world have investigated this sham,' Pete said, shaking his head. 'We're talking everything from tax evasion to the legality of their servitude contracts that bind the faithful like slaves for a billion years. The whole world knows they're a cult, but they're Teflon. Nothing ever sticks.'

'They're a religion,' Laura corrected. She reached into a drawer and pulled out a thick hardback book with The Shepherd's face on the cover and the words *Fork-Tongued Saviour* across it. 'Just like the Mormons, Scientologists, and Jehovah's Witnesses.'

'One made-up space fairy is just like another, you mean?' Pete said, remembering one of the first conversations he'd had with Frankie when she'd asked him if he was religious, because one way or another everyone brought their own preconceptions and prejudices to the table when they were investigating. He certainly had plenty of those.

'I mean that despite thorough investigations, no one has been able to *prove* they've committed any crimes, and they've tried. That has to mean something.'

'Sure it does. They've never been investigated by me,' Pete said, picking up the book. 'You heard about this book, right? What happened to the writer? The guy was taken out in the middle of London at closing time, someone leaned him down in the gutter and reversed a fucking Range Rover over his head. They really didn't want this book coming out. The publisher reported all sorts of harassment and intimidation trying to get him to pull the book.'

'Again, nothing was ever proved. Bray's death was considered an accident—'

'The guy was an alcoholic nine years sober and he suddenly took it upon himself to get out of his skull and stumble conveniently into the street right in front of a Range Rover they never managed to trace because its licence plates were obscured by mud. Mighty fucking accidental, Law.'

'And despite lawsuits they're recognized by the EU as a religion.'

'Look, people are free to believe what they want to, I get that, and if they get excited by a great volcano burning aliens alive, well, good for them. I'm not going to piss on their parade, but I'm not grabbing hold of the E-meter and confessing all my sins, either. Call it what it is, a cult.'

'You are such a cynic,' Laura smiled.

'That I am. But you've seen that Ricky Gervais thing? If you took every holy book in the world and burned them, in two thousand years' time they wouldn't come back. They're stories. Some other stories might replace them, but the ones we have now would be gone for good. But if you took every science book in the world and destroyed them, removing the knowledge from our collective conscience, in two thousand years' time all of that knowledge would be back, because science we'd rediscover, because no matter how you look at it, science doesn't change, it's fundamentally the truth of our planet. You drop an apple, it's always going to feel the force of gravity bringing it down.'

'Just like you,' a voice said from over the partition, earning a couple of chuckles around the squad room.

'Funny fuckers,' Pete said, but he was grinning.

It felt good to be back.

'Here's the thing: sure, maybe they're squeaky clean goody two-shoes by the letter of the law, but what they do is disgusting. They target the at-risk, the young, the vulnerable, and they brainwash them. And once they sign that indentured contract, they give up all of their worldly possessions, are given a couple of quid a week to live on, and charged double that for each confession, meaning they get deeper and deeper into a hole with One World, and there's no getting out.'

'I get all that, Pete, but they're still not breaking the law.'

He shook his head. 'It's immoral.'

'It's their choice. Free will.'

'How many of those kids would leave if they could?'

'How many kids get buyer's remorse when they sign up for the army and want to quit during basic training? How many more want to bail when they hear their first posting is a war zone?'

'I don't want to fall out with you, Law. These people are scum.'

'I'll have to take your word for it.'

'OK, riddle me this, why have the local cops excised all mention of One World from their reports?'

'Pass. Ask me one on sport or arts and entertainment. I'm a killer when it comes to eighties music and B-movies.' She was smiling, but it was a serious point, and he was going to say it out loud, because . . .

'Because their reach is long and their influence pernicious. There's no getting around the fact that interviewing officer either chose to exclude Annja's statement, or was ordered to leave it out. And frankly, either way stinks. Gut instinct? Either one, or both of them, have been got at.'

'Or they're members of One World,' Laura said. And that was the nightmare scenario, cult members on the inside, screwing with the investigation. 'So, you want to turn this into a rat-catcher investigation into the Estonian police?'

Pete sighed. 'A bit too far outside our remit to sell Akardi on that, I reckon.' But the fact that they'd turned a blind eye gnawed at him – and not for the obvious reason. Annually, across Europe, thousands of people joined One World. Most were young and impres-sionable. When he'd been young it had been the lyrics of The Pixies and REM those kids looked to for direction, now it was The Shepherd and his pseudo-spiritual bollocks. So why hide it? Why cut that reference from the file? It wasn't as though Irma Lutz was the only young woman who thought the black hole in the middle of her life could be filled by a fake religion – and that was why it rang every alarm bell, because you only cut it if there was something to hide.

'So, where's Frankie now?'

Laura made a show of checking the time on her watch against the clock on the wall as if it were a matter of minutes and not days that Frankie had been gone. 'As of eight days ago, Tallinn.'

'She's gone there alone? What the hell was she thinking? You knew I was coming back today. One week and she had back-up. One week.'

Laura lowered her voice, pitching her answer softly enough that her voice wouldn't carry to the next cubicle. 'You want the official version, or the truth?'

'You tell me?'

'Officially, she's visiting her cousin, the mother of the missing girl. She's also going to speak to Annja Rosen again and take a new statement, so she can close the file at our end, too.'

'And what the fuck is she really doing out there?'

'She's going undercover . . .'

'She's what?'

Laura reached inside her desk drawer and withdrew a white envelope. 'She asked me to give you this when you came in.'

The envelope had no name on it. Inside was a single sheet of white paper, the message handwritten. Meaning it wasn't on any database or system back-up, meaning it wasn't vulnerable to security breaches or hacking, or a paper-trail audit if the shit hit the fan.

Or maybe he was being paranoid and it was the easiest way for her to give him a message?

Pete read it slowly, digesting the implications of Frankie's recklessness.

'One . . . two . . . three . . .'

'What are you doing?'

'Working out how long it takes you to find an excuse to join her.'

'Funny bugger.'

'I know the way your mind works,' she said, a smug smile creeping across her face. 'If you'd like to step in the briefing room I'll show you everything you need.'

'Are you trying to seduce me, Miss Byrne?'

'You should be so lucky.'

*   *   *

'Is this strictly necessary?' he asked as she switched on the large screen. Laura tapped out a series of commands on the laptop.

'Why don't you make yourself useful and turn down the lights?'

Sometimes it was just easier to do as he was told. Plus, the office was Laura's domain. The only difference to River House was that she had more toys to play with here. Like the projector.

'You've heard about the forest fire raging through Estonia, right?'

He shook his head.

'Have you been living under a rock?'

'I've been watching a lot of porn. Since Stormy Daniels and the Orange One, I figure porn is how the world ends.'

'Sometimes you're just weird, Pete.'

He nodded. 'That I am. So, catch me up.'

A series of images appeared on the screen. They showed the scale of the fire and the devastation in its wake. 'Every time they think they're starting to get it under control there's a fresh outbreak somewhere else. This thing is raging. There are lives at risk every day, and not just the fire-fighters, and yet four days ago someone was arrested for deliberately lighting a new fire.'

Which was all well and good but had nothing to do with Frankie disappearing into the wilderness in search of a made-up god. Or did it?

The image changed.

This time it showed scorched earth and the wisps of smoke still seeping from charred roots and branches.

It took a moment for Pete to realize what he was looking at.

'Not the best quality, it was taken on a mobile phone by a fire officer.'

'It's a body,' Pete said as the image focused on a protruding arm. The flesh had been charred in the fire. The bone was visible in places where the meat and fat had rendered down to nothing.

'No flies on you.'

'So, what has this got to do with Frankie?'

More images, this time of the body lying naked on a pathologist's slab. The fire had done some damage, as had time in the earth, but it was a good bet the bullet hole in her stomach was the cause of death.

'OK, a wild fire uncovers the body of a murdered girl?'

'She's Russian.'

'Which isn't exactly strange in Estonia given they're neighbours. Hardly an international incident.'

Laura sighed and shook her head. 'And there was me thinking you'd be looking for a reason to go to Tallinn.'

The penny dropped.

'Do we have any identification?'

'Not yet, but they're working on it.'

'So how do we know she's Russian?'

He could see her smile in the dim backlight from the projector. 'The pathologist believes she'd had a number of procedures in Russia, including a titanium plate for an injury. The engraving on the plate, including serial, is all Cyrillic. We haven't sourced the manufacturer yet but the odds are good it's Russian in origin.'

'Flimsy, but fair enough. So how do we get it past the suits upstairs?'

'Peter, Peter, Peter, don't you ever read your emails?'

'Not if I can help it.'

'They sweetened my move here with something of a promotion. I say if something is worth following up, and I think this is worth following up.'

'So, you're my boss now?'

'If you insist on putting a label on it,' Laura said.

'With great power, comes great responsibility.'

'*Spider Man*?'

'An unnamed French revolutionary writer.'

'I never had you down as a historical soul.'

'Daytime quiz-show addiction.'

'OK, so, you'll follow this up? With luck you won't need to make contact with Frankie, but having you in place as back-up for when the shit hits the fan would make me feel better.'

'I like the fact that you say "when".'

'I told you, I know you, Peter Ash. And I'm starting to know Frankie. That woman is a magnet for trouble. There was no way you weren't going out there after her.'

'You seem very sure of yourself.'

'I am. You're on the next flight out. Your boarding card is preloaded on your phone app.'

'Welcome to the new world,' Ash said.

'We've been here for six months, it's time you caught up.'

FOUR

It was getting late.

It has been over a week since Frankie stepped off the ferry. She had twenty euros left in her pocket and no easy way to lay her hands on more. But that was the point. She needed to make herself vulnerable.

There was a pay-as-you-go phone in the bottom of her rucksack along with a fake passport that shaved almost ten years off her true age and named her Ceska Volk, which was close enough to who she had always been for her not to be thrown by someone calling her it. She couldn't risk carrying anything that even hinted she wasn't who she claimed to be.

And to sell the idea that she was a vulnerable young girl sleeping on the streets, she needed to be a vulnerable young girl sleeping on the streets.

The one advantage she had over those other girls like the one she was pretending to be was that if things went south she had Laura to get her out of there.

The twenty euros would probably buy her a night in a hostel, or a half-decent meal, but not both. But that kind of luxury wasn't going to help her look street-worn fast enough. She needed this beaten-down look if she was going to pass for homeless when she finally turned up at the soup kitchen's door.

As it was, she would be marked out as a newcomer. People remembered faces when they saw them for the first time, especially when they were the kind that looked to help. You never knew who might slip through the cracks, or how long you had to catch them before they fell. So, tonight's bed was going to be another uncomfortable doorway, huddled up under a bridge, or, if she was accepted, the cardboard city where the homeless congregated for safety. It was different in every city, and very much depended upon the identity of the place itself. She'd seen black-masked hooligans smash one up in Stockholm a few years back when football fans had taken it upon themselves to purge the streets.

Frankie resisted the urge to head towards the waterfront to bed down for the night.

She'd spent her first night there and quickly learnt her lesson. There were good and bad places to sleep. There was nothing good about the isolation that part of town offered. It was far too risky.

Plenty of those homeless gravitated to the waterfront in big cities, but in her experience it wasn't a natural first port of call. New arrivals gravitated towards the brighter lights and stayed there for a while. They didn't venture away from those shop doorways until the desperation forced them to. Some kept to the same doorway every night, but Frankie had moved on to pastures new every time darkness fell. It didn't take long to find a new doorway for tonight. She pressed herself into the shadows and pulled the sleeping bag she'd brought around her. It was still early, but with nowhere to go she wasn't going to wander. Exploring wasn't natural. She needed to do everything right. She settled in for the long wait.

She scrawled an 'I'm homeless, helpless, and hungry' message on a scrap of cardboard and set it down by her feet.

She wasn't expecting sympathy. A week of living like this had drummed that naivety out of her. Life was hard. Kids flocked to the big cities in the hope of changing their lives or finding a future they didn't think they could have back home. Kids ran here because they couldn't stay where they were. Kids ran here to hide. There were as many reasons as there were kids sleeping rough. And that meant that people were becoming inured to the plight of others.

Still, the sign gave it an edge of realism, not least because she was at least one of the three.

She placed a few coins on the card and closed her eyes.

The concrete was painfully uncomfortable, but she was tired enough that she managed to drift in and out of a light sleep that offered no sort of rest.

Footsteps came and went, keeping their own rhythms. Every now and then she heard the dull clatter of coins landing on the cardboard. Frankie pretended not to hear them rather than having to look up and show gratitude. It was better that way. Maybe better for those giving the money, too.

Time didn't have much meaning here.

It was dark.

It would still be dark for a long time to come.

The footsteps slowed and faded away, wider and wider gaps between them until they stopped altogether.

She drifted again, trying to ignore the pain in her back.

Some nameless hour in the night Frankie startled awake to an unexpected sound. She looked up into the gurning face of a drunk looming over her. It took her a moment to realize it was piss splashing over her sleeping bag.

She was up in an instant, forgetting all about the character she was playing.

The movement panicked the pissing man. He tried to turn, flaccid cock still in hand, a ribbon of urine still flowing, and tripped over his own feet. He went sprawling to the ground, the urine soaking into his trousers.

The smile was gone from his face.

Frankie saw three other young men standing nearby, delighting at the misfortune of their friend, and realized what was going on.

'You bastards!' Frankie snarled, lashing out wildly at the man on the ground as he tried to put his dick away and zip himself up at the same time as he splashed around trying to stand. It would have been funny if it wasn't so disgusting.

The others just laughed at him.

The man got to his feet and staggered away without looking back.

On the other side of the street a gaggle of girls had stopped and stood watching. Frankie ignored them. She turned her back on the drunks, surprised to see the generosity of coins that had been dropped onto her cardboard sign. There was more than enough for a decent breakfast when morning came, though some of the coins were wet.

Most of the piss had missed her sleeping bag. Even from close range the drunk's aim had been piss-poor. Most of it soaked into his designer-label trousers.

She swallowed down her disgust, knowing that it only added to the authenticity of her bag. You lived rough, this was what happened to you.

'I'm sorry,' one of the young men said, taking a ten-euro note from his pocket. He pushed it into her hand and set off after his friends. Frankie took it without a word. It would keep her alive for two more days. That was how little it took to make a difference.

She waited until they'd all gone, then sat down with her back to the doorway and gathered up the coins.

She was more angry than upset, and she'd had to bite down on her instinct, otherwise she would have hospitalized the drunk, which whilst being satisfying would have been a mistake, all things considered.

She was on her guard when the next figure approached.

'You OK?' the young woman asked as she crouched down in front of her. She offered Frankie a paper cup of coffee, which she accepted with gratitude, savouring the warmth that immediately bled into her skin even before she took a sip.

'Thanks,' she said, letting the steam warm her face. 'I'm fine.'

'You shouldn't have to put up with that kind of shit.' Unlike most of the young people who had walked along the street, she wasn't dressed for a night out, which marked her out as a do-gooder. There were always a few on the lookout for people to help.

The coffee tasted half decent.

'My name's Tasha,' the woman said.

'Ceska.'

'Russian?'

Frankie shook her head. 'Czech.' It sounded like a Czech name rather than an affectionate nickname her grandmother had given her.

'Long way from home.'

Frankie shrugged. 'Not sure I have a home any more.'

'Ah,' Tasha said, then took a sip of her own coffee, and fell into a comfortable silence.

'Thank you,' Frankie said eventually. 'Not just for the coffee. For the company. It gets pretty lonely out here.'

'It's OK,' Tasha said.

'You do this a lot?' She'd seen them a couple of times over the last week. They set up a table and offered coffee in paper cups and badly buttered cheese sandwiches to people who lined up for the handouts.

'There are a few of us out most nights. There are too many kids living rough. Not enough shelters. We try to help. We run a soup kitchen, down by the docks. You might want to come and find us if you get hungry. The food's not fancy, but it's hot and filling.'

'Sounds good.'

'Ha, well, you might want to reserve judgement until you've tasted it, but it's better than nothing.'

First contact.

Frankie had to resist the temptation to ask questions. She wasn't a cop here. She was a vulnerable young woman. She needed to think like one. That meant not looking a gift horse in the mouth. How many soup kitchens could there be in a city the size of Tallinn? Two, three?

'Hope to see you in the morning,' Tasha said, pushing herself back up to her feet. 'Look after yourself, Ceska.'

'I will.'

'I say this to all the kids I meet out here, so even though you aren't a kid, don't be offended: if you can go home, you really should. This life is hard enough without putting yourself through this. And if you can't go home, well . . . just be careful.'

'Thanks.'

'See you in the morning.' This time it wasn't a question.

Frankie settled herself back down a doorway along from the faint lingering smell of urine.

FIVE

The next flight out was at five thirty in the morning, which meant being through customs by four thirty, which meant trying to sleep was a pointless exercise with the journey to Cologne-Bonn airport taking thirty minutes door-to-door. Four in the morning was a strange time. A mortician had once told him that more people died in the hour between three and four a.m. than any other time of the day. That little factoid had stuck with him, and he found himself thinking about it as the taxi drove him through the deserted streets. He got it. It made sense. Four a.m. was a lonely time. It wasn't about ghosts or things that went bump in the night. It was about being alone and not wanting to carry on. It didn't matter if you were sick or lost, it was just harder at four a.m.

He read through the dossier Laura had put together for him, including more details about his excuse for being in Estonia. As with everything she did, it was beyond thorough. He knew they were deliberately grasping at straws, but the more he read the more it felt like it might actually be possible that there was a link between this dead body in the forest fire and more young women from the old Eastern Bloc who were being trafficked to the West. Young, in this case, meant kids as well as seventeen-, eighteen- and nineteen-year-olds. One name he saw was thirteen when she'd gone missing.

His blood ran cold.

He hated shit like this, when kids were involved.

He knew logically it went back to his father. Those guilt trips around children's homes and orphanages come Christmastime, and rooted deeper, the horrors the old man had fled as a child. Peter had learned about his father's second life when he was hunting Karius. That had cast a different light on his own childhood. It was all just so flimsy. Even so, it was a massive leap from the burned body to the rest of it, and any cop worth their salt would call him out on it, so he worked up a whole 'You know what the bosses are like, wanting to cover their backs' speech.

He woke her up. The phone only made it to the third ring before she answered. He didn't bother saying hello. She knew who it was.

'OK, fess up, what's your secret?'

'I have no idea what you're talking about, but then it is nearly four in the morning and I was in the middle of a very hot Gerald Butler dream, so that's hardly surprising.'

'This stuff in the file.'

'What about it?'

'It's convincing. I mean seriously convincing.'

'That's because it's true,' she said. 'Girls are being trafficked through Latvia, Lithuania, and Estonia. Tallinn is a logical staging post, it opens the way into Scandinavia via Sweden and Helsinki, and there are direct ferries into St Petersburg. It's a gateway to Europe with good road and rail links. You can drive to Berlin in seventeen hours, and thanks to the Eurozone you're not getting your cargo checked by customs once it's loaded up. Frictionless borders.'

'I can hear the Brexiteers' mocking laughter from here.'

'There's nothing to link the dead girl to the human railway, but frankly, that's a detail. You need an excuse, this is an excuse.'

'Ah, Law, you little subversive. You've only been the boss for five minutes and you're already screwing with the system.'

'No choice. If we told the truth we'd have to flag One World in the system, and worst case, if they do have someone on the inside, then all sorts of alarm bells will start ringing somewhere. Maybe not inside Division, maybe not even in Bonn, but that doesn't mean they won't be heard somewhere. Who knows what kind of influence those bastards have got. Put it this way, better to get a slap on the wrist for sending you on a wild-goose chase than getting Frankie cut up and dissolved in a vat of lye.'

'When you put it like that, I can see just how much hanging around me has damaged you.'

'Is that supposed to be a compliment?'

'Of course. You're one of us.'

'One of us, one of us,' she said, in an eerie monotone like something out of an old horror movie. That made him smile.

'When is Frankie meant to check in?'

'She isn't. She's got a burner phone for emergencies.'

'But you're tracking her?'

'Of course. I've got eyes on her most of the time.'

'I don't like the way you say "most". You going to let me have her number?'

'Only if you promise not to use it.'

'Well, that's a promise I won't be able to keep.'

'I'm serious. No calls on that number unless we are desperate. I'm your point of contact out there, Pete. I'll direct you to her once you touch down. Keep the burner I gave you on at all times.'

It looked like it was at least a decade behind the technology curve, barely capable of stringing together multiple texts, with no MMS functionality, because that was exactly what it was meant to look like. The brains trust inside Division had modified the unit so that it could do everything a modern smart phone could, and work as an independent tracker which relayed its GPS signal back to the Galileo satellite system run by the EU. The tracker had its own four-week battery which would continue to function even if the main battery and SIM card were removed. The device was paired with Frankie's and would work like a homing beacon, allowing them to find each other. Laura had set up a three-digit activation code.

Zero. Zero. Seven.

It was as close as he was ever going to get to feeling like James Bond.

SIX

The call from Frankie Varg weighed on Annja Rosen's mind far more than she thought it would in the week that followed it.

On one level she still felt sad that she'd lost her friend, but on another she was pissed off that Irma had done something so utterly stupid.

Annja felt like she'd been abandoned.

What stuck in her mind was the note of surprise in Frankie's voice when Annja told her she'd already given a statement to the police. It jarred with her because surely if she'd been a cop she'd have known that? But Annja was beginning to think she'd been played. She'd taken the woman at her word. But what if she wasn't a cop? What if she was some sort of muck-raking journalist? The kind that hacked the phones of dead girls trying to get a story?

Annja played the conversation over and over in her head.

Had she told the woman anything she shouldn't?

Did she even know something worth knowing?

She couldn't think of anything.

Sure, she knew some of Irma's secrets, but nothing of any worth. She knew friend stuff, like the name of her dog, her secret crush, her best friend when she was growing up and just how badly she'd screwed things up there, the first boy she had kissed, and just how much of a disaster that had been. She knew about the first time she'd kissed a girl and how different it had been, and how hard Irma had struggled to work out who she was and who she wanted to be. But apart from a few photographs on her phone it was if Irma had never existed. And that was what haunted her: just how easy it was for someone to completely disappear.

Annja's first thought was to tell the police about the call; it couldn't hurt. If they already knew someone was investigating Irma's disappearance, then great, she really, really hoped this Frankie woman would find a way to bring her home; and if they didn't, well then they would now, either way there was no need for it to weigh on her mind.

The problem was, since Irma had left, Annja had lost touch with their shared friends. It hadn't taken her long to realize they weren't really shared at all. They were Irma's friends.

But then she'd found the slip of paper and that had taken the indecision out of it.

She knew what the right thing to do was.

Annja stood outside the police station for a good ten minutes staring at the word stencilled on the glass before she mustered the courage to go inside. She'd spent most of the morning convincing herself she was making a fool of herself. But it was also the right thing to do.

And she owed it to Irma to do everything she could. Maybe then she could move on?

Annja took a deep breath and walked inside.

A couple of people sat in the cheap plastic chairs, waiting. A sad-faced woman clutched a shopping basket on her lap. A small dog peered out of the opening. Annja gave her a nervous smile before going up to the glass screen.

The desk officer didn't look up.

'Can I help you?' he asked, still fascinated by something else.

'I need to speak to Detective Kask,' Annja said, a little too softly for her words to carry. She repeated herself.

'What's it concerning?'

'He came to see me a few months ago. My friend disappeared. He said to get in touch with him if I remembered anything that might help find her.'

The desk officer nodded. 'What's the name of your friend?'

'Irma Lutz.'

He made her spell it out.

'And yours?'

'Annja Rosen.'

'Take a seat. I'll see if he's available.'

Ten minutes later she was being ushered into an empty interview room.

Kask was older than she remembered, nearer to the grizzled desk officer's age than her own. He still had that roguish smile she remembered though.

'OK, Annja, how can I help?' He leaned towards her across the wooden table. It was all about body language. He was telling her he was one of the good guys, here to fix her problems. He was interested. And for a moment at least she was the centre of his entire universe.

Which didn't make it any easier for Annja to find the right words. Face to face with Kask, it felt like such a waste of time. 'It might be nothing,' she said. 'It probably is. But you said to get in touch . . . so . . . I'm not really sure where to start.'

'That's OK. Take your time.'

Slowly, Annja explained about the call she'd received from Frankie, and the special European police agency she supposedly represented.

She produced the slip of paper from her handbag and slid it across the table.

'I thought you might want this. I started to worry that maybe she wasn't a cop, you know?'

He reached out and placed a finger on the paper, drawing it the last few centimetres towards him. 'Frankie Varg,' he said, reading the name written on it.

'You know her?' He inclined his head slightly. She took that as an answer. 'That's a relief. But now I'm beginning to think that I'm wasting your time. I'm sorry.' She closed her bag and started to get to her feet.

Kask held up his hand to stop her.

'You're not wasting my time. Believe me. It's always better to let us know about your concerns. Keeping this to yourself won't help Irma. So, tell me why you're worried.'

Annja slumped back down into the seat. 'I can't really explain it, it was just that she seemed surprised that you'd already spoken to me.'

Kask leaned back this time, inclining his head slightly. 'We've sent her a copy of our files.'

Annja nodded. 'That's what she said. I guess she missed my statement.'

'It's possible. Pages stick together, or maybe we missed something when we mailed them over – it happens, we're only human,' he said with that warm smile of his. 'But thank you.'

'That's what I thought. That's why I didn't think there was any harm in telling them just what I'd told you in my original statement.'

Something changed in the man's face, just the slightest shift in the set of the muscles under the skin. He didn't say anything for a moment. 'It's fine. You didn't do anything wrong, Annja. All you've done is save me the trouble of digging up your original statement and sending it over. Don't worry.' He got to his feet and opened the door for her, offering his hand as he thanked her again, and repeated the promise that if she thought of anything else, no matter how insignificant she might think it, to get in touch. Annja promised she would. She left with the distinct impression that he couldn't get her out of there fast enough.

The woman with the small dog still waited, offering her own uncertain smile to Kask this time.

Annja felt a curious sense of unease as she stepped outside again, and looked back over her shoulder to see Kask watching her through the glass door.

SEVEN

Maksim Kask watched the woman leave.

He was glad to see the back of her.

With luck he'd never see her again.

He'd known that she was going to be a pain in the arse from the first moment he'd met her. He took no pleasure in being proved right.

A woman in the plastic seats gave him a hopeful smile, but he ignored her and headed back towards his office. He exchanged a nod and a grimace with the desk sergeant.

The other man understood.

Back in the office he shared with three other members of the team, Kask unfolded the slip of paper the girl had given him. It took all of a second to decide what he was going to do with it. He screwed the paper into a ball and threw it into the trash. That was where it belonged.

What were the chances that Frankie Varg would realize the significance of the girl's statement? The absolute last thing he needed was her digging too deep. He reached for the phone on his desk then changed his mind. Another officer sank into the battered leather chair at a neighbouring desk. The man nodded then drew his computer keyboard a fraction closer and began to type.

Kask reached inside his desk drawer and retrieved a packet of cigarettes and his lighter.

He needed to make a call, but not where he could be overheard.

Kask shook his cigarettes in the direction of his colleague who grimaced but showed he understood. Being a smoker gave him the opportunity for time alone without anyone thinking to question him.

He headed back out into the street.

The back door led into a parking area. There were half a dozen marked vehicles, a mixture of cars and vans, ready for use at a moment's notice. No one else was getting their nicotine fix.

Rather than making the call straight away, he lit a cigarette and took a couple of deep drags to calm his nerves before he fished the phone out of his pocket.

Kask let the cigarette hang loose in his lips as he punched in the numbers, smoke wisping up across his face and stinging his eyes.

The phone was answered on the third ring.

'It's Kask,' he said, ignoring the fact that every phone had caller ID these days. 'I think we've got a problem.'

There was only silence.

He felt the need to fill it.

'That girl is back. The flatmate. I kept One World out of the statement we have on file from her, but there's someone sniffing around from Eurocrimes Division. It might be something and nothing, but she's been talking to the flatmate. I've got no idea if she named One World again or not. I couldn't push it without looking like it was important.'

Silence.

'I don't think they've met face to face.'

'Then why are you telling me now?'

Kask's collar felt a little too tight around his throat. A bead of sweat formed on his forehead. He regretted making the call. All he was doing was drawing attention to his own fuck up.

'I thought it was under control.'

'And clearly you were wrong, or you wouldn't be calling me now looking for me to deal with your mess. You disappoint

me, Kask. I don't like being disappointed. I suggest you deal with
it and don't bother me again until the problem has gone away.' The
call was ended before Kask could defend himself.

He knew exactly what The Shepherd meant when he said deal
with it.

EIGHT

F rankie woke to a chorus of brushes dragging across the paving
stones as a street cleaner got too close to her doorway. The
brushes swept up the debris, leaving a trail of damp pavement
behind it, barely visible in the dull early light.

The pre-dawn city was a strange beast. There were none of the
late-night revellers and none of the early morning commuters,
meaning for once in its day it was empty.

Or at least near empty.

There was always someone on the move, somewhere, even if it
was just the street cleaners and the taxi drivers. Tallinn was no
different to any other city in the civilized world.

It might have been more than a week, but Frankie wasn't used
to sleeping in a piss-soaked doorway. It was soul-destroying.
Dehumanizing. Every muscle in her body ached. But it went so
much deeper than that. There was a chill in her bones.

She glanced down the street, seeing other shapes in doorways
beginning to stir.

She thought about the woman from the night before. Tasha. She
assumed it was an affectionate form of Natasha, or a Russian variant.

Another rough-sleeper was on his feet, gathering up his meagre
possessions. She watched him roll his sleeping bag and tie a frayed
piece of rope round it to make it easier to carry. A small dog fussed
around him, then ran ahead as he started along the road towards
Frankie. The dog came up to her, slowing as it got to within patting
distance, and paused to sniff her, its stub of a tail wagging
furiously.

'Come on, Tino,' the man urged. He offered Frankie a brief smile.
'The police will be around in half an hour or so to move everyone

on. They can get pretty rough,' he said, touching a fading bruise on his left cheek. 'You might wanna be gone before they turn up.'

She nodded. 'Thanks for the warning.'

'We're going down to the docks. The holy rollers run a little kitchen down there. It's worth a few minutes of their religious nonsense for a decent breakfast.'

'Most important meal of the day,' she said.

'Only meal of the day more often than not,' he said.

'I spoke to someone last night.'

'That'll be Tasha,' he said. 'She never seems to stop, but she means well. And who's going to say no to that hot coffee she always has? Not me. We can wait for you if you like?'

'That's OK, I'll see you and this handsome little chap down there. Save a seat.'

He nodded. 'Tino's got you covered. Come on, mate,' he said to the dog, and together they walked off into the sunrise.

Frankie glanced down the street. A couple of others were starting to move out. Like Tino and his master, they headed the same way, drawn by the lure of the free breakfast like moths to a flame. Tino kept turning back as he padded forward, craning his neck to see if she was following. Eventually he lost interest in her.

Frankie slid out of her sleeping bag. She stood a little unsteadily as she stretched. It took her a couple of minutes longer than the others to pack her things away, but they'd had a lot more practice. By the time she moved out of her doorway the sky had grown brighter and the last of the homeless were making their way off the street. She was wrong, they weren't moths to flames, they were rats being lured down to the water by some Pied Piper. The street cleaner made its way back down the path toward her.

Given the tide of humanity moving toward the docks she didn't think it'd be too difficult to find Tasha's soup kitchen.

The benefit of not being the first through the door was that it'd make her seem reluctant to accept charity. That was the kind of little detail that filled out a character and helped sell it. So she followed another homeless man – older than many of the others she'd seen – with his bed under his arm and a torn plastic carrier bag filled to overflowing with all of his worldly goods in the other hand. Frankie's bag and sack were far from new, but they were both high quality. She couldn't help but feel privileged, not least because

she was doing this through choice, not necessity. It was humbling
that in just those few possessions she carried with her, Frankie had
so much more than the others who'd spent the night on the same
street with her.

The coins she had been given weighed heavily in her pocket.

It took longer than she had expected to make it down the long
winding road to the opening between towering warehouses and the
small hole-in-the-wall joint where Tasha and a couple of other
women were warming up porridge oats and ladling out bowls
filled to the brim. They even sprinkled cinnamon on the top, just a
little flourish that made it feel more than it really was. There were
twice as many people in the queue waiting to be fed as there
were inside, chatting over hot drinks.

The skeletal limbs of the dockyard cranes towered over them.

There was a camaraderie here, she realized. A sense of together-
ness. She hadn't expected that. Maybe it would disappear as they
dispersed, each left to fend for themselves? Or maybe not, she
thought, looking at what Tasha was creating here. She wasn't just
feeding people. She was creating a society.

As Frankie neared the front of the line she got a decent look at
the young women running things. She realized she'd made a mistake,
it wasn't Tasha handing out the bowls. Tasha was working out back
and came through the swinging doors carrying another steaming vat
of porridge. The women were so similar they could have passed for
sisters: tall, slim, long blonde hair and sharp cheekbones and noses.
It was a strong Slavic or Scandinavian look.

It was like she'd stumbled upon Stepford's soup kitchen.

It gave her the creeps.

NINE

T he plane was in the air for little more than two hours, but
the journey took more than twice that thanks to the rigmarole
involved in getting through the two airports.

Pete had always assumed freedom of movement would make a
journey like this so much faster. And maybe it had, pre-bin Laden

and Shoe Bombers, but the state of the world today meant full-body scans, little plastic bags for liquids, and struggling with belts and portable devices at the scanners. He was all for security. His entire life was based upon the notion of it. But the inconvenience still fucked him off a treat and it was only going to get worse if he had to join the Other Passports line, which never seemed to move out of its gradual glacial creep.

Maybe Division could invest in fancy private jets. A Gulfstream or two for the field agents, their own pilots and cabin crew? He smiled at the thought, and realized he had a better shot at convincing the suits to invest in a Nespresso machine to feed Law's addiction than he did of travelling anything but economy.

Laura had booked him into a hotel and lined up a hire car.

The hotel she'd chosen was close to the centre of the city, and for once it wasn't the cheapest place on the block. He assumed she was thinking about the legwork. It was better to be slap bang in the centre of the action if he was going to be walking the streets at night. The decor was tired but clean, with a slightly old-worldy charm about it, and the woman on reception seemed genuinely delighted to check him in and tell him all about the sights her city had to offer. He watched her talk fluently to three different sets of guests in three different languages with the kind of ease that mocked the British school system. It never failed to amaze him just how relaxed and natural language skills were once you stepped off the island.

She handed him his key – an actual honest to goodness key, brass, about the size of his hand, with a huge wooden fob with the room number embossed on it.

His room – number 213 – looked out onto the busy street, which he'd been promised would be a little quieter at night. He wasn't sure he believed the receptionist, but that was OK. It was why he was here.

It was still early, but even so there was a steady flow of road and foot traffic, though nothing compared with the hustle and bustle outside his new Bonn apartment every night. That place was worse than his flat back in London. He tested the bed. The mattress was like a bed of nails.

He fished out the phone Laura had given him and punched in the three-digit code. She knew him far too well. Just hitting 007 put a smile on his face. It took a few seconds to pick up the signal from Galileo and connect, then he saw the two red dots on the screen, like something out of an old Atari game. One was him, the other Frankie. It was as simple as that.

It would have been nice if there was a proper map he could expand around her location to give himself a better idea of where she was, but that was beyond what the technology had to offer.

He used an old-fashioned paper map instead.

It took him a moment to orientate himself, then he realized Frankie was down in the docklands.

She was a couple of miles from his hotel.

He didn't need to make contact.

The last thing he wanted to do was draw attention to her.

His plan was pretty basic, do some digging around while he waited for nightfall. Then he'd try to find her.

That meant he had a whole day to fill, and despite the promised charms of the city, he had no great desire to spend it sightseeing.

First thing on the agenda, act like an investigating officer – that meant developing the cover Law had established for him. And the only way he was going to do that was by making himself known to local law enforcement.

He had the contact details for a female officer, Mirjam Rebane, who was dealing with the discovery of the body in the woods. She wasn't in the same jurisdictional territory as any of the officers working Irma Lutz's disappearance. That was a plus.

He also had Annja Rosen's contact details so he could verify her statement, but that could wait until tomorrow. He'd call later to make arrangements. Today was going to be all about the body in the woods.

He'd seen the smoke and scorched earth from the plane. The fire was a hungry bastard. The damage was brutal. And it was still burning. From up there, it still looked like it was out of control, but the news reports promised that wasn't the case. The sky was full of heavy smoke. He'd felt it in his lungs as he walked to the hotel; even though the air in the city itself looked fine it was obviously thick with smoke particles. What they needed was rain. A proper biblical flood to really drown the fire and reduce the risk of it picking up again.

Rebane wasn't surprised to receive his call, though she was unsure as to why he needed to visit in person given the fact she had nothing to tell him that wasn't already in the files. Nevertheless, an hour later he was drinking coffee on the other side of a table from the woman. The cafe promised better coffee than the homogenous chains that littered the city with their green-tailed mermaids. It was also quiet, meaning they could talk.

'It's a long way to come for a cup of coffee,' Mirjam Rebane said, her English flawless, though Peter caught a trace of an unexpected accent. She raised the cup to her lips even though the contents must be too hot to drink. Europeans, he was quickly coming to realize, all had asbestos-lined mouths when it came to their coffee-drinking. 'All the way from London?'

'Bonn.'

'You were in Germany?'

'We're based there now. Long story. Centralized investigation. It's meant to make the job easier.'

'You don't sound convinced.'

He shrugged. 'Judging by your accent it seems like you're a long way from home, too.'

'The curse of family, I'm afraid. My mother. She was from Liverpool. I've never set foot outside of Estonia. Not even to go and worship the sun. So, tell me, Mr Ash, how do you think I can help you?'

'It's a long shot,' he said, 'and there's no real reason to think your girl in the woods is mixed up in this in any way, but we've had reliable intelligence that young girls are being trafficked through Tallinn into the Eurozone.'

The woman pursed her lips. 'What do you need from me?'

'Anything you can tell me about Tallinn, really. Russian communities in the city. Places where girls might take refuge if they managed to escape the traffickers. Support networks. Anything that might be relevant. This isn't my patch. I'm coming in here blind.'

She nodded again. 'It's possible. But we must be honest for a moment, Peter, even if my colleagues were aware of such survivors, I'm not sure that they would be willing to talk to you.'

'It's got to be worth a shot.'

'I can make a few calls, but no promises.'

'That would be something. The Russian authorities aren't being particularly cooperative.'

'I can imagine. Do you need to see the body?'

'Only if you think I'm going to see something the pathologist missed.'

'Do you perhaps have superpowers? X-ray vision?'

'I have Laura,' he said, earning a laugh from Mirjam.

'Is she your boss?'

'We work together, let's put it that way,' he said, feeling that reflected a more accurate position. 'I'm a field agent, she's support staff, but the reality is she runs the show.'

She drained her coffee. 'Ah, so you just don't want to admit she's your boss? I know plenty of men like you.' Her grin took the sting out of the words. 'I'll give you a call this afternoon and let you know how I get on, who knows, you might get lucky?'

Peter resisted the temptation to say anything stupid, and instead, said his goodbyes.

When she was gone, he leaned back in his chair.

He fished out his phone and called the number he had been given for Annja Rosen.

There was no reply.

'Hi, Annja, my name is Peter Ash. I work in Eurocrimes with Frankie Varg. I'm in Tallinn and would like to meet up with you for a chat tomorrow if you're free? You can reach me on this number, any time. Thanks.'

Done, he punched in the 007 code to check on Frankie's position.

She was still down by the docks.

IN THE DARKNESS . . .

*T*he girl felt a sense of panic as she was lowered into the darkness, the harness cut tight beneath her arms. She accepted it. This was her test. Her challenge. The hole would not break her. She would stay true. All she wanted in this world was to be accepted, to be part of the family. John had promised her this was the final test, the hardest of all. So many had failed, but she was special. He promised her that, that she was special, that she could do this.

And she believed him.

She had arrived wearing a blindfold that covered her ears and nose as well. They didn't remove it until the door closed behind them and she stood in a narrow corridor.

She faced a stranger.

He was a brute. A giant of a man. But his voice was soft. Gentle even. Like his soul. 'We are all one family,' she said, trustingly.

'One World,' he assured her, even as he buckled her into a harness and lowered her down into the hole.

It was deeper than she could have imagined. Impossible for her to claw her way out of if she panicked.

'It will be over soon,' he promised, no more than a silhouette now. And still she felt herself sinking lower.

Fear.

She had to overcome her fear.

That was the test, surely.

But it was hard.

She clung on to the rope so desperately her knuckles hurt. Even as she hit the dirt floor she couldn't let go.

She struggled to stand, trying to orientate herself in the darkness. She craned her head upwards, to the opening where the brute looked down on her.

'Release the harness and step away from the rope,' he told her. A moment later the rope grew slack.

She unclipped the karabiner and let the rope dangle free.

Without a word the brute began to raise the rope into the last circle of light she feared she'd ever see.

'How long?' she called up.

He didn't answer.

An iron lid clanged down over the hole with a weight of finality as it slammed closed, burying her down there.

There was no light.

Her ragged breathing filled the darkness.

She heard the muffled sound of retreating footsteps, and the closing of a door, putting a second barrier between her and the world. No one was going to hear her scream.

She would not be afraid.

She wouldn't allow herself to give in to fear.

She would control her breathing, her heart. She would centre her

*being. She would survive this ordeal. She would please The Shepherd.
She would not fail him.*

But all she wanted to do was sob.

Would they hear her?

Would they punish her failure?

*No. She dug deep, casting aside any last remnants of doubt and
fear. She would leave the past completely behind her and be born
again, emerging from this hole when she was whole and new and
ready to embrace the family body and soul.*

She was hungry for that.

*She had come such a long way. All she wanted out of this life
was to find contentment in the loving arms of her family. To be one
with them. One world. One family. She didn't need anything else.*

*She took a shuffling step, her arms outstretched, feeling for the
limits of the space that had become her entire universe. One, two,
three, four, five tiny steps before her fingertips brushed against the
cold damp clay wall.*

*She brushed her hands over the surface. There was something
harder to it, old clay bricks, the coarse mortar and plaster exposed
around them dragged beneath her nails. Slowly, she inched along,
exploring. The wall was curved, like a well. She felt disorientated,
struggling to work out the size of the hole. There was only darkness
and confusion. All it had taken to remove the foundation of her life,
numbers, from her mind, was a few minutes in the dark.*

She fought down the panic.

*Her foot caught something. It clattered and rolled away from her.
She crouched down, fumbling around to try and find whatever it
was.*

*Her hands rubbed against a hard earth floor, feeling out, questing.
Eventually she found the metal bucket. It carried the faint aroma
of disinfectant that masked something more unpleasant.*

She hadn't considered the practicalities of the hole.

*It was her toilet, the reek that still clung to the metal a reminder
of the hole's last inhabitant.*

She set it down, close to the wall.

And then she heard the moving rats in the darkness.

The test really had begun.

TEN

Tasha spotted her eventually.

She waved and beamed a big smile at Frankie. Her own smile was a little smaller, a little more tentative.

The queue moved quickly. It was not long before it was her turn to be given her bowl of porridge and mug of coffee. As the woman had promised last night, it was nothing fancy but it was warm and filling.

'Glad you found us,' Tasha said.

'You were the best offer in town,' Frankie said. 'It was you or a couple of hours in the company of a particularly talkative tree in the park.'

She glanced over her shoulder. There were only a couple of people remaining in the queue. She stepped to one side to let them get to the counter to be served.

'Don't rush off when you've finished,' Tasha said. 'Maybe we could have a chat?'

'Sure.' Frankie grabbed a spoon and made her way back outside to where crates were being used as chairs like this was some hipster chic little coffeehouse down by the water.

The man with the dog, Tino, sat nearby, surreptitiously feeding the animal a spoonful for each one he took. He gave her a nod. Tino took it as an invitation to wander over and say hello. It was a simple little thing, but as she leaned down to scruff at the nape of his neck, she felt like she belonged, as though she'd passed some sort of test and become part of this group of kindred souls.

She felt like such a fraud.

She looked around. There were a few subtle signs that suggested the soup kitchen was being supported by One World, but no big overt signs or banners. The logo was printed on the mug she drank from, and no doubt she'd see it mirrored at the bottom of the bowl once she'd finished. It was clever. Not exactly subliminal, but not in your face, either. It got the word out without ramming it down anyone's throat. No one wants to be preached at when they're taking charity. It's humbling enough just to cross the threshold and hold out your hands for help.

There were a few flyers on a trestle table, but no one took one.

Most of the homeless had begun to drift away by the time Tasha came to sit with her, carrying a mug of her own.

'Time to close up?' Frankie asked.

'Soon,' Tasha said. 'There will be a few more stragglers over the next half an hour or so. That's the usual pattern.' Tasha took a sip of her coffee. 'We've always been able to give everyone who turns up something at least, we pride ourselves on that. There's always something for the hungry, even if we've got to run to the store for bread and cheese so we can make toasted sandwiches. Everyone gets something inside them.'

'What you're doing, it's really important.'

'Thank you.'

'How long have you been feeding people?'

'Here? Almost a year. Some people come back twice a day, they've come to rely on us. Others we see now and again. Some we only ever see once. Everyone deserves a little help to turn their life around. Some are just passing through, like you.'

For one fleeting moment Frankie wondered if the woman had seen through her and somehow knew she wasn't what she claimed to be.

'And *you're* here every day?'

'There's always a team of us, not always me. We're always looking for people to lend a hand, if you're hanging around.'

'I don't know how long I'll be here.'

'That's OK. Honestly. But if you think you could give us a hand tonight, well, that would be great. Added bonus, you wouldn't have to sleep in a shop doorway.'

Frankie looked up from her mug, not entirely sure what was on offer here.

Seeing her confusion, Tasha smiled. 'Don't get too excited. We'll be here until late, probably two, two-thirty, so a couple of us usually sleep in the back of the van for a few hours before we open up again for the morning. It's the same team tonight and tomorrow morning, then tomorrow night another team relieves us. It makes sense.'

'Women only?'

'In the van? Of course. There are men involved in the organization, but we find that it works better this way.'

'OK, I'm going to be rude now, but honestly, how can you afford
to do all this? It must cost a fortune to keep this going twice a day,
even if the day-to-day is run by volunteers.'

'We're funded by a charitable organization,' Tasha said. She took
another sip of her coffee. The logo was there for all to see. She
waved goodbye to one of the rough-sleepers over Frankie's shoulder.
'Have you heard of One World?'

'One World? Is that some religious thing? I'm not big on the
whole God thing,' she said, shrugging an apology.

Tasha offered Frankie a slightly patronizing smile. 'Not religious,
I promise you. It's more spiritual. They do a lot of good work in
the community. We're not their only initiative in Tallinn. There are
shelters, a women's refuge, all sorts of things aimed to try and
provide some little comfort to the lost. There'll be someone here
tonight if you'd like to find out more about what they do.'

Frankie shrugged, noncommittally.

'No catch, I promise.'

'In that case, it can't hurt, I suppose.'

ELEVEN

Annja Rosen listened to the message as soon as she left the
lecture hall.

She had found it hard to concentrate, and harder to follow
as the professors worked through their coding challenges. Irma, on the
other hand, had always been a bit of a savant with a computer in front
of her. She was just naturally gifted and understood the structures of
good code. More often than not she'd go over it with Annja back in the
flat, talking it over with her until she finally understood. And she always
made it seem so easy. She could see the strengths and weaknesses of a
single piece of code and extrapolate it in ways that Annja couldn't. She
could plug holes in a system's defences before anyone else even understood there were holes, whereas Annja had to work hard and bend her
brain to deal with this stuff. Still, as a graduate she'd get a good job.

The university attracted students from all over Estonia and beyond, laying a strong claim to being the best of the best as far as these ex-Soviet states were concerned.

'Hi, Annja,' the man's voice said. He spoke in English, no doubt a little slower than he would normally speak, but she had no trouble in understanding him. 'My name is Peter Ash.' He explained how he wanted to meet up for a chat.

She had hoped she was finished with it all after she'd talked to Kask. He hadn't seemed concerned or all that interested about Frankie Varg's initial approach. Indeed, he'd confirmed she was law enforcement so she couldn't see any reason not to meet Ash.

She called him back as soon as she was away from the rush of bodies trying to make their way across the quad between buildings.

'It's Annja,' she said. 'Annja Rosen. I can meet you tomorrow at eleven if that works for you. There's a cafe opposite the cathedral, the Alexander Nevsky. I can take my break at eleven, but I won't have long I'm afraid. Fifteen minutes or so. Is that OK?'

She had blurted it all out without taking a breath.

'That sounds fine,' he said. 'I'm sure we can get it sorted in fifteen minutes, probably less. As long as this place serves good coffee we're good. I'll be there early. There's a slice of cake in it for you.'

'No need.'

'I insist, really.'

'No, I meant there's no need to get there early,' she explained. 'I work there, part time. Coffee and cake on the house. I'll make sure there's a quiet table.'

'Perfect. See you at eleven then.'

TWELVE

It was mid-afternoon by the time Mirjam Rebane called back.

Back in his hotel, Peter had spent a couple of hours catching up on stuff Laura had sent through from Division.

'Good news,' she promised him. 'I've managed to find someone willing to talk to you.'

'That's great, I can't thank you enough,' he said. 'When and where?'

'I'll pick you up outside your hotel. Seven.'

'There's no need.'

'There's every need. He's only prepared to talk to you because I'm vouching for you. You don't see him without me there with you.'

'Fair enough. I'm staying at the—'

'Don't worry, I know where you're staying,' she said with a soft chuckle. 'You're not the only detective in town. I hope you're on expenses. You'll be buying dinner.'

He could still hear her laugh long after she had hung up. She'd got some cheek, which, to be honest, he liked. He was quite happy to pay, even if it wasn't on expenses. Not that he expected the conversation to lead anywhere. Still, what was it they said, fake it until you make it? That worked with a bust, too.

It wasn't like Frankie was sending up the Bat Signal, which meant she had everything under control.

He intended to take a walk around the city after dark, get a feel for the place. If Frankie was still sleeping rough he'd make sure she had something to eat and drink. They didn't have to chat. He could just drop twenty euro in her lap like he was trying to clear his conscience if it looked like she was making inroads.

Peter still had a couple of hours to kill, but absolutely nothing to fill it with. According to her geotag Frankie had spent most of the morning down by the docks. The little beacon that marked her presence had barely moved. If it wasn't for the fact he'd picked up her signal around the city centre a few hours later he'd have worried she'd ditched the phone and was out there, cut adrift. But she'd obviously made some sort of contact down there, because looking at his phone now it was pretty obvious she was heading back towards the docks.

He switched modes and put a call through to Laura back in Division.

'Evening, Law.'

'How's the Baltic?'

'Bracing.'

'And the digs?'

'Nice enough, but next time maybe we can spring for a sea view?'

'In your dreams,' she said.

'Has Frankie checked in?'

'A few minutes ago.'

'Anything of interest?'

'She's already cosy with a woman from One World. They made contact last night, invited her to visit their soup kitchen this morning. They've asked her to help out this evening.'

'Lucky break.'

'No such thing. Frankie had to sleep in a doorway and get pissed on to make contact, Peter.'

'Pissed on? The fuckers.'

'Yep. The guy doesn't know how lucky he was to walk away. She told me she barely stopped herself from chasing him down and breaking both his legs.'

'That's the Frankie we know and love.'

'This One World woman obviously saw it happen. So it bought Frankie some sympathy. What about you?'

'I've touched base with Annja Rosen. We're meeting tomorrow morning.'

'Good. How did she sound?'

'Shy, nervous. Like this was the last thing she wanted to be doing. We're meeting in the cafe where she works. I'm hoping the familiar surroundings will relax her. You know me, kid gloves.'

'I know you,' she said, though it didn't sound like that was a hundred per cent positive thing. 'Anything on the body from the woods?'

The call had very smoothly turned into a debrief. Laura was settling into her role, he realized. He wanted to say good for her, but figured it'd just make her self-conscious so kept his cheerleading to himself.

'I met the investigating officer who's been lumbered with it.'

'Mirjam Rebane.'

'She spoke *very* highly of you.'

'You know, I'm never quite sure whether you're taking the piss.'

'Deadly serious. You've got a fan. I think she wants to be you when she grows up.'

'Funny man.'

'She's picking me up later. We're going to meet someone from the Russian community. A runaway, I think.'

'OK. Keep me looped in.'

THIRTEEN

Maksim Kask was starting to think he was shit out of luck. He didn't like that feeling.

He'd been watching the bus stop for the best part of an hour with students coming and going.

It was a long shot. It had always been a long shot. There was nothing to suggest the girl was even in the university right now, never mind that she'd go straight home. For everything that it wasn't, Tallinn was still a capital city. There was life in it. She was young. She could have been out half the night screwing some stranger up against a wall for all he knew, or passing around a bong with a handful of other computer nerds talking about the latest madness of gamergate. It was a different life.

But she had to come this way, either by bus or walking. He hadn't missed her.

As far as he knew, now that Irma Lutz was gone, Annja Rosen lived alone.

That would make things easier.

He would have preferred longer to prepare, but he didn't have the luxury. She had to be taken care of tonight.

Eventually he saw a lone student walking towards him, burdened with a stack of books almost as big as she was.

The heavens opened above them. A single slash of lightning jagged across the sky, and immediately in its wake, in that echoing silence that followed the crash of thunder, fat rain drops came down. Hard.

He had to wait until she was closer before he could be sure that it was Annja Rosen, but as soon as he was, he turned the engine over and moved slowly towards the bus stop.

Kask rolled down the window and called, 'Annja!'

She ignored him, hurrying along.

He called again, and this time she turned. There was a moment where he thought she was going to bolt, then she recognized him.

'Can I give you a lift?'

He reached over and released the door, taking the choice away from her. It was the tiniest thing, but on such tiny things life and death pivot.

The splash of rain across the leather interior made her mind up for her.

She struggled to get inside, balancing the books, then managed to spill half of them into the footwell.

She started to apologize, but he stopped her.

'It's fine. Buckle up. I'll have you home in no time. Nice and dry. Lucky I saw you there.'

She fumbled with the seat belt and finally managed to get it to click into place. 'Lucky?' she asked as he pulled away from the kerb.

'Yeah, nothing important, really. I just wanted to let you know that I've managed to locate the statement you made and I've sent it over to Frankie Varg's office. She's probably got it by now.'

'That's good,' Annja said. 'But you could have called me. You didn't have to drive all this way.'

'It's fine. It was on my way.'

She didn't reply.

Annja stared straight ahead as the wipers tried to sluice the rain from the glass. In the couple of minutes they'd been in the car it had turned from a downpour into a deluge.

A woman in a yellow coat ran into the road in front of him, not looking or not seeing him through the torrential rain. Kask hit the brakes, hard. Annja reached out a hand to brace herself against the dashboard. There was a moment when he thought the rubber wasn't going to grip on the road and they were going to aquaplane into the woman, but mercifully, the wheels caught and the car stopped no more than a foot short of her.

'Jesus,' he said, not moving.

The woman in the yellow coat turned to stare in through the windscreen like she was daring him to hit her.

He just shook his head.

'Are you OK?' Annja asked, and for a moment seemed to mistake the headshake for an admission that he wasn't.

Kask waited for the woman to get out of the road, then pulled away. He put the radio on. Neil Finn insisted that everywhere he went he took the weather with him, which was just about the most ludicrous juxtaposition the deejay could have managed if he'd been trying. He would have laughed, but his mind was very much on other things.

Annja didn't say anything when he indicated to turn left. They were already halfway down the street before she said, 'This isn't the way I usually go home.'

'There's been an accident,' he lied, smoothly. 'I had to take a detour earlier. It didn't look like it was going to get cleared any time soon. I know a workaround. It'll only take an extra couple of minutes, don't worry.' Why would she? He was a cop. She trusted him. He was one of the good guys.

But that trust was only going to last so long.

'Did you speak to Frankie?' she asked.

'No,' he said. It was better not to get caught in any specific lie. The trick was to keep as close to the truth as possible. That made it easier. 'We just sent the files over. I put a note in the email, apologizing that it was all my fault, even though it wasn't, you know, keep those international relations smooth.' He tried to make it sound conspiratorial, like he was letting her in on a big secret that he was a really great guy.

'Ah, I may as well cancel the meeting.'

'Meeting?'

He tried not to let the sudden swell of panic he felt inside reach his voice. He wasn't sure that he succeeded.

'Another officer from Eurocrimes wanted to talk to me about Irma. I figured they just wanted a new statement. I'm meeting him tomorrow.'

'He's coming here?' Kask's grip tightened on the wheel as his foot pressed a little harder on the accelerator.

'Tomorrow morning.'

It was all going wrong.

He needed her to buy his story. He needed the world to just forget all about this girl. Otherwise he'd never be able to sleep at night again. The Shepherd had made that pretty fucking obvious. It was her or him. And he had no intention of dying for a very long time.

'I can walk from here,' Annja said, even though she was further

away from her apartment than she had been when she'd got into
the car.

Her hands fumbled at the seat-belt clasp, ready to get out.

He couldn't let her do that.

He realized that the traffic lights up ahead had just turned red.
If he stopped she was going to get out. He tried to think. He needed
to make sure she stayed in the car. The only thing he could think
of was to move faster, and risk running the red light, hoping nothing
was coming the other way. He floored the accelerator, crossing the
junction to a chorus of blaring horns and the screech of crunching
metal. There was no impact. No collision. The rear-view mirror was
filled with two cars locked in an expensive dance of crushed metal
and burned rubber in the middle of the junction.

'Let me out!' Annja screamed at him, but he ignored her.

The second scream broke something inside his head. 'Shut
up!' He lashed out, a single punch slammed into the side of her
mouth. Her head jerked back, hitting the passenger window every
bit as hard as he'd just hit her.

She wasn't moving.

He checked her seat belt. It was still locked.

The half-formed idea that had been running around his head
started to solidify. A missing piece fell into place.

He knew what he had to do.

FOURTEEN

T he rain looked like it could fall for ever.
It was exactly what the wildfire needed, but it was the
very last thing Frankie wanted.

She'd barely reached the row of old customs warehouses that
opened up into the docks when the heavens opened. In the three
hundred metre dash to the soup kitchen the entire road had trans-
formed into a shimmering lake. The rain drummed on the surface
so hard it bounced ten centimetres back into the air on each tiny
impact.

Tasha was already there, along with another couple of young

women. She couldn't be sure if they were the same ones from that morning. As much as she hated to admit it, they all looked the same. Rain hammered on the roof of the van and filled the awning that extended from the side building to provide a little shelter for anyone who did brave the conditions.

'We won't get many tonight,' Tasha said, looking out through the rain-streaked window. 'At least not while it's like this. If it lets up later we might see some familiar faces. Plenty of people would rather go hungry than get soaked. People tend to forget they've got to sleep in those clothes, and it's not just that it's uncomfortable, they're risking pneumonia.'

'What do you need me to do?'

Tasha introduced her to the two other women. It didn't take more than a couple of stumbled sentences and muddled meanings to know they had little in terms of a common language. Still, a juggling act of English, French, and German, along with plenty of pointing and miming, got them working as a team.

Frankie's next few hours consisted of trimming, peeling, and chopping vegetables, most of which looked like they were past their best. Tasha explained that it was stuff that had passed its sell-by date and been donated by supermarkets – it was still good, she assured her, and this was much better than throwing it away. Once it was chopped and mixed into the massive vat of soup they were making, it could just as easily have been Fairtrade eco-friendly natural produce for all anyone could tell.

Occasionally one of them would venture out to push the gathered water from the awning that sagged under the weight. By the time they'd finished the prep and had the vat of soup simmering away the rain had at least eased a little, downgrading from biblical to tropical storm. It was hard work. She could tell the others were grateful for the extra pair of hands.

Tasha produced coffee as they cleared the scraps away.

The two girls who'd been working alongside Frankie disappeared out into the rain, running, hands over their heads like that could possibly keep them dry, across the road to the van.

'You've done well,' Tasha said as she handed Frankie a mug. She saw Frankie's puzzled look and added, 'Smoke break. You want to join them?'

'I'm OK.'

'I'm glad you came back.'

'I'm sure you would have managed without me.' She saw the first patches of blue sky through the rain. 'Maybe tonight won't be a washout after all.'

'That's good. We want the speaker from One World to see how much good we're doing. I hate when they come and there's no one to feed. You know. It makes it look like they're wasting their money and we need them to keep funding us if we're going to do any real good here.'

'I can understand that,' Frankie said.

As if on cue a couple of bedraggled men shuffled around the side of the warehouse across the way. She'd noticed that a lot of homeless people seemed to have the same beaten-down walk.

'You want me to give the others a shout? All hands on deck?'

Tasha shook her head. 'I'm sure we can manage for a while. Let them have a break.'

Frankie nodded. It was the answer she'd hoped for; keeping Tasha to herself for a while, now she was talking, meant she had a better chance of hearing the One World spiel and what it was that convinced kids like Irma Lutz to sign their lives away. Because she didn't get it, and she was never going to get it. She'd see half-forgotten celebrities making a fool out of themselves on television proclaiming how One World had saved their lives, how they'd been in the grips of barbiturate abuse before the drugs programme had helped them kick the habit and find themselves, and all she could think was that they'd swapped one drug for another. They all seemed so happy; but that could just as easily be said for the turkeys on the way to the slaughterhouse for Christmas.

The men came in from the rain, stamping their feet on the mat and apologizing as they left a trail of wet footprints up to the counter. Tasha grinned and told them they could mop up after they'd eaten if they felt that bad. That earned a couple of grins, which they exchanged for generous helpings of stew and a couple of crusty bread rolls.

Almost as soon as they were in their seats another man arrived, and another.

Before long there was a steady flow of people coming and going. The two smokers seemed to be on the longest cigarettes ever, but Frankie and Tasha coped fine by themselves.

After maybe an hour, the rain was down to a drizzle. There was a fine mist in the air that fogged the sea out beyond the docks, making the little hole-in-the-wall soup kitchen seem like it stood on the edge of civilization and out beyond it, in the mist, there'd be dragons.

She heard it before she saw it – a limousine. It came slowly around the corner, between the bonded warehouses, and pulled up a hundred metres or so away, the engine idling before the driver killed the lights. Visitors. Tasha took a moment to straighten her apron and hair, making it pretty obvious she wanted to look her best for whoever was in there.

Frankie ladled out another helping of soup as the two girls returned from their cigarette break.

Tasha stepped out from behind the counter and walked out to greet the two men getting out of the car. The fact that it also meant she had a minute or two alone with them to talk wasn't lost on Frankie.

She watched the exchange. The passenger greeted her warmly. Hand on shoulder. Not quite an embrace, but definite familiarity and ease. They talked. Tasha mostly, it seemed. Then she pointed in the direction of the window and the still rain bowed awning. The driver said little. There was no hand on the shoulder, no hugs, and he remained with the car. So, just a driver, not a bodyguard.

The two girls primped and preened themselves. It was embarrassing to watch. They were so painfully eager to meet the man, though how he was supposed to tell them apart given the whole might-as-well be twins thing they had going on, Frankie had no idea.

Frankie busied herself with stirring the vat of simmering stew and tidying the counter. Once he reached the van, the newcomer exchanged pleasantries with the women. She assumed that meant he was fluent in at least a few of the hundred and twenty languages spoken in the ex-Soviet states. That in itself was noteworthy.

Tasha brought him inside.

'And this is Ceska,' she said, once they were through the door. 'She's only just joined us.'

Frankie felt a sudden urge to deny having joined anything, but she let it slide.

Right now, all she could see was the good that Tasha and the others were doing, and how much it was appreciated by those who needed it the most. This kind of thing, where people fell between the cracks, it should have been down to the authorities to keep them safe, but it wasn't. Governments couldn't cope when things left the realm of theoretical poverty and austerity. It was normal people who did that. People like Tasha. They gave of themselves. Their time, their friendliness and honesty. But most of all, their souls. They were just good people.

And that didn't fit with what she'd been expecting. She'd be the first to admit that. She'd come in prepared to judge them by the crackpot doctrine spouted by their so-called preachers. But that was a mistake. People like Tasha weren't all bug-eyed religious fanatics. They were just good people who wanted to help.

Lesson learned.

Frankie looked up from what she was doing, making eye contact with the man for the first time. His eyes were a striking blue steel. It was as though they looked *inside* her, that somehow he could tell what she was thinking simply by staring into her soul. Without the disarming smile he offered, that look would have been enough to ice the blood in her veins.

Frankie reached out, shaking his hand when he offered it.

'Hello, Ceska. That's a beautiful name,' he said, his voice rich with a softness and warmth that was both kind and sensual without the words themselves being seductive. He was a charming man. It was easy to imagine him as a politician or a preacher, someone that inspired dedication and love by charisma alone.

But then, he was a man of faith.

FIFTEEN

I f anyone had seen her as they drove along they would have assumed she was asleep.

For a moment Kask thought, or rather hoped, that she was already dead. He didn't want to think about what he was going to have to do to her otherwise. But he was never going to be that lucky, was he? A single punch to silence her and save himself? Never.

It wouldn't be the first time he had taken a life, but it would be the first time he'd done it like this, like a murderer. The words they always used made it sound so detached, in cold blood, ruthless killer, but it was nothing like that. He felt like his skin was on fire. Because this wasn't just. This wasn't in the line of duty. This was different. The only other person he had killed had deserved it – as much as anyone could deserve death. Killing him had saved the country tens, maybe hundreds, of thousands of euros in a trial and sentence, and more in terms of lives and the human cost. The man was a monster. He didn't deserve a prison cell. He didn't deserve to stand up in court and spout his racial hatred and supposed genetic superiority. No, killing him had done the country a favour.

And that was how he slept at night.

But the girl was different. Nothing that applied to that monster of a man could be said about her. Her only crime was being friends with the wrong person.

If she could have just shut up . . .

But he couldn't trust that she would, not now she had another visitor from Eurocrimes coming to stir things up. He had to do something. And something meant silence. He drove on, telling himself he had no choice. The radio mocked him, this time the Gin Blossoms promised to follow him down. Meaning hell, they were telling him he was going to hell. He wanted to shriek – not just scream, shriek – something really primal, just let it all out. But he couldn't. He had to think smart. He had to protect himself. It was absolutely key that he could never be implicated in her death. He couldn't worry about his soul.

He knew a strip of waste land on the edge of the city. The place was free of CCTV. He knew it would make a good dumping ground for the body because he'd been there on the other side of the job, an investigator staring down at a mutilated corpse and realizing just how little the place offered in terms of help for his investigation.

He would have preferred to make her body disappear completely – acid or lye – then dump the waste with the other toxic crap the petro-chem companies poured out into the sea. But another disappearance, two girls from the same flat, would raise too many questions, and questions didn't bring closure.

Kask took a circuitous route through the outskirts of town, cutting through residential areas he knew were CCTV black spots.

The rain had almost stopped by the time he reached his destination. The tower blocks on the edge of town disappeared in mist. He killed the wipers, changing the quality of sound inside the car immediately.

The woman gave another groan and shifted in her seat. She made no move to fight the belt or struggle to escape, but that didn't mean she wasn't fully alert and faking it.

He pulled the car to a halt and jerked the handbrake on.

Annja shifted in her seat, turning her head.

He didn't want her to open her eyes. That was going to make this so much worse. He needed to get it done before she came round.

Kask slipped out of the car.

He ran around to the passenger side.

Before he could reach for the door, she threw it open, slamming it into him. The impact was enough to send him slipping and slithering back in the mud as he lost his footing. She tried to make a run for it, but the rain had turned the ground into swampland. Every step was a half-slide, the mud sucking up around his ankles as he chased her.

She didn't get far.

He drove his fist into the base of her spine. Her head went back, her back arched, her legs buckled as she stumbled, but didn't fall. The blow cost him precious distance in the chase. Somehow, Annja found the strength to carry on running, the mud gripping her trainers as her arms and legs pumped furiously. No onlookers were going to mistake what was happening this time. Kask stumbled after her, and for a second thought about taking his service weapon out and shooting her in the back, but that was a dumb fantasy that would have put him in prison before the week was out.

It needed to be more intimate than that.

Face to face, like lovers do . . .

Kask found a burst of speed as Annja began to flag, muscles burning, and hit her again – higher this time, in the base of the skull. She fell and he was down on top of her in a heartbeat, straddling her body, using his weight to pin her. She looked up at him. She looked into the very heart of him, her eyes seeing the darkness before it descended.

He had to do it now.

He had to end it.

Kask slipped both hands around her throat, all of his weight pressing down on her, and squeezed. Tighter and tighter, saying, 'Sorry,' over and over, as he willed Annja Rosen to stop breathing.

She didn't die quietly. She fought desperately, her heels scrambling against the mud, cutting channels. Her hands thrashed wildly, clawing at his arms as she tried to throw him off her, reaching for his face, trying to mark him, to get a scratch, anything that might mean she could fight him from the other side.

But then it was over.

Kask kept his hands locked around her throat long after she fell motionless.

He knew she was dead.

But he couldn't let go.

What came next was worse.

But it had to be done.

SIXTEEN

Peter Ash was watching a busker playing the Beatles on piano-accordion as Mirjam Rebane's car pulled up at the kerb.

He wouldn't have recognized the driver but for the fact she said, 'Get in.' Out of her work wear she was a different person. He felt seriously underdressed in his jeans, shirt with plain white T-shirt underneath. She gave him the once over as he clipped his seat belt into place, but made no comment.

'So, who are we going to meet?'

'You can call him Ivan.' Though she pronounced it Ee-vahn, he knew it was going to come out of his own mouth sounding much more British.

'And that sounds like made-up name if ever I heard one.'

'He only agreed to meet you on the condition you were not told his real name.'

'But knows that I'm a cop?'

'He does.'

'And he knows you're a cop, too?'

'He does.'

'So what's the difference?'

'He trusts me. He doesn't know you. And given the treatment some of his fellow Russians who've spoken out against their countrymen over the last few years have received, I think we can forgive him, don't you?'

'Former KGB,' Peter said. It wasn't a question. It was a logical leap, and he wasn't entirely sure what had tipped him off to it, but he was sure that's what they were dealing with. It would explain a lot, including Mirjam's role. She didn't confirm or deny, which was confirmation enough for him.

The KGB itself might no longer exist, at least in name if not nature, but there were plenty of former officers who had chosen to live out their lives away from the country they had once pledged themselves to when the alternatives included Novichok.

'So, how much have you told him about me?'

'Just that you work for a cross-border force, and that the scope of your investigations is on stuff that moves from country to country. He's smart enough to work out what that means. He said he couldn't understand why Europe would want to repeat the mistakes of the Soviet Union.'

'Really?'

'Ha. No, not really,' she smiled. 'He said it was his duty to stop girls from his country being exploited by the West. I think you should hear the rest from his mouth. And don't worry, his English is better than yours.'

Peter smiled at that. 'Are you sure you aren't related to Laura?' Before she could answer, he asked a second more realistic question, 'Where are we meeting him?'

'There's a little Italian I know.'

'Is it Frankie Dettori?'

She turned to look at him, brow furrowed in confusion, not getting the joke.

'Close?'

'Almost there,' she said.

Peter was sure that he caught a glimpse of a smile at the corner of her mouth.

SEVENTEEN

Karl Tamm lived in a bedsit in the worst part of the worst part of town. Everyone around him was looking to get out. Not Karl. This place was a little slice of heaven for him.

Kask hadn't needed to look up his address, he had been there often enough on official business.

Tamm had been out of prison for almost a year, but all that meant was that he'd had a year of giving them the runaround. The guy was a serial recidivist. He had a taste for girls he couldn't have. Back in the old country he would have been gelded like a horse, but Kask wasn't so sure the guy needed his balls to fulfil the kind of sick cravings he had.

Estonia didn't maintain a sex-offenders register, but that didn't mean they didn't monitor the activities of ex-cons who'd served their time if they'd done a certain kind of crime.

Anything else would have been wilfully naive. They weren't stupid. They knew what he had was a sickness and that he wasn't about to suddenly be healed. There were no miracle cures for people like Karl Tamm.

He was always one of the first they pulled in when a violent sexual assault took place.

Kask was convinced Tamm was on the hook for the deaths of two women they hadn't been able to prove – and almost certainly others they didn't know about yet. Which was the whole reason for his visit now.

Tamm's battered yellow Volvo was parked up kerbside, a few metres away from Kask's rear window. It had a thicker layer of rust than the last time he had seen it, he was sure.

Kask waited in his own car.

He took the time to carefully put on a pair of latex gloves from the box he kept in the glove compartment for crime-scene investigations. Sooner or later Tamm would leave his place. He wasn't going to stay in there all night. He needed to eat, and Tamm didn't cook. He was a takeaway junkie – though more often than not it wasn't food he brought home with him. But then, this part of town had the broadest menu when it came to meat. Ten minutes in either direction he'd have his choice of Asian, Scandinavian, Russian, or local whores. Ladyboys and twinks cost a little more, because they were rarer. Paying someone to piss on them or fist them or whatever his kink was bought their discretion, too. None of the working girls complained about him, even if he liked the rough stuff. Last time, Kask had searched his computer and found all sorts of torture porn, the kind of stuff that made the gut churn. As far as Kask was concerned some of the stuff was one step from snuff, but it obviously did it for Tamm.

The other thing about Karl Tamm was that he liked his mementos.

That had stuck in Kask's mind.

He sat back, listening to the music. He caught words like sulphur, vultures, and the dark star of his heart in the lyrics and couldn't be sure if the promise of 'something good' that the singer promised him wasn't actually his own mind fracturing to create some sort of black personality to goad him on.

The song changed, and changed again, before Tamm came down the steps to the street. At the bottom, he turned away from Kask's car, showing him his back. He wasn't sure Tamm would have recognized him, but fate removed that concern.

He didn't have long, but he didn't need long.

Kask watched the brute of a man turn the corner at the end of the street and gave it a silent count of thirty before he got out of the car. He crossed the road, heading for Tamm's building.

The man lived on the top floor, which increased the risk of him being seen going up and down the stairs, but that couldn't be helped. The thing about places like this was that people kept to themselves. No one was big on eye contact. They didn't tend to know their neighbours. It made sense. They all had their secrets and they wanted to keep them secret. Friendships almost always resulted in saying something you regretted in an unguarded moment – and with someone like Karl Tamm that regret meant cleaning up the mess. It was just easier if strangers kept away from their own door. They weren't going to press their eyes up to the fish-eye lens of the peephole to spy on whoever was coming and going. No one wanted to be a witness.

Kask kept his head down as he entered, heading straight up the stairs, taking the risers two and three at a time, like he belonged. No hesitation. No looking at the names on the board downstairs to work out who lived where.

He heard someone moving about on the second landing.

He hesitated, missing half a step, then heard a door slam and carried on up.

There were only two doors on the top floor.

Kask slipped a bump key off his wallet and was inside in a moment. That was the thing about places like this, they weren't locked up tight. Most of the landlords fitted cheap locks because they were easy to break into without causing any damage, so when their tenants defaulted on their rent, getting them out was less hassle. The only people who fitted decent locks were the drug dealers, which always amused Kask because anyone breaking into their places was signing their own death warrant.

He pushed open the door and slipped inside, closing it softly behind him.

It had only been seven weeks since he'd last searched the room, and very little had changed because Karl Tamm had very little. Even so, his proclivity for collecting pretty much guaranteed there would be something tucked away here that would link him to another crime. It was habitual. There was no way he wasn't doing what he'd always done. Kask didn't care. He'd care later, when he came back following the leads he was laying down. And he'd enjoy himself when he did, because people like Karl Tamm deserved all the shit the world threw at them.

He caught a glimpse of himself in the mirror and nodded.

He was a good man. Getting Tamm off the streets was good for everyone.

Dim amber streetlight filtered in through the grubby windows. He didn't need to turn on a light. He hadn't come to steal anything.

He saw what he needed: a place to hide something.

It didn't have to be a good place, just somewhere Tamm wouldn't look for a few hours.

He squatted down in front of a battered chest of drawers, pulling the bottom drawer all the way out and putting it down on the floor beside him.

He felt into the void beneath it, hoping he'd stumbled upon Tamm's secret place, but there was nothing in there. It didn't matter.

He pulled the polythene evidence bag from his pocket and upended it, emptying its contents into the bottom of the chest before sliding the drawer back into place.

Kask was done here.

It would be more than enough to convince any judge that Karl Tamm had killed Annja Rosen.

EIGHTEEN

'So you're our fresh blood?' the man said.

'I guess I am,' Frankie agreed. His personality was strangely compelling. She'd been in his orbit less than a minute, but already she had an idea of what it was that drew the lost and lonely to him. And he was smooth. Slick. She doubted they'd have a clue they were being manipulated. They taught this kind of stuff back in the academy for use in interrogation; it was harder to walk away from something you had agreed to than it was to say no in the first place, so the skill was in getting that first yes out of someone. It was how a lot of places, like gyms, recruited and held on to their members. It was a running gag how tough it was to leave a gym, but the same could be said for everything from mobile-phone contracts to satellite TV. They all used specialist customer-retention teams. It was almost cult-like in how they clung on to the not-so faithful.

She wasn't sure of his accent, but then it wasn't always easy when it wasn't your mother tongue. American? Maybe. Canadian? He'd addressed her in English rather than Swedish, and she knew she'd told Tasha she was Swedish, so despite being an accomplished polyglot he'd chosen the language he was most comfortable with. Was that telling?

'That's right. Ceska Volk.'

'John,' he said. 'It really is a pleasure to meet you, Ceska. And it looks like you're fitting in well.'

'Just helping out,' she said. 'It's good that there's something like this around to help people. You can see how much we need it.' By we she meant the lost. 'And it's so good that you're helping to fund them.'

'I agree. And I'm really glad you think so. I like to come down here and visit Tasha, to see her working on the front line, to see how much of a difference she makes every single night. She's a special lady.'

'She is,' Frankie smiled.

The more he spoke the more she was convinced that John was Canadian rather than American. The differences were subtle without him hitting any of those obvious tells like 'aboot', which were a dead giveaway.

'May I ask you something, Ceska?'

'Sure.'

'Had you heard of One World before you met Tasha?'

'I'm afraid not, I'm sorry.'

He waved away her apology. 'Oh, don't apologize, Ceska.' She noted the repeated use of her fake name, like a hostage negotiator trying to form a bond between them. He was good. 'Honestly. We don't go out of our way to seek publicity. We aren't doing this for thanks or praise. The work is enough.'

Frankie had to stop herself from glancing at the stack of leaflets that Tasha had put on the table a few minutes before he arrived. She'd taken the time to read one, not surprised to find that it extolled the good work that One World did not only in Estonia but in many other countries around the Baltic States, along with vague but impressive-sounding statistics from the African nations.

'Well, you know, maybe you should,' she said. 'If people knew how much you were doing it might shame the authorities into action.'

'Perhaps,' John said, holding her gaze for a moment. His piranha-smile even wider than it had been just a moment before. 'You might have a point there, Ceska. It's certainly food for thought. Tasha is right, you're exactly the kind of person we need to help us make a difference here.' He was nodding as he spoke, like he was having the best idea. 'I really do hope we'll see you again. There is so much that needs to be done. We run training camps to help our volunteers fulfil their potential. I have no idea if you'd be interested in that kind of thing, but if you think you might be, I'm sure Tasha will be able to tell you about them.'

He shook her hand again and moved on to speak to a couple of the men still at their table drying out.

One thing about John speaking to her in English, given the

seeming communication barrier between her and the smokers, was she was almost sure they had no idea what she'd just been offered.

Through the window, she saw a homeless woman, popsocks down around her swollen ankles, approaching the soup kitchen. She gave John's driver a withering look as she waddled past him. Frankie remembered her from breakfast and greeted her with a warm smile as she came in through the door. She realized she wasn't playing a part; she was genuinely glad to see her. She'd made it through the day, and for people like her every day was a win.

For the next few minutes Frankie was deep in conversation with the woman. She spoke in faltering English and mainly had complaints about the stupid weather, burning up the countryside and drowning them at the same time. Frankie nodded along and almost missed John's departure. The car was obviously some kind of hybrid, the engine was virtually silent as it was summoned into life.

She watched him drive away.

'I think he likes you,' Tasha said as she placed a hand on Frankie's shoulder.

'Of course he does, look at her, she's an angel,' the old woman said, offering a toothy smile. She offered the two smokers a considerably less approving glower as they disappeared for another cigarette.

'That she is,' Tasha agreed. 'You can see where she cut her wings off.' She winked at the old woman as she waddled over to an empty table with her hands cupped around the bowl of thick stew.

'John was right, though. Think about it. There's a place for you here. And a bed. You could be a real asset. You've got a wise head on those shoulders of yours.'

'If I had a wise head do you think I'd be sleeping on the streets?'

'Sweetheart, not having a home doesn't mean you're stupid. It's just circumstance. You see Leon over there? The guy with a ring of hair like a monk? He used to be a university lecturer. Smartest man I've ever met. And yet he's down here eating my soup because without it he'd starve. Sometimes life just takes a wrong turn. A run of bad luck and you end up in freefall. Sometimes we can't help people. We have two hundred suicides a year in this country, which doesn't sound a lot for a country, but the reality is we have a relatively small population at 1.3 million people. By population size we're the 157th largest country in the world, but with a rate of twenty suicides for every 100,000 people we've got the seventh highest suicide rate in the world.'

'Jesus . . .'

'It gets worse when you break it down. Ten per cent of all school children are reported to have suicidal thoughts. Think about it. Ten per cent. That's the future of this country, and ten per cent of them don't want to be here tomorrow. A third of all girls in Estonia are reported to have mutilated themselves in some fashion. The waiting lines for help are months long. The state can't help. I just wish there was *more* we could do.'

'John mentioned a training camp? Is that for counsellors and stuff like that? To help these kids? I'm not a psychologist,' Frankie said, hoping she wasn't pushing too hard, too soon. It was a delicate balancing act between being keen and being natural. They'd expect her to have questions. But it was important she came across as the kind of person they wanted her to be.

'Psychologists know nothing, not really, they're charlatans. They pretend they can help you by getting you to share your secrets, but they're not helping anyone but themselves get rich.' She said it with surprising vehemence. 'There's a place in the forest, we call it the compound, but it's more like a training camp where you take instruction and get to learn more about what One World does. The Shepherd helps us to truly grasp our full potential and realize the possibilities this life has to offer. I think you'd love it, Ceska. You get to share ideas, talk to people like you, brilliant, vibrant souls, you get to think about what you would do if you could change the world.'

She resisted the temptation to make a crack about song singing and holding hands. Hanging out with Laura and Peter all the time was having an impact on the way her mind worked. 'Have you been there?'

'I have. A long time ago.'

'How long do the camps last?'

'A week or so usually. But if they see something special in you, a skill, or talent, you might be chosen to join a second group, for more intensive training.'

'Can I think about it?'

'Of course you can, there's no hurry. But – and you might want to consider this, but don't think I'm pushing you – John mentioned that there's one starting tomorrow. I can ask him if there's a space if you're interested?'

'Tomorrow?'

'Don't fret,' Tasha said with a smile. 'It's not now or never. They run a lot of these retreats. It's just that if they're short-handed some of the activities don't work so well, you know?'

'Can I sleep on it?'

'Of course you can, Ceska. I can give him a call after breakfast if you fancy it. And if not, well, then we can worry about what we're cooking tomorrow night. It's all good.'

Frankie nodded, noticing a few more stragglers shuffling their way towards the door.

'Action stations, kiddo,' Tasha said, grinning. 'We can talk about it later.'

NINETEEN

The restaurant was closed, but that didn't stop Mirjam walking straight to the door and rapping on the glass.

A few seconds later it opened.

The man who let them in had obviously modelled himself on the Italian plumber from that old video game. He hugged Mirjam and kissed her on both cheeks. His welcome for Peter Ash was less effusive. He shook Peter's hand, pumping it a couple of times, both of his own meaty hands closed around Peter's. The smile never left his face.

'Come in, come in,' he said, accent thick in those repeated words, and led them to the only table that was occupied.

'Hello, Ivan,' Mirjam said. 'This is my colleague, Peter Ash, the man I was telling you about.'

Ivan rose and stepped out from around the table to embrace her like a long-lost friend. He nodded to Peter, then returned to his seat.

The Italian left them to it, scuttling away to the clatter of pans in the kitchen.

'So, shall we get right down to it, Mr Ash?' Peter nodded, taking a seat at the table. 'First, you need to understand, I'm not in touch with any of my former colleagues, so I cannot broker a meeting if that is what you were hoping?'

Peter shook his head. 'I've got zero interest in the old country, Ivan. What happens there is someone else's problem. What I am concerned about is what's happening here, in Estonia, and how it spreads into the rest of Europe.'

The big man nodded. 'You think that Russian girls are being trafficked? And you think I can help?'

'Mirjam thought you might be in a position to.'

'Well, I can tell you this much, everything you can imagine is true. Or it was. What I don't know is if it's still happening.'

'And you have evidence?'

'A witness.' Peter nodded, but didn't say anything, letting the man talk. 'I know a girl who came into the country this way. She managed to escape the traffickers.'

'Is there any way I could I speak to her?'

'With your mouth is usually the easiest way,' Ivan said, earning a snort from Mirjam. Peter just smiled, it was the kind of smart-arsed crap he'd come out with right before someone gave him a slap. 'But all in good time. The issue, of course, is that she's here illegally. No papers. No visas. No permission to stay. I wouldn't want to cause her distress or make her life any more difficult than it already is, you understand?' His flicked his gaze towards Mirjam and back.

Peter took that as his cue. 'We're only talking hypothetically.'

'Mr Ash has limited jurisdiction here, Ivan, and no powers of deportation or repatriation without the cooperation of the member state. He can't simply overrule the Human Rights Act.'

'As inconvenient as that can be at times,' Peter said with a wry smile.

'That is good to know, but you have considerably more power here,' Ivan said.

'I do,' Mirjam agreed. 'And there is a limit to what I can turn a blind eye to, so if you do arrange for Peter to sit down with your contact I don't want to be there. It's better not to know than to have to lie.'

'Then perhaps you have a craving for nicotine?'

She nodded and left them to it.

'She doesn't smoke,' Ivan said.

'She's good people,' Peter agreed.

'That she is. If I were twenty years younger I would *still* be too old for her, but I'd happily make a fool out of myself trying to convince her otherwise.' Ivan laughed for the first time since Peter had entered the restaurant. His demeanour shifted. 'I am very protective of Mirjam. I was forced to leave my daughter behind. She has taken the brunt of my parental guilt. I would hate to think you might be abusing her good nature.'

Peter met his gaze and knew he was looking into the eyes of a man who had both tortured and killed people he didn't believe. 'I'm not interested in punishing victims. I want to stop the people behind this.'

Ivan said nothing for a moment, seeming to weigh his honesty on some invisible scale, then said, 'I believe you.'

'You'll arrange for us to meet?'

'I will reach out to her, but I won't force her to talk about anything she doesn't want to.'

Peter nodded. 'She can walk away at any time. You have my word.'

'If you betray either of us I will find you, and I will kill you.'

'I don't doubt that for a moment,' Peter said, holding his gaze until finally the big Russian finally laughed, his face broadening into a wide grin.

'I like you,' Ivan said. 'I don't say that very often.'

He raised a hand as if summoning a waiter, and a few moments later Peter heard soft footsteps coming up behind him.

He didn't turn around.

A thin, waif-like girl barely out of her teens joined them. She carried her ghosts in her face.

'This is Tanya,' Ivan said, and to the girl, 'This is Peter.'

Peter nodded, but made no move to make contact. The girl stood with her arms wrapped around herself. She sank down into the chair beside the Russian.

'Peter would like to ask you a few questions. You don't have to answer any, do you understand?' She nodded. Ivan inclined his head slightly, turning the conversation over to Peter.

'Hello, Tanya. Can you tell me how long you've been here?'

She shrugged. 'Six months.'

'Did you know where you were going when you left Russia?'

'Ukraine,' she corrected. 'I came from Ukraine, not Russia.'

'I'm sorry,' Peter said.

She shrugged. 'Not important. Most English people don't know the difference. I was supposed to be going to London. I had been learning English for two years so I could start a new life there.'

Peter nodded. It wasn't a surprising story. 'You speak it very well,' he said, earning a flicker of a smile.

'Some of the other girls thought they were going to other places. Then we found out the truth.'

'The truth?'

She chewed on her bottom lip, a curiously innocent gesture given what she was about to say. 'They said we owed them money. More than we had. They told us we were going to have to work it off. At first they said they had places for us as cleaners, and looking after children, but that was a lie. We were going to be made to have sex for money until they decided we had paid off our debt.'

It wasn't the first time he'd heard a similar story. It was a crude trap, but it didn't need to be any more sophisticated than that – take their passports, hold them hostage, keep them frightened, isolated, break them until they were willing to fuck strangers for money, thinking they were earning their freedom.

'How many of you were there?'

'Eleven to begin with,' she said. 'But one of the girls ran on the first night.'

'She got away?' Peter said, though it was much more likely that the opposite was true. Six months fitted the timeline for the burned body that had turned up in the wildfire. He needed to be careful with what he said next. The forensics division had reconstructed the dead girl's face, creating a digital model. The picture was in his pocket. He could put it on the table and ask her if it was the same girl, but it was a case of weighing up the cost of it. The moment he put that picture down on the table she'd know the other girl was dead. But didn't that girl deserve a name? Didn't her parents deserve to know what had happened to their little girl? Didn't they deserve closure?

Of course she did, but the best way to bring that about was to be careful now, to earn Tanya's trust and keep Ivan onside.

'Do you know where they took you?' he asked, before she could answer his first question.

'They called it the compound, but it was really just some cabins in the middle of the forest. We were there for a few days, they said they were training us, then they were going to move us somewhere else. They put us on a ferry. I don't know where they were taking us.'

'How did you get away?'

'I threw myself overboard. They thought I drowned,' she said. 'Do you think you can find the other girls? Can you save them?'

It was the kind of promise he didn't want to make, because there was absolutely no way he could keep it. 'I'll do my best. I can promise you that much.'

'I'm glad you didn't lie to me,' she said. 'People think that they should lie when you ask something like that. They think it makes things better. It doesn't.'

'Can I ask how you got involved with these people in the first place?'

'You mean: how was I stupid enough to get trapped in that mess? That's what you want to ask, isn't it? That's what I've asked myself every single day for the last six months.'

'I don't think you're stupid. Sometimes we want to get away from something so badly we don't give much thought to where we are running to, or how we're going to get there. Getting away is all that really matters.'

'And maybe that's when you realize that what you left behind wasn't really that bad,' she said.

'Sometimes, but not always. Sometimes what you left behind is a lot worse,' Peter offered, conscious that there was nothing to be gained by telling her there was a better life waiting for her in Ukraine. He had no idea what she'd run away from.

'And sometimes it takes a lifetime to realize you were in the wrong place all along,' Ivan said with a shrug, taking ownership of his own mistakes. Peter was surprised that he'd remained silent for so long.

She nodded and gave him a smile, a more certain one this time, but she still couldn't look him in the eye for more than a second before her eyes darted down towards her hands. 'This life might not be perfect, but it is better than the one I had before. I have friends here. But to answer your question, there were people who used to come round handing out soup and hot tea when I was living on the streets.'

He nodded. 'They offered you a way out?'

She sniffed, still looking down as she nodded. 'At first they just offered food, but the more I got to know them the nicer they were to me. I thought we'd become friends. I'd help out, making food, serving people, then after a while they said they could help me move to London, they had people there. I could have a new start. They could help me get work. I might need to start with stuff like picking fruit and cleaning toilets, the kind of work that no one in your country wants to do, but they could help me find somewhere to live. Like they said, a new start.'

'Thank you, I know it can't be easy to think about this again. Just one last question, the girl who got away? Do you remember her name?'

She looked up hesitantly, her eyes going to Ivan before she answered.

He nodded.

'Maria Bartok.'

TWENTY

'Did you get what you needed?' Mirjam asked as they drove away from the now shuttered restaurant.

'Apart from food,' he said. 'Not to sound ungrateful, but I could eat a horse. I'd kinda thought we'd get something to eat.'

'Do you think I got my glad rags on just to play chauffeur?'

Ten minutes later Mirjam pulled up outside another Italian restaurant, considerably more up-market than the one they had just left. 'Like I said, I'm just going to assume you are on expenses.' She offered a slight smile.

'It's that or the overdraft,' he said.

'Second mortgage might be more appropriate,' Mirjam said, leading him in. Half of the staff seemed to recognize her. Again, there were hugs and kisses, and genuine affection. He caught a couple of diners looking his way as they were led to a table in the corner where candles had already been lit. He was the only man in the place wearing jeans. Mirjam talked her way through the place, exchanging songbird sentences with the staff, until they were left with a couple of menus and a beaming smile from the departing waitress, who looked him up and down then nodded approvingly.

'Friends of yours?' Peter said when they finally had a moment alone.

'Something like that. The chatty one was my baby sister.'

'You might have said.'

'And spoil my fun?

'Fun?'

'I told them you were my new man. They are most impressed.' Now her grin was wide.

'I'm flattered, I think.'

'You should be, I'm out of your league.' Mirjam burst out laughing. 'You know what families are like. Mum and Dad have been on my back for ages, nagging about grandchildren and finding a nice man to settle down with. I thought I'd kill two birds with one scandalous stone.'

He nodded. 'There are worse fake girlfriends to be set up with,' he said.

'That there are. So, want to tell me what happened with Ivan when I was gone?'

'I'm putting two and two together here, but Tanya gave me the name of another girl. They were in some forest compound together six months ago. The other girl escaped on the first night.'

'And you think she's our victim?'

He shrugged. 'How many bodies can there be out there in those trees?'

'That's not a question you want to ask.' He couldn't tell if she was joking or not.

'Like that, is it?'

'Every country has its secrets,' she said, and all of a sudden he remembered that it was less than thirty years since Estonia had regained its independence from Russia. Sometimes it was too easy to forget just how radically the geopolitical world had changed since the early 90s.

'I've got a name. Next step is to try to find a picture and compare it with the electronic reconstruction we've got.'

'You didn't show it to her?'

'She's already been through enough.'

She looked at him then. He wasn't sure what was behind the look. Disapproval?

'A man with a heart,' Mirjam said, finally.

'Don't tell my partner that.'

'You did the right thing. If she'd walked into the police station to report a missing person, that would be different.'

'We both know that's not going to happen. You want me to run the name through the system here?'

Ash hesitated for a moment. 'Probably best if we leave it to Laura. I don't want to drag you into this.'

'I think I'm pretty much dragged into it, don't you, given that it's my corpse you're talking about. I'm beginning to think you don't trust me.'

'Would that be such a bad thing?'

'You're not going to tell me, are you?'

He shook his head.

'But you swear you'll tell me if there's anything I need to know?'

'Of course.'

While it seemed to satisfy her it was painfully obvious his refusal to share had damaged the level of trust between them. Her smile had faded a little. It wasn't going to be an easy fix.

'I did discover that old Russians have a certain way with death threats,' he offered with a straight face.

'He's a teddy bear,' she said.

'An ex-KGB teddy bear,' Peter said. He made a decision. 'It seems pretty clear that girls are being trafficked through Tallinn. They're being promised new lives in the West, then being trapped in the sex trade. We're at the gateway here. Once they're inside the EU anything becomes possible. A trip over to Sweden and then on to the UK, or south to warmer climates.'

'And they burn girls who try to escape them.'

It wasn't a question.

'I've got a feeling they do a lot worse than that,' Peter said.

'Are you sure there's nothing more I can do? I want to help, Peter. I'm not some fragile flower. I'm a damned good cop.'

'Well, right now there is one thing you can do for me.'

'Name it.'

'You can order for me, because I can't read a word of this.'

'You're such a dick,' Mirjam said, shaking her head.

'And there was me thinking I was being charming and a little funny.'

'I really should just say fuck you, Peter Ash, get up and walk away.'

'And yet you're still sat here.'

'You're really not that charming, you know?'

'But a little funny? Give me that, at least.'

She just shook her head. 'The *ossobuco* is to die for.'

TWENTY-ONE

K ask didn't sleep.

He knew that he wouldn't, so he'd spent the night sitting in the leather chair in his study that his ex-wife had bought him for his fortieth birthday. That was a different life. Or at least it felt like a different one. So much could happen in six years when it came to the world falling apart. He didn't recognize the man he had been when he looked in the mirror these days. Kask stared at the whisky bottle, knowing that if he opened it, he'd empty it, and that would be a dumb mistake this late in the game.

He needed to keep his wits about him.

Dawn's early light crawled slowly up the window frame. He needed to make the call before someone else found the body. He'd planned it out meticulously, setting things up like dominoes so that once one fell it would bring all the others down, but so much could still go wrong.

Twenty minutes later he pulled to a halt beside a payphone a couple of kilometres from where he'd dumped Annja Rosen's body.

Wearing a fresh pair of latex gloves, he dialled 112.

The emergency line was picked up on the second ring.

'There's a body,' he said without preamble. 'I was walking. I didn't realize what it was at first. My dog wouldn't leave it alone. Then I saw the arm and I realized . . .'

'Can I take your name, please, sir?' the woman on the other end of the line asked. He ignored her, pretending shock. It was a natural response to the discovery of a corpse.

'I don't . . . She's on the wasteground. She's dead. It's a she. I've never seen a body . . . I . . . I saw a car.'

'What kind of car?'

'A Volvo. Not a new one. An old model. It was rusty. Yellow.'

He gave her directions to the place, deliberately not perfect, because witnesses made mistakes. It was important that he was close enough for police find the body, but he wanted them to search. Laying it up on a platter was a mistake. 'I have to go. Find. Her. Please. She's alone out there. Please.'

'Can I have your name, please, sir?'

'I left my mother on her own.' He hung up before she could ask for his name again.

Kask headed back to the car to the sound of the payphone ringing. He had no intention of going back to answer.

He could still hear it ringing as he clambered back into the driver's seat. He turned the engine over and turned the music back on and pulled away, driving for a few minutes.

The police radio squawked into life.

He listened to the general calling all cars alert, until he was sure the dispatcher had the location right, before he began to circle back towards the scene. He had no intention of being first responder, or second, or even third.

He radioed in, 'I'm in the vicinity. I'll swing by and check it out,' and made sure he sounded just disinterested enough that it felt routine, then thought to add, 'Send an ambulance just in case.'

'Already en route,' the dispatcher told him.

As he turned towards the wasteland he realized that he was first on the scene.

He pulled up about three metres from where he'd parked when he'd dumped Annja's body.

In a moment of perfect irony he saw a dog walker approaching the corpse, being dragged towards it by a small, excitable dog. Kask thanked whatever god or devil looked after people like him. He watched the man approach the body, and saw that moment of understanding.

He had two choices now, drive away, and risk the old man describing his car to the first officers on the scene, or getting out of the car and going over to flash his badge. It wasn't much of a choice.

He walked across the field toward the old man and his dog.

'There's a body,' the old man called, seeing him.

Even from this far away it was obvious he was shaken up. Kask could see that he was trembling. He didn't know what to do, but then who did? Who stumbled upon a body in the wasteland and knew what they were supposed to do? Kask reached into his pocket for his badge and called, 'Police,' much to the relief of the old man.

'Have you touched her?' Kask asked, wincing inwardly as he realized he hadn't seen the body. He cast a glance in Annja Rosen's direction, unsure if it was actually possible to identify her sex from where they stood. Although the scrub grass was calf-high and higher in patches, there was no mistaking the fact they were looking at a naked woman.

Kask took a deep breath, steeling himself. He needed to be utterly professional about this, go through the procedures step by step, keep it straight.

In the distance he heard a siren from a squad police car and the different tone of an ambulance haring through the cramped streets. They couldn't know that they were wasting their time.

'Stay there please, sir,' Kask said, holding out a hand like he was dealing with the dog, not the man. He stepped onto the grass, careful to follow the same path he had used to dump the body, deliberately confusing the muddy footprints by walking in them.

He'd get a slap on the wrist for disturbing the crime scene, but he'd plead ignorance. All he needed to do was get to the girl, crouch down, and make a show of checking to see if she was dead or not before reinforcements arrived on the scene.

He had all the time in the world.

Kask walked in a slow circle around her, then again, this time not looking at the body but rather staring out over the wasteland as though trying to get a fix on where her killer could have come from and fled. It was good. Better than he had a right to hope for. His god was working overtime.

He crouched down beside Annja Rosen, and put his fingers to her throat. Her skin was already so much colder than he'd expected it to be.

He heard the first car pull up, followed a few seconds later by the ambulance.

He rose slowly to his feet, raising a hand to signal the uniform.

The officer shouted to him, but his voice didn't carry. The paramedics were unloading a stretcher from the back of the wagon as he shook his head, sure the gesture would carry more effectively than any shout.

He watched the man struggle across the muddy ground, another set of footprints to fuck with the tracks. Perfect.

'Can you step away from the body please, sir,' the officer repeated.

Kask didn't need twenty-plus years on the force to recognize someone who'd never seen a corpse before.

The fresh-faced young officer was already reaching for his service weapon, which was a mistake.

'I'm just going to get my identification out of my pocket,' Kask said, moving slowly to reach into his inside pocket for his badge.

'Keep your hands where I can see them,' the uniform said. 'Move away from the body. Walk back to the road.'

Kask shrugged and held his hands up, 'You're the boss,' he said, very deliberately following the same path back to the road he'd already walked twice.

He tried to keep the smile off his face.

A second uniformed officer waited beside the squad car. He was talking to the dog walker. Kask knew him.

'Maksim Kask? What the fuck are you doing out this way, man? This isn't your patch.' Which was the one flaw in his plan, but he had an answer. The Estonian Police and Border Guard was divided into three agencies, Central Law Enforcement, Central Criminal, and the Forensic Service, and divided into East, South, North, and West prefectures, with him operating out of Tallinn East, and this field being squarely in the jurisdiction of Tallinn South.

'Saving a girl from the walk of shame,' he said.

'Ever the fucking gentleman, eh, Max?'

'Not sure the ex-wife would agree,' Kask said with a wry smile.

'You know this guy?' the baby-face officer asked.

'You might wanna call this guy *Sir*.'

Kask turned around, his hands still raised. 'OK if I put these down?' He was happy to let the smile show now. They were all friends here, despite the macabre circumstances of their meeting.

'Sorry, sir, I had no idea,' the young uniform said.

'No harm, no foul,' he said. 'You did the right thing. She's several hours dead. We need to secure the scene and get on to the Forensic Service Centre, get the lab boys out here before things deteriorate.'

'Of course, sir. Straight away. I'll put the call in.'

He let the older officer take a brief statement from the dog walker, who couldn't really tell him much more than the fact his dog had dragged him through the scrubland, driven wild by the scent of the body. He hadn't seen it until he was on top of it. He looked down at his shoes, covered in mud, and seemed to realize he'd trampled all over the crime scene.

'Don't worry, when forensics get here we'll make sure your prints are eliminated,' Kask assured him.

He went back to his car and called it in, then settled in to wait until forensics arrived, along with the coroner.

By the time they arrived half a dozen officers had trampled across the muddy track making it all but impossible to distinguish one print from another. They weren't happy, but he really didn't give a shit. He was pretty sure he'd just got away with murder.

TWENTY-TWO

They talked through much of the night into the early morning. Tasha evangelized the camp and, to be honest, did a pretty good job of selling Frankie on it. But what was most interesting was how she danced around certain phrases, though she couldn't help but get carried away with her enthusiasms every now and then. That was the curse of the converted. She was so used to talking to those who shared her secrets, and saw the world through those Kool-Aid tinted glasses.

It wasn't until they were clearing away, the last mug of tea drunk, and they were on their own that Tasha asked, 'Can I trust you, Ceska?'

Frankie didn't immediately rush to say yes. She wanted to take her time with her answer, giving it the weight it deserved, because for a runaway trust was not lightly given. She had to force herself to be less decisive and assertive. More humble. Unsure.

She nodded.

'He saved my life,' she said. 'I was young and stupid. I was a runaway, like you. I'd packed my entire life into my car, an old battered estate car held together by sticky tape and a few prayers. I didn't know where I was going, only that I had to get there. So I drove. And, I'm ashamed to say, I drank. I drank a lot. It was easier than being sober. One thing you probably know about this country, there are a lot more trees than people. It was the heart of winter. We'd just had snow for three days solid. I was deep in the forest on a single-lane road that was just twists and turns and more twists when I lost control of the car on the ice and started to slew sideways, and no matter what I did, I couldn't stop. The car rolled onto its roof, and over again, and went off the road into a deep ditch. Something broke free, some bit of metal from the steering column or something, and it punched right through me. I knew I was going to die. There was no one out there, not in a million miles, and there was no way I could get to the hospital. I was just going to bleed out.

'But then he came to me. The Shepherd. He got me out of that car with his bare hands. I don't know how. God was on his side. He laid me down on the side of the road, and I swear, he healed me. It's his gift. He laid his hands on the wound where the metal was still spearing out of my stomach. I can still remember the incredible heat of his hands as he healed me, Ceska.'

And Frankie didn't for a moment doubt that the woman *believed* what she was saying. Stress, shock, blood loss, there were lots of reasons to explain away a miracle.

Tasha looked at her like she knew what she was thinking, and said almost exactly the same thing. 'There are lots of ways to rationalize what happened out there, but I was there. I know what he did, Ceska. It's his gift. He healed me. And I've been with him ever since.'

She untucked the hem of her blouse and lifted it to reveal a mess of scar tissue, which seemed to back up her words.

'He's a very special man. I've seen him heal a girl of her burns with my own eyes. She was in so much pain, but he took that out of her. He is God's mercy on the earth, Ceska. We are blessed to have him in our lives.'

Frankie nodded.

Feeling self-conscious, Tasha busied herself washing up the last of the dishes while Frankie wiped down the tables.

Part of Frankie wondered why they didn't just let some of the regulars bed down for the night here. It was warm. It was dry. But it wasn't a shelter. She had no idea what sort of problems that would cause for One World. So instead, they wandered off to their own spaces. She'd heard a couple of them refer to them as home, which was a heartbreaking reality.

Finally, they locked up, and went out to the van. The air had that wonderful post-storm crisp freshness to it.

She opened up the van. There were a couple of inflatable mattresses in the back. As Tasha got in, she did a magic trick and produced a bottle of wine.

'We're worth it,' she said, reaching for a corkscrew. She produced two more One World mugs and filled them. No rules against alcohol, then.

Tasha didn't push the training camp on her. Instead they talked about dreams. What did Frankie want to do with her life? What would she change, fix, that kind of thing, and Frankie found herself being as honest as she could be because despite everything, she liked the other woman.

Eventually they fell silent.

A little while later Tasha rolled over. And after that her breathing settled into alcohol-induced snoring.

Frankie took the opportunity to fish the phone from the bottom of her rucksack. She slipped out of the van, gently closing the door so as not to wake the other woman.

The moon was incredibly bright in the sky. Some sort of super-moon. There seemed to be one every couple of months at the moment. She'd never heard the term until a few years ago. In the distance she heard the clang and clatter of work going on further down by the docks. She couldn't see any movement.

She walked away from the van to lean against a wall, and keyed in the three-figure code that would unlock the phone's true purpose. It only took a second for it to connect with Galileo, a single blip registering on her small screen. Her heart sank. She'd been banking on Peter being in Tallinn by now.

She wanted a face-to-face debrief with him, because she'd got plenty she needed to tell, and stuff she wanted to ask about the so-called training camp, but wishes and fishes and all that.

She was going to have to say yes and gamble that the others kept up with her.

She'd missed the significance of the single dot.

'Over here,' a male voice whispered from the shadows, soft enough to not disturb anyone who wasn't meant to hear it, loud enough to spook Frankie. The man stepped out of the shadows, the moonlight showing half of his face to the world.

'Peter.'

'I was beginning to think you'd fallen asleep. So, what's the score?'

Frankie kept it brief. 'Going well. Maybe too well.'

'Too well?'

She shrugged. 'It's too easy. They seem too desperate to befriend me. I can't help feeling like I'm being set up. I was found by Tasha.' She pointed to the van. 'She runs the soup kitchen. She fed me this morning, then asked me to help out tonight. She introduced me to someone from One World, they call him The Shepherd. I guess he's some sort of spiritual leader.' She told him the story of the miraculous laying-on of hands that had saved Tasha's life, and shrugged at her own scepticism. 'He's invited me to some kind of induction camp out in the forest.'

'I've just left a girl who escaped from human traffickers who was kept in a place called the compound – that was a place out in the forest. You do know what you're doing, don't you, Frankie?'

'I've got you looking out for me,' she said.

'We need to be realistic here, there's only so much you can do.'

'It might be nothing, but if that compound is their staging post we need to know where it is. And we need to know what's there. I'm not letting them get away with this, Pete. We're talking about vulnerable young girls. I'm ending this. You understand?' She knew he did. He'd almost lost his life six months ago because his own father had failed to protect the children he'd promised to, even if he was only a kid himself at the time. Those kinds of promises stick with you, like inheritances from one generation to the next. It was why Peter Ash was a cop. He wasn't that complicated, but what men were?

'When do you go?'

'After breakfast. I've just got to tell them I'm in.'

'Anything you need from me?'

'Fill Laura in. I want to be able to relax knowing her eyes are on me.'

He nodded. 'Want me to follow?'

She shook her head. 'No need to risk it. The last thing I need when I'm in there is you triggering some sort of perimeter alarm or getting spotted by a patrol. Trust me, Pete, I'm a big girl. I can look after myself.'

'Mitch told me,' he said, with a grin. It was the first time he'd mentioned his old partner, Mitch Greer, in a while. She didn't know if invoking his name now was a good thing or not.

'Quid pro quo,' Frankie said.

'Clarice,' Peter finished for her. She was about to ask who Clarice was, then she remembered the movie. 'We've got a dead girl in the forest. She'd been there six months before the wildfires exposed the body. I've got a name, Maria Bartok. Next job is to find out who she was, and how she wound up murdered in the woods outside of Tallinn. Pound to a penny we're going to hear the magic words One World. That whole fucked-up cult thing gives me the creeps.'

Frankie listened as he walked her through it, including his scheduled morning meeting with Annja Rosen, Irma's flatmate.

There was movement inside the van, the vehicle creaking on its suspension.

Peter Ash disappeared into the shadows.

Frankie quickly slipped the phone back into her pocket and was back at the van door before it opened.

'Sorry,' she said, seeing Tasha's sleepy face lit by the small interior light. 'Didn't mean to wake you.'

'Everything OK?'

'Needed a pee,' Frankie laughed. 'Too much wine.'

Tasha nodded, and settled back into her sleeping bag.

Frankie clambered in beside her. 'He saved your life,' she said, meaning The Shepherd. 'Do you think he could save mine?'

'I know it.'

'Then yes, I'm in. More than anything I just want to feel like I belong,' she said.

'I promise you, you've found somewhere worth belonging,' Tasha said.

Frankie was convinced she could see the smile on her face despite the darkness inside the van.

TWENTY-THREE

A sh walked back to where he had left his car.

It was more than fifteen minutes from where he'd met Frankie, up a steep staircase that ran alongside one of the old bonded warehouses, cutting out a lot of the twists and turns of the road for the old dock workers. It was a staggering climb that left him breathless. Halfway to the top he was cursing his own stupidity for taking the crow-flies shortcut to save maybe five minutes of more gradual climbing. At the top his thighs and lungs were burning and he felt like he'd dropped half a kilo of water-weight.

But Frankie was good. That was the key. She'd infiltrated the first ring of One World – and the second ring sounded like the same compound Ivan's girl, Tanya, had escaped from, which put Frankie directly in the line of fire, quite literally.

He'd have felt better being on hand, even if it meant sleeping rough in the forest for a few nights with nothing but a camping gas stove and a one-man tent, but she was right, his being there put her at risk. She could get to places he couldn't in this case purely because these bastards preyed on vulnerable women. He got that.

But he didn't have to like it.

It wasn't about her being a woman. She was right when she said she could handle herself. She was his partner. That meant something to him. He imagined Mitch's spectre shaking his head and offering the old joke: *Losing one partner is unlucky, mate, but losing two would be downright fucking careless.*

'Fuck you, Mitch,' he said to the empty street.

Frankie had dragged him out of that fire six months ago. He'd be dead without her. That was the reality of what had gone down in the ruins of that Parisian orphanage.

He'd definitely used up one of his extra lives.

*   *   *

Laura was hunting Maria Bartok's past.

If she wasn't the girl in the forest, then they had a survivor to find, and if she was they had closure to bring. Knowing where she'd come from could give an idea to the flow of traffic.

Standing here, looking out over the docks and across to the ferry terminal, it made sense that girls would be trafficked from here through Sweden. Sweden might look like it was on the periphery of Europe, but driving from Malmö across the Öresund Bridge into Denmark, and down to Roedby you could be in Puttgarden, Germany, in two hours, without showing your passport once. You could move anywhere in Europe without having to identify yourself as long as you didn't try to fly. It made tracking people near-impossible.

Getting into the UK was more difficult, being islands, but going through Dublin you could disembark without showing any ID, so it was doable, even if the Channel Tunnel and major airports were out of the question.

He wasn't sure what more he could do here, but heading into Sweden without a solid lead would be worse than chasing shadows. There had to be a way in, though. A way of attacking this from the other side. Frankie from the inside, him from the out. Trafficking was like any business in that there was a supply line, buyers and sellers. If Tanya was right and the girls were being used as sex-workers on the other end, there'd be the equivalent of cards stuck in phone boxes and listings on websites where hobby escorts were advertised side by side with organized crime. Since the FBI had shut down Backpage, the main site for sex-workers, a lot of this stuff had been driven back out onto the streets, of course, putting the power back into the hands of the scum that ruled those back alleys. But it wasn't as though he could just turn up in Stockholm and start asking the girls working the streets, 'Hey, did you end up here because you had a religious revelation? Spend any time in a forest compound in Estonia? Know any girls who burned to death trying to escape?'

Peter had seen a few rough-sleepers on the walk down. They didn't make eye contact. He knew they needed to be invisible. Being seen meant they risked the kind of crap Frankie had gone through, being pissed on, beaten, or worse. Invisibility was armour. On the walk back, he counted the huddled shapes in the shadows.

He stopped counting long before he reached the hire car. There were just too many of them. It was soul-destroying. He drove slowly back up towards the hotel. The streets were almost empty until he reached the centre of the Old Town, and even there it was quiet. He saw a few people staggering home, lovers walking hand in hand or kissing up against the walls of brightly painted buildings with the kind of frantic need of those first alcohol-fuelled encounters. He couldn't remember ever being like that, so desperate to consume and be consumed that he hadn't been able to make it halfway home before he'd had to start tearing at the woman's clothes in the street. But then, he'd always kind of hated himself and doubted anyone would actually want him, so that blind spot in his memory was hardly surprising. He saw a couple of taxis trawling for trade.

It would be busy again as people returned to work, but for a few hours more at least, Tallinn slept.

He parked up outside the hotel, then went for a walk, covering many of the same streets he'd just driven, looking at the faces, looking for the saviours walking those same streets with their coffees and warm soups, but they weren't out that night.

He sat on a bench in the centre of town and took his phone out of his pocket, opened the web browser, and used his thumbs to type: *escort tallinn*. The search returned about thirty ads for used cars, as well as listings for prostitutes. He saw that they used a k instead of a c and quickly adjusted his search, turning up hundreds of more listings promising OWO, CIM, and other acronyms, with the usual disclaimers that any money that changed hands was purely for the companionship and any sex that happened was a bonus. There was an element of organization to it all, he realized, with very similarly worded listings being repeated for a lot of the girls. A disproportionate number of the listings were for girls from Ukraine, Latvia, Lithuania, and Estonia, but there were several listings for Russians, too.

So many of the girls looked the same, too, but that was hardly surprising seeing as they were using stock photographs and glamour shots of complete strangers. Either there was some serious fiddling of the genetic lottery going on, or six of the thirty girls on the first page had stolen the same set of shots for their own use.

It wasn't going to be any help, so he killed the browser and started walking back towards the hotel. In the morning he'd call Laura and see if she'd had any luck tracing Maria Bartok, and update her on Frankie's situation.

Right now, everything felt like it was in a holding pattern, not least because the investigation that had brought him out here wasn't supposed to be real – no matter how real it felt talking to Tanya and Ivan and Mirjam Rebane. He was only here for Frankie, all the rest of it was window-dressing, and if she said wait, he waited, and just hoped that the One World compound turned out to be what she needed it to be.

It was easy to forget that she was looking for family.

For Frankie it wasn't about naming the body in the forest or finding the men running a supply line of sex-workers into Europe. It was about Irma Lutz, a kid who had disappeared from university because she'd found God. If they focused on that, then maybe, just maybe, it was a problem they could solve. Because the alternative, going down that rabbit hole and trying to tackle the sex and slave trade across twenty-eight – soon to be twenty-seven if the Government in constant flux didn't derail the whole withdrawal process – member states, was lunacy of the highest order.

But then Peter Ash had never been that smart. It was his weakness; white-knight syndrome.

TWENTY-FOUR

K ask left the scene to the forensics unit, grimly satisfied that they'd have a suspect in custody before the mud had set.

He went back to the office.

As much as he would have liked to witness Tamm's fall he needed to be elsewhere. He trusted his own cunning. Each piece of his plan would fall into place – he knew that because he knew how cops thought. He knew what they looked for and how they processed an investigation because there was a way of doing things. A methodology. He'd always thought cops would make the most dangerous criminals if they set their minds to it. Not only did they have the resources, they had the specific knowledge needed to get away with murder.

And now he was about to put that theory to the test.

When the emergency dispatcher had mentioned the dog-walker's call putting a rusty yellow Volvo at the scene it had taken all of five minutes for someone to mention Karl Tamm's name. That was the joy of being well known to the police.

Within an hour they had Tamm in custody.

He'd run, or at least tried to, which made it even better.

It didn't matter that they always ran. It was all about perception. Tamm wasn't just in the frame, he'd bolted, which painted a target squarely on his back.

News spread through the station quickly.

'Looks like you missed out on all the fun,' Jaan Puhvel said, coming into the squad room, coffee in hand.

'Fun?' he said, looking up. He needed to keep the smile off his face.

'That body you found.'

'I didn't exactly find her,' he said.

'First officer on the scene, that makes her yours,' Jaan said.

'Sure. But not on our patch. South are doing just fine.'

'If you call the fastest murder arrest on record "fine", then yep they're doing just fine.'

'They've got someone *already*?' Just the right amount of surprise in his voice.

'Oh man, I thought you'd have heard it on the jungle drums. They brought Karl Tamm in. He's downstairs in interrogation.'

'Jesus, that's fast.'

'We got lucky. His yellow Volvo was seen driving away.'

'A yellow Volvo. C'mon, that's thin. There must be dozens in the city, and more passing through every day.'

'Lucky break. It was enough for a warrant.'

'And?' As he said it, the image of the girl lying naked in the grass filled his mind. He felt sick.

'They found a girl's thong hidden in his room. We've always suspected Tamm was a collector, but we've got him this time, Max. He's not walking away from this.'

'They've got a positive match?'

'Not yet. Forensics sent them back to central labs for DNA testing. But they're hers, my friend.'

'Do we have an ID on the girl?'

'They found her bag and a load of books near the body. There was no ID anywhere, but South ran a check with the library and the only student who had checked out the exact list of texts is Annja Rosen, a computer-studies undergrad.'

'I know that name,' he said, knowing he was playing a dangerous game now. 'I know I know that name. Give me a second. Yes. It came up in a disappearance case a while back. I'm sure that was it. Annja Rosen. Her flatmate was reported as missing, but if I remember right she'd signed up to some holier than thou cult and gone off to find herself.'

Now, if anyone spotted the link between Rosen and Irma Lutz, and that he was the bridge between the two, he was covered. He hadn't tried to hide it. It was the first thing he'd said when he'd heard the girl's name.

TWENTY-FIVE

The cafe was busy without being full.

He saw no sign of Annja bussing tables, so figured she was out back. As far as Peter could tell there was only the one woman working the counter, and she was struggling to keep up with the orders for frothy coffees, warm paninis, and breakfast bagels and keep the tables cleared for new arrivals.

He took up residence at an empty table and waited for the woman to make her way around to him.

Peter passed the time people-watching; and there was a good slice of life to be seen. It never ceased to amaze him just how diverse culture was capable of being, despite feeling like you were surrounded by a hundred variants of the same blonde hair and blue eyes, sharp cheekbones and ridiculously thin bodies, the reality was that more than half of the seats in the place were taken up by the young, the beautiful, and the fiercely intelligent, but under those blanket descriptors he saw fierce dreads, and hipster beards, alabaster-pale cheeks, and ebony black skin. There were three Asian girls sharing a table, arguing about some sort of ethical debate which probably came down to people are shits. At least that was Peter's understanding of ethics. It was all great in theory, until you introduced people into the mix, then it all went to fuckery.

The waitress finally reached him, and asked, 'What can I get for you?' in English.

'Actually, I'm looking for Annja,' he said. 'But a decent Americano would hit the spot.'

'You and me both,' she said. 'She hasn't turned up this morning. And she didn't even call in so we could get cover. Do me a favour, if you see her, tell her that she needn't bother coming in tomorrow. Anyway, I'll get that coffee for you. Anything go with it? Assuming you still want it?'

'Please,' he said. 'What's good?'

'Everything,' she said, 'but then I'm biased.'

'OK, how about—' He looked up at the chalkboard for the daily specials, with its list of creative croissants, sourdough sandwiches, baked goods, and healthy delights, and opted for, 'That black bean and sweet potato hash sounds good.'

'With scrambled or fried egg?'

'Fried.'

'Coming right up.'

Alone again, he tried Annja's number.

It went straight to voicemail.

'Hi Annja, it's Peter Ash.' He glanced at his watch to double-check the time. 'It's almost eleven. I'm here, but your boss says you haven't arrived yet. If you need me to rearrange, I can do that. I can come out to you, if that would help? Give me a call.'

His coffee, craft-brewed, arrived faster than he'd expected. He'd only just hung up when the woman put it on the table in front of him. 'Enjoy,' she said. 'The hash will be a few minutes.'

He drank his too-hot coffee and checked the tracking to be sure Frankie was still down by the docks. Eleven o'clock. They were probably cleaning up after the breakfast run.

His food came a few minutes later.

He ate like a condemned man, wolfing down the meal. It was better than good.

He left a twenty-euro note under the saucer, which covered a decent tip. She was clearing away his table and collecting the cash before he was halfway to the door.

Peter stood outside the cafe for a moment, annoyed at having been stood up, and frustrated that Annja had set her phone to go direct to voicemail rather than just answer and tell him she'd changed her mind about talking. It happened. People got antsy about talking to cops, even when they'd done nothing wrong.

He was thinking about taking a walk down to the campus to see if she was there when his phone rang.

'Law. What's the good word?'

'There isn't one.'

A shiver ran up the ladder of his spine and, in that moment, the silence between her delivering the bad news and that last second when his life was normal, Peter felt a tide of weakness flow through his body, buckling his knees as he tried to say, 'Frankie?'

Realizing her mistake, Laura was quick to say, 'No, she's fine. It's Annja Rosen. She's dead. They found her body this morning. It was out on some wasteland on the edge of the city. The initial report suggests sexual assault. South Tallinn already have someone in custody.'

'Fucking hell, Law. This is all just a bit too convenient.' He shook his head, looking back through the cafe window to where the woman was busy serving another customer. 'This stinks. We arrange to talk, she turns up dead. I don't buy it.'

'No such thing as coincidence,' Laura agreed. 'And do you want to know what stinks the stinkiest?'

'Hit me.'

'The first officer on the scene? Maksim Kask. And what, pray tell, is special about Maksim Kask? Why, Officer Kask is the same officer who took and buried Annja Rosen's statement.'

'Fuck that shit.'

'Fuck that shit indeed.'

'And Frankie's about to go off into the woods with One World to play happy campers.'

'It's one thing for a Church to use their influence to keep their name out of an investigation, but killing a witness?'

'They're not a Church, Law. They're a fucking cult. They're capable of anything. You saw the piece HuffPost did on them a while back? That woman separated from her own kid, forced to kidnap it from one of their temples to get it to hospital. That baby was malnourished and suffering from neglect. It had been left on a mattress in its own faeces for days, dying, and the only medicine those bastards allowed was the magic touch of their fucking Shepherd? When these fuckheads think they're doing it for a higher purpose, then yeah, anything is possible. These fuckers think they're untouchable.'

His mind was racing. He didn't have many friends out here. Not ones he could confide in when it came to asking awkward questions like: *Is one of your most decorated detectives a corrupt religious fanatic capable of murder?*

But there was one.

Maybe.

Even if talking with her was going to involve expenses.

'Pete, do me a favour before you go charging off half-cocked,' Laura said.

'What?'

'Try not to get yourself half-crucified and almost burned alive.'

'I shall make that my top priority,' he promised, and killed the call.

He couldn't shake the feeling that this was the fracture in One World's facade that those who railed against the cult had been looking for; it wasn't taxes, or something vague like a billboard asking a daughter to come home. It was the body of a girl dumped on wasteground. It was a corrupt cop in the pocket of their holy man. It was compelling. It was front-page newspaper visual. It was the kind of thing that could bring down a house of false gods and fake prophets. If he didn't get himself   or Frankie   killed trying to get to the heart of it.

TWENTY-SIX

Laura was shaken.

She wasn't a field agent, but that didn't mean she was immune to the stuff they were investigating. A kid had just lost her life because she'd told the truth. And if Laura hadn't noticed the statement was missing from the file she might still be alive. It was as simple as that. Cause and effect. Sending Peter Ash out there to interview her had got her killed.

And that was on her.

No one else.

She needed to do something. And that wasn't just guilt driving her. She was separated from the mess. She could dig in different ways to Peter. She had the entire weight of Division behind her. She could monitor traffic on a local level, looking for patterns on a global one. She could listen to chatter, cross-reference reports from all sorts of jurisdictions, and maybe, just maybe, see something he'd miss down at the sharp end.

The first thing was to take that name he'd given her, Maria Bartok, and find out once and for all if she was the body in the woods.

And it would keep her mind off Annja Rosen.

But, assuming it was Maria Bartok, and she'd come over the border from Russia, then finding where she'd been picked up by the traffickers was going to be a nightmare. Russia wasn't like the EU. She didn't have access to their systems. There was no cross-jurisdictional border cooperation in place. And the idea of hacking into Russian databases to get at that stuff . . . was likely to set off a diplomatic Cold War, or at least earn her a stretch in the Lubyanka.

There could be breadcrumbs, of course, the most obvious being if she'd use her own passport to enter the Eurozone. That at least ought to offer a point of entry. But there was nothing to say the traffickers hadn't found another way to get her across the border, including the use of facilitators.

There was a whole lexicon for this stuff, she'd discovered. Facilitators came in all shapes and sizes; they were the legitimate businesses that ran alongside the trafficking and provided the support structure that made it possible for the people trade to function. Stuff like hotels and motels, property landlords, taxi drivers and haulage drivers, advertisers like Craigslist, banks that brokered the transactions. And then there were the Lot Lizards, Loose Bitches, and Gorillas. Most of it was self-explanatory. Some of it made her sick to the stomach, like references to Kiddie Strolls, Seasoning, and Branding which were dehumanizing even if they sounded relatively innocent; psychological manipulation, intimidation, sodomy, gang rape, food and sleep deprivation, isolation. and physical beatings. Stuff designed to break the girl's will and turn her into a malleable sex-worker who wouldn't put up a fight. Ninety-nine times out of a hundred the girls would never find the money to pay their exit fees, making it a form of slavery, which was reinforced by the use of tattoos to brand the girls as the property of a certain pimp, though the phrase 'modern day slavery' was loaded with a lot of problems, not least the fact that in an attempt to protect the victims many countries had turned to the aggressive punishment of anti-prostitution laws, which seemed to mean that salvation came in the form of arrest.

It was a fucked-up world they were living in.

But then, she'd never thought anything different.

Laura set to work.

It was going to take time to put all the searches in place, but all she could do was be systematic about it. Back in London she'd been working on a crawler bot that could trawl through every database she had access to – and a few she shouldn't have been able to touch. It was still fairly crude, and guaranteed to dredge up a lot of irrelevant hits, but this seemed the perfect time to test it.

The risk was that somewhere down the chain there was another Kask keeping an eye out for people taking an interest in Maria Bartok.

Any sort of search that pinged back with her name was fine, but actually initiating one with it and risking tripping any alerts Kask might have put on her name to monitor outside interest was dumb. So, avoiding the obvious risk, she worked with Maria's presumed nationality, took a broad age range of fifteen to thirty, and used the digital reconstruction to map out noticeable features. It was a gamble, but by not deliberately searching out Bartok's name she should still turn up the woman without triggering any alerts. Theoretically. It depended on how good or paranoid Kask was, and how invasive her dive into their system went. Limiting the key features would help with the initial response, but there was always the risk doing so would exclude the right girl.

It would have been so much easier if she could just put Maria Bartok's name into the crawler, but for now she didn't want anyone watching to know they knew the girl's name.

She hit search.

It didn't take long for the search engine to warn her she was looking at a six-to-eight-hour search time for full access to all of the member states. Any number of precise details would slash that time dramatically, not just the name, even so it seemed like a ridiculous amount of time to compile the data given a Google search was essentially instantaneous.

The difference was this was far from a simple search, but if it worked, by the end of it she'd know if Maria Bartok had used her own passport anywhere in the world, registered to work and pay tax, or received medical attention within the countries of the European Union. She'd know what kind of medical attention she'd received, including things that breached doctor–patient confidentiality. She'd have her hands-on personal information, including voter registration and credit-card usage, if Maria Bartok had made it as far as using a credit card or finding a job that paid tax. And that was a big if, given she was almost certainly lying in an Estonian morgue with her skin burned off.

TWENTY-SEVEN

T his time breakfast was more relaxed affair.

They had each other's rhythm, and when they were joined again by the two girls who'd been there yesterday things dropped into a comfortable routine.

While the girls set up, Tasha made the call to let John know that Frankie was interested in the camp. She gave Frankie the thumbs-up a moment later, like it had ever been in doubt. Frankie offered her a smile in return and carried on with brewing the coffee for the first breakfast guests.

Tasha finished her call. 'All good,' she said, coming over to the serving hatch. 'John will swing by and pick you up at ten thirty.'

'That means I'm bailing on you right when the dirty work starts,' Frankie protested.

'Don't worry about it, we can manage. We've done it often enough.'

'Are you here again tonight?'

Tasha shook her head. 'I'm done for the day. Got a couple of days off now.'

'Nice. Any plans?' Which was a very subtle way of asking just how much One World controlled her existence.

'Sleep,' she laughed, not giving anything away.

'No partying then?'

'Ha, the chance would be a fine thing. I'm too old for discos. Hell, do they even still call them discos? Yeah, I'm that old. Besides, I don't know many people here. The only real friends I've got in Tallinn are either working here tonight or they'll be on the shift with me when I take over from the crew here.'

Which sounded like an empty existence. 'No family?'

Tasha shook her head. There was a moment. A flicker of something in her face. If Frankie hadn't known better she'd have thought it was distaste. 'No family,' she said. 'They turned their back on me when I needed them, so I've done the same to them. I have a new family now, and our bonds are stronger than blood. They are from love. Sometimes we need to cut our losses, move away from relationships that don't work, that impact on your state of mind and well-being. It isn't about being passive or accepting. It's about realizing where the fight actually is. One World helped me understand that. For all the strength and energy I wasted trying to force my mother to love me enough to stop my stepfather from *loving* me and just be on my side for once, I realized I could channel that pain and grief into good. I could make a difference for kids who were like me, but not as strong, or didn't have people like The Shepherd to help them.'

'I know what you mean,' Frankie said. 'My mother kicked me out,' which was so far from the truth it would have needed satnav to find it, but was just the kind of thing that would forge an added bond between her and Tasha.

Tasha reached out and touched her arm in response, a small but significant gesture.

'Go to the camp, listen to what people have to teach you. Go in with an open mind. Use what helps you. You don't have to become a devout follower of The Shepherd. We're not like that. But if you find something there that helps you, then maybe One World will make your life better. That can't be a bad thing, can it?'

'No,' Frankie agreed.

'And if you come back to us, well, maybe we can be the family you deserve?'

She leaned in and gave her a hug, holding Frankie tighter than anyone had in a long time.

'Will you still be here when I get back?'

'Of course,' Tasha said. 'But there's always the chance you will decide your future isn't here, serving soup and cleaning tables. Maybe your journey will lead you elsewhere. It's a wide world.'

Frankie tried to look surprised, as if the possibility of being moved on elsewhere had never crossed her mind. Her brief conversation with Peter had pretty much convinced her this camp was some sort of test, the good girls go to heaven the bad go to hell, kind of thing. She needed to make sure her face fitted. But was hell always the same place? And if it was, was that where she'd find Irma?

The next couple of hours passed through a filter of treacle, moving slower than any since she'd set foot in Tallinn. Frankie recognized a few of the returning faces, and met them with genuine pleasure, happy to make even this small difference to them. And in their faces she saw something else, too. Hope. Not theirs, but hers. And it was a hope she'd never expected to find down here. It was the hope that when she got to the end of this road she wouldn't find anything wrong with One World, and that all her time away in the woodland compound would do was prove to her these were good people doing everything they could for the homeless of this city and who knew how many others. Because if she was the reason they stopped helping, how many of these people smiling back at her now would survive the coming winter?

IN THE DARKNESS . . .

Time passed slowly, if it passed at all.
      The only light she saw was when they lowered food down to her.

Her life up until that point had been measured in the rising and the setting of the sun, in the anchor points of minutes, hours, and seconds. Lacking this was another level of disorientation.

She hated the bucket.

The sound it made when she peed into it. The way the dehumanizing stench of her shit was enhanced by it.

It was worse than the rats brushing up against her.

She slept.

Not well.

Sometimes sitting up, sometimes curled into a foetal ball. She never felt refreshed. There was never any change in the darkness.

She couldn't hear them any more, moving about above her. They had forsaken her.

But that was the test, wasn't it?

A test of faith.

She would not fail him.

She would not surrender to the darkness.

Her world was silence.

She pressed her hand against her heart to feel something. To mark the passage of life in those desperate panicked beats.

All she could do was think. Let her mind race. Run.

John posed a computer-related puzzle on the journey from the compound to the hole. It was the last thing she'd expected from him, truth be told. It was very specific in application, almost mundane really, like the kind of challenge her professors would pose on a Friday to keep them busy over the weekend, which felt peculiar as One World seemed so distant from mundane demands. But it had seemed so important to him. She wanted to please him. That was all she ever wanted. She focused on those words now, ignoring the cold and the damp.

But how could she solve his puzzle without a computer?

She needed to see the code. To visualize it. She tried to create the lines in the darkness, imagining them as brilliant bright flashes in the black, scrolling in front of her.

And in her mind they were bright enough to light her face, banishing the darkness.

She sought refuge in the code, looking for answers, for a way to do what John had asked of her.

She would not fail him.

Not now. Not when she was so close.

He loved her.

More lines of code, looking for the break, the weakness. It had to be there. And in that relentless search she hoped to find her sanity, because even as the instructions filled the darkness she felt her sense of self slipping.

Food was lowered down.

Empty plates taken away.

Water in a slop bucket.
Moments of disorientating light.
She didn't call out.
She didn't beg.
She knew better.
She needed to be strong.
She needed to solve the problem he had set her, then and only then could she call out.
She felt the rats brush up against her, used to her intrusion in their home now.

TWENTY-EIGHT

Another lunchtime in another cafe.

Peter Ash was beginning to think he'd make a killing if he saved those loyalty card stamps all the coffee chains offered.

That half-thought kick-started a chain of possibilities versus probabilities in a filling-time kind of way: for some of those reward schemes surely you'd be able to track someone? It wasn't that he expected it to be of any use in this particular case, but it could be an angle. But knowing Laura, they were already in her database crawler. She was always half a dozen steps ahead of him when it came to technology.

'Sorry I'm late,' Mirjam Rebane said, slipping into the seat opposite him. The radio was playing a version of 'Every Time You Go Away' he'd never heard before. She was barely ten minutes late, which in his world was as good as being early.

'Busy morning?'

'You know the job, same, same, but different. A naked corpse might not be an everyday kind of occurrence, but it's not a one-off, sadly. I take it that's what you want to talk about? Annja Rosen?' He nodded. 'It's all anyone's been talking about since they brought Tamm in,' she said.

'Tamm?'

'Local sex-offender. Nasty piece of work.'

He nodded again, letting the silences live.

'As soon as I heard the name I knew it was tied up with your case. Question is, is the universe fucking with you, or is it more twisted than that?'

'Half the time I'm convinced the universe hates me.'

'But not this time? Even though they've brought in the killer.'

He looked at her. 'Don't take this the wrong way, Mirjam, but I need to ask you something – just because I need to hear you say it.'

'OK, I'll do my best not to get offended.'

'Are you one of the good guys?'

'Well, that's a dumb question.'

'It's not. I don't know who I can trust here.'

'Are you serious? Shit, you're serious.'

He nodded. 'I told you, I need to hear you say it. I need to know you're not part of One World. I need to know you're not on the take.'

'I should just get up and walk out,' she said, but she didn't move.

'Don't do that.'

'I'm not mixed up in any cult. I don't believe in God. I don't fuck on a first date and I'm not into drugs. I don't gamble. My biggest vice is I'm a bit of a daddy's girl. If you don't trust me that's your call, Peter, I won't lose any sleep over it. But I was beginning to think—'

'That's all I needed to hear,' he promised. 'And when I tell you why, I hope you'll understand. The first officer on the scene was Maksim Kask.'

'So?'

'The same Maksim Kask who took Annja's statement about Irma Lutz's disappearance.'

'I'd say "So?" again, but I'm assuming you've got something else to tell me?'

'Annja's statement was omitted from the files sent over to my Division.'

'Clerical error?'

'It was the only statement in which Irma's connection to One World was mentioned.'

'OK, I can see why you might wonder, but Kask? You really think one of our most decorated officers could be involved in this?'

'I was due to meet her this morning, just a few hours after she died. Why can't I shake the feeling she was being silenced?'

'Wait, you think Kask killed her . . .? Seriously? Even though they've got a perp bang to rights?'

Peter held up a hand. 'I know what you're thinking. I know all of your objections, because they're the same ones I'd have. Cops don't become cops to get away with murder. They just don't. But what if One World had something on him? Something enough to make him cross the line? It's not out of the question. He doesn't even have to be the one to pull the trigger. He could just be the one who offered up the sacrificial sex-offender so it's all wrapped up nice and conveniently. I mean, two girls from the same apartment, months apart, are the subject of major investigations, both with Kask slap bang in the middle of them? I'm not saying you're not great detectives here, but this is way too convenient. The girl's panties hidden in the guy's apartment because some random passer-by saw a yellow car?'

'You know a lot about this,' she said. It wasn't a question. 'Laura. Does she have access to all our systems?'

'Major cases, certainly.'

'But not missing persons?' Mirjam asked.

'Not everything is going to end up in the system. Summary details. The written report. But when it's deemed no crime has taken place? The temptation is to let things slide. That makes it an imperfect system. So talking to the people on the business end is just good police work. Our job is always more difficult simply because we're dealing with stuff across national borders. Everyone gets quite territorial. Computers don't. At least that's what Laura says. It's all about patterns. Sometimes it's more about the things that aren't there than those that are there. Like Annja's statement.'

Mirjam nodded. 'Makes perfect sense to me.'

'Which is why I like you.'

'Why, Peter Ash, are you hitting on me?'

He changed the subject without missing a beat. 'So you know Kask. What's your hot take on him? Could he do something like this?'

'Don't really know him. I've heard stories, though. He's got a bit of a reputation.'

'The kind of stories worth sharing?'

'OK, well, one black mark, given what we're talking about here: he's the religious type. Claims to have some kind of divine moral compass that guides his work.' She didn't look happy to be telling tales out of school. He said nothing, letting her work her way through her own moral quagmire. 'I've heard him say he gets a thrill out of nailing the dealers, and getting the prostitutes and perverts off the streets.'

'Plenty of cops get a buzz out of putting the bad guys away.'

'You weren't listening to me, were you? I said the dealers, prostitutes, and perverts. The girls are victims not villains. They need help. But Kask is on some kind of crusade where they all need to be burned.'

'OK, so he's a poster boy for One World by the sounds of things.'

'Even if that's the case, you know this is outside of your remit, don't you? This is a murder in my country. A capital crime. The victim is Estonian. The man we have in custody is Estonian, and the officer you suspect of being corrupt is Estonian. I don't know how involved you can be in this.'

Which was true.

'Which is why we're talking.'

'And there was me thinking you wanted me for my body.'

'Stir the pot.'

'I'm not following?'

'Rattle Kask.'

'You want me to deliberately try and draw him into making a mistake?'

'Assuming he's the bad guy here, yep.'

'I don't know.'

'All you need to do is ask a question. It'll get back to him.'

'What sort of question?'

He prefaced his plan carefully. 'You're a good cop. A good cop is going to want to make sure any conviction is safe. This is murder we're talking about. One flatmate disappears, another winds up murdered, and he's point man on both? What's that saying: "God doesn't play dice with the universe?" A decent lawyer is going to have a field day with the level of coincidence here. So, a good cop asks: how did they get so lucky? A dog walker called in to say they saw a yellow car. What time was the call logged? Where was the call logged from? Caller's identity? You know the sort of stuff. Look for what's not there as much as what is.'

'Hold on,' she said.

He stopped talking, waiting for her to explain.

She didn't.

As he leaned forward a little, about to ask, Mirjam Rebane shook her head.

'Coincidences,' she said finally.

'That's what I've been saying,' Peter said.

She shook her head. 'No. Coincidences,' she said again.

'What are you thinking?'

'The dog walker.'

'The one who called the report of the car in?'

'Yup.'

'What about them?'

'It's what's not there, right?'

'More often than not,' Peter agreed.

'I need to check something before I say it out loud. Give me a minute.'

'Go for it.'

She left him at the table disappearing outside for closer to ten minutes before she returned.

She wasn't smiling as she slipped back into her seat.

'I called in a couple of favours. Got a friend to send me a transcript of the emergency call. Easier than me translating Estonian for you.' She put the transcript on the table and turned it so Peter could read it.

> *'There's a body. I was walking. I didn't realize what it was at first. My dog wouldn't leave it alone. Then I saw the arm and I realized . . .'*
>
> *'Can I take your name, please, sir?'*
>
> *'I don't . . . She's on the wasteground. She's dead. It's a she. I've never seen a body . . . I . . . I saw a car.'*
>
> *'What kind of car?'*
>
> *'A Volvo. Not a new one. An old model. It was rusty. Yellow.'*
>
> *'Can you give me your location, sir?'*
>
> *'It's the wasteland on the edge of the industrial estate*

out beyond the ring road. The far side of the railway line.
I have to go. Find. Her. Please. She's alone out there. Please.'
   'Can I have your name, please, sir?'
   'I left my mother on her own.'

It wasn't much.

'I'm not seeing whatever you are,' Peter admitted.

'I have to go. I left my mother on her own,' Mirjam said.

Peter nodded.

She handed him a second sheet. It was a situation report. A detailed situation report. Including the time officers arrived on the scene, and the time the one witness, Sten Christof Semjonov, had been released, nearly three hours later.

Semjonov's statement was attached.

'What isn't there?' Mirjam asked as he pushed the transcript back towards her.

'He doesn't mention calling it in,' Peter said.

'He doesn't mention calling it in, but he's thorough about everything else. Meticulous detail, really. An ideal witness. He reports seeing Kask's car, and waving him over. And then he talks about the two cops arriving on the scene and the moment when the first uniformed officer is so wound up he nearly shoots Kask. There's no gap in the testimony where he leaves Kask with the body and walks across to call it in, and he doesn't once say he called it in and then returned to Annja's body to wait. He specifically claims he saw Kask standing by his car and called him over, while Kask claims he was responding to the dispatcher's call. Now maybe he forgot to mention he placed a call . . .'

'Maybe,' Peter said, entertaining reasonable doubt.

'But that's not the kicker,' Mirjam said. She brought another image front and centre on the screen and passed the phone back to Peter. 'This is.'

He read the name on the death certificate: Mari-Liis Semjonov.

'His mother wasn't there waiting for him. She died seventeen years ago. What's not there? Two different dog walkers found the same corpse and the first one walked off after they called it in? Or Kask's lying.'

'You ever talk to Kask?'

'Sure.'

'Did you hear the logged call?'

'I did.'

'And did it sound like his voice?'

'It sounded eerily like his voice,' Mirjam told him.

'Sometimes I hate being right,' Peter said.

'No you don't.'

'No I don't,' he agreed. 'Will he be able to tell you've accessed this stuff?'

'We'll find out soon enough.'

'Well, I did ask you to rattle his cage.'

'Consider it rattled.'

TWENTY-NINE

The black limo returned for Frankie much sooner than she'd expected. There was no sign of John this time. The driver was alone.

'Ceska? John sent me to pick you up,' he said. 'He'll join us out at the compound.'

Frankie looked to Tasha. The other woman nodded as if to say, sure, this is how it's supposed to be. 'Tomas will take care of you, don't worry.'

'OK, I'll just grab my things.'

'It's fine. You won't need any of that stuff,' Tomas assured her.

Frankie shook her head. 'They're my things . . .'

She didn't care about the change of clothes, her sleeping bag, or even her rucksack. The only thing she did care about was the burner phone at the bottom of it. That was her lifeline.

'Trust me, you won't need it. We've got everything you need out at the compound. Tasha will look after your stuff for you.'

'It'll be right here waiting for you when you get back, promise,' Tasha said.

'You don't understand, it's my stuff . . . the only stuff I have in the world that's mine.' She shook her head. She wasn't getting into that car without her rucksack. Even without the phone, this determination to cling onto her few possessions felt genuine.

The man shrugged, gave a sigh, and said, 'Suit yourself,' as he made a show of looking at his watch. 'But we don't want to be late.'

Nodding, Frankie hurried to the van to stuff her sleeping bag into her pack, wishing she had a couple of seconds to send a message to Peter to let him know they were moving out. She just had to trust that Laura was monitoring her tracker.

By the time she returned to the car the boot was already open for her to drop her things into. Tomas stood beside the car. He looked thoroughly unimpressed by her treasures as he slammed the boot closed.

'In you get,' he said, opening the rear passenger-side door.

'Can't I sit in the front?'

'Just do as you're told, eh?' He didn't move aside, so she slid onto the back seat.

It was only when he closed the door with little more than a click that she realized the tint on the windows was so dark she couldn't see out, and that there was a glass divider between the rear and the front of the car. She reached over to try the handle, but it didn't open. The child locks were in place, meaning she was essentially being held captive in the luxury car. She straightened up as Tomas got into the driver's seat.

Without being able to see out, she was quickly going to lose any sense of direction, making it hard to guess where Tomas was taking her, or how far they'd travelled. It wasn't ideal.

'If you lift the armrest next to you,' Tomas said, his voice coming through a small speaker built into the fascia beneath the glass divider, 'you'll find bottled water and sandwiches if you get hungry. Settle back and enjoy the ride. If you want music there's a stereo system built into the speaker; no radio, but it's hooked up to Spotify and I've got some decent playlists sorted.'

'How long will it take us to get to the compound?'

'A couple of hours, depending on traffic. Kick back, relax.'

There was a silence then as the speaker disconnected and she was left alone. *In the back of a limo, no one can hear you scream,* she thought, the thought coming alive with Peter Ash's voice inside her mind. His bad sense of humour was rubbing off on her.

She found the touchscreen beneath the grille and brought it to life with the heat of her fingertip, and searched through the playlists for one with songs she recognized. It wasn't that she was eager to hear the tunes, she needed them as a way to mark the time.

She felt the car pull away and settled back in for the ride. She was more comfortable than she'd been in days. And bone-deep tired. It wasn't a good combination. She promised herself she was only closing her eyes, that she was going to listen to the songs and commit them to memory.

THIRTY

F rankie was on the move.

Laura chewed on her bottom lip as she watched the signal move across one of her monitors. The refresh rate was moving a lot faster than walking pace. She'd been waiting for this to happen. As plans went, it went. She wasn't happy with it, but she'd always known Frankie was going to take that shot. It didn't matter if she had backup in place or not. That wasn't who she was. Hell, it was in her name. She was a hunter. A lone wolf.

Laura sent a short text to Peter Ash. All it said was: 'She's on the move.'

She got a reply back seconds later that simply said, 'OK.'

Peter was on a hunt of his own. She'd known he would do it properly when she'd sent him over there armed with an excuse. The reason her research for his cover story had been so good was because it was real. There were dozens of girls a year being moved through the Baltic States to feed the demand for sex-workers in Europe. She'd known from the moment she'd chosen the cover story that Peter was going to dive right in. She was gambling he'd chase the truth right to one of those pimp circles, or whatever they called those houses where the girls were basically held hostage, and save a few lives in the process, because that was who he was.

What she hadn't expected was the seeming overlap with One World, which was a whole different level of disturbing.

Her crawler churned out a steady stream of results, most of them useless. It was just too big a data set, meaning too big a result pool. And once she'd collated everything and dug through the results there was still zero to guarantee there'd be anything even remotely usable. It didn't mean her logic was flawed, either. You couldn't find what wasn't there to be found. It was pretty much that simple. Crossing the Iron Curtain, no matter how many years it was since it had supposedly come down, posed no end of problems for data mining.

She looked out across the Operations Room. There were twenty-seven other teams in here, all of them working their own cases, sharing resources and pooling knowledge. Over a hundred people were assigned to Division now. It wasn't like it had been in River House. She could walk across the floor to where Etienne Reynard was hunched over his terminal and ask him for a favour even if France wasn't involved. That pooling of resources, the idea they were stronger together, was new.

She liked it.

Even so, she did kind of miss the broom cupboard back in London. There were a lot of memories tied to that place. And ghosts. Or ghost. One. Mitch. He'd never been here, there was no link to him in this glass-and-steel custom-built monstrosity. She kept a photo of the three of them on her desk. Peter hadn't commented on it when he'd seen it.

She went to get herself a decent cup of coffee, and smiled to Zanya and Anoninia, the Polish team. They were the odd ones out in Division. Most field teams were male–female, or male–male partnerships being run by someone like her. Poland brought two women to the table, and they had a clearance rate that shamed most of the boys. Sem Dekker was at the machine, struggling with one of the little foil capsules which appeared to be jammed in the machine.

'If you've broken it I will kill you,' Laura said, coming up beside him.

'It's all good,' he assured her.

The sheer amount of coffee grounds across his fingertips suggested otherwise.

'Out of the way, pretty boy,' Laura said, and set about getting the damaged capsule out of the machine.

It took her a couple of seconds.

Sem just shook his head.

'Hey, this is my element,' she said, and skipped ahead of him in the line to brew up first.

All around them the Operations Room was a Babel of languages; so many different sounds they all blurred together into one incredible fusion where words ceased to be.

It was enough to drive her out of her mind when she was trying to concentrate, but at times like this she rather enjoyed the sheer multicultural cross-section the open-plan Operations Room offered.

It did however make her feel incredibly isolated at times, and ignorant, given so many of the people in this place spoke three, four, and five languages fluently.

Even Peter managed to mangle some high-school French.

She was, she thought, quite possibly the only person here who was monolingual.

She returned to her desk, coffee in hand.

The red dot marking Frankie's route had made progress through the grid of streets that carved up the Old Town of Tallinn. Unlike the portable devices Frankie and Peter carried, she was able to see the snail trail of Frankie's route going all the way back to the docklands. She could also switch the dates and look back at her various routes over the last few days if necessary.

The signal weaved its way through the streets, turning left and right, but always heading in the same general direction.

Laura switched the view to overhead satellite and zoomed out for a moment until she picked out the wasteground where Annja Rosen's body had been discovered.

The car was heading in the same general direction, which did nothing to set her mind at rest.

After the outer ring of the ring road, beyond the industrial estate and the wasteland, was a significant amount of forest that was as yet untouched by the forest fire. It did, however, offer the flames a direct route into the heart of the city if the wind should turn before the firefighters had it under control.

She had to assume the compound was hidden away in there somewhere.

It wouldn't be too far from civilization; that made transportation an issue. The further from the docks and the routes out of the country the more room there was for things to go wrong.

That was one of the more unexpected things her research into trafficking had turned up. Facilitators. Those landlords in and around the key checkpoints – or chokepoints as the trafficker's lingo termed them. They might be geographic or trans-regional, crossing from water to land, a bridge, a port, or other points of egress where customs and immigration agents came into play. Where the trafficked girls flowed they turned a blind eye for regular cash. The thought process is simple: what they didn't see didn't hurt them. Which is a long way from not hurting anyone, but money trumped some stranger's pain.

She could try to use satellite imaging to locate any hot spots, but it was a stretch given the whole country was basically burning. The compound wouldn't use mains electricity, it'd be off the grid, meaning generators. Was she looking for a significantly sized clearing, or had the compound been built among the trees, retaining the cover that the canopy provided? She had so many questions and nothing in the answer column. Realistically, all she could do for the time being was watch Frankie's flashing red signal on the monitor and wait.

And she hated waiting.

THIRTY-ONE

P eter Ash left Mirjam with plenty to think about. More, in truth, than he wanted to. There was something happening. He wasn't ready for that. He needed to be all about the dead girls, not thinking about how much he enjoyed her company. That way lay madness.

So, now they had an idea what they were dealing with, and that was at the very least a corrupt cop, which meant Mirjam taking things through official channels risked tipping Kask off. But not taking the hunt through the proper process risked a lot more.

Sometimes he hated his job.

On the list of shit things in his life, a corrupt cop was right up there with the shittiest of the shit.

But they had to rattle him.

They couldn't let Kask just go through the next few days complacent and content that he'd got away with murder. These were key hours. These were where he was likely to trip up, especially if he thought he was under suspicion. But how to do that without tipping off the higher-ups given they thought they had the right man in custody?

Through that fringe Church of his.

It was One World.

It had to be.

But they needed to get proof of that. Part of him half-hoped that particular rock remained unturned, if they were part of a bigger conspiracy to commit crime. In truth, he didn't know much about One World beyond the usual gossip he'd heard about the stuff with their missionaries out amongst the *Big Issue* sellers in Covent Garden trying to spread the word of The Shepherd. He didn't have a clue what they actually believed in.

Peter figured the internet could offer up some of that. But like it or not, places like Wikipedia were rife with self-edits and agendas and telling a fake news website and propaganda hole from the real deal was just about impossible. The internet might offer the world in your pocket through your mobile phone, but it also opened up that whole world of crazy, too.

He needed to talk to someone – maybe a journalist who'd spent time digging to try and find the cracks in the perfect face they presented the world, or a man who knew a man, and when it came to that sort of interconnectivity there was only one man Peter Ash knew who even remotely fitted that bill.

Ernesto Donatti, the Vatican fixer.

He wasn't about to make that call until he had some privacy though.

They hadn't spoken since the fire, and what felt like the great betrayal of their friendship.

Ernesto Donatti had almost died in that chapel, side by side with Ash. Without Frankie they both would have. They should have been bonded by that. But they weren't. They had too many burned bridges between them for it ever to be that easy.

It was going to be a difficult call.

There was no chance he was making it without a drink first. He needed to steel himself, because at the very least, it was him taking the first step to rebuilding those bridges, and even after everything they'd been through together, Peter still thought of himself as the victim, not both of them as victims. Maybe that would come. In time. Maybe it wouldn't.

So, how did you lay that first foundation stone?

By calling in a favour.

Peter poured himself a cup of instant black coffee that would have had Laura calling in the exorcist to cleanse him of evil spirits and settled into the armchair.

A notepad and pen rested on the small table beside him. Both had the hotel logo on them.

'Peter Ash? As I live and breathe. I felt sure you had left this earth, because I couldn't believe my friend would go six months without reaching out to tell me otherwise.' The familiar voice was both warm and friendly. And in that one teasing line, Donatti had done his best to thaw the ice between them. 'More seriously, how are you, Peter? I have talked to Laura. She is quite the lady. Tell me, are you working again?'

'Yep. In Germany,' he said, not entirely sure how he felt about Laura and Donatti bonding. 'What about you? In one piece?'

'I seem to be on the mend, though I am not sure I will ever get used to being tied to a desk.'

'I hope there's no expiry date on those air miles,' Peter said, earning a chuckle. There was a brief pause beyond that. Peter wouldn't have noticed it but for the fact he knew his old friend better than he knew himself. There was a shift going on, the bonhomie shifting into practicality as Donatti's tone changed. 'As much as I am glad to finally hear your voice, I'm assuming this isn't a social call?'

'No, it isn't. But it's good to hear your voice, Ernesto. It's been a long time.'

'Not entirely my doing, Peter. The road goes both ways.'

'I didn't call for a lecture.'

'And I will not offer one. But tell me, what *can* I do for you?'

Peter thought about it, wondering the best way to broach the subject, and decided to go at it head-on. 'I'm trying to find out what I can about one of these new Churches. They call themselves One World. I want to get an idea of what they're like, what they believe in, what they're doing, that kind of thing.'

'Related to a case? Or are you thinking of conversion? I can do you a good deal with the Holy Father if you're thinking about coming home.'

'Purely work,' Peter said.

'Well, you can't blame a man for trying. Can I ask about the case?'

Which was exactly what he'd expected from the other man. One thing his dealings with Donatti had taught him was that it went both ways. Donatti traded in information. Nothing came free. You wanted to know something? He wanted to know something in return. Still, he was guessing that getting Donatti to dish the dirt on One World shouldn't bring him into conflict over protecting the reputation of the Catholic Church, which was normally what kept his lips zipped up tight.

'Not yet. I'll fill you in as we go, but first of all I'm hoping you can give me a bit of a Bluffer's Guide because I really don't know much about them.'

'Where to begin,' the Italian said. 'Well, as you might imagine we tend to be interested in anything claiming to be a new religion—'

'Competition for souls?'

He could hear the smile in the other man's voice as he said, 'More of a shield from charlatans. One World. Let's see, I think I first heard the name ten years ago. They are a Christian sect whose main priority is charitable work. Their focus was small scale. It wasn't about trying to change the world with sweeping gestures. They set up food banks and soup kitchens and dedicated their efforts to trying to help the hungry. This, remember, was at a time when the focus was on improving living conditions in Third World countries. They made a point of preaching that we had a duty to help our own.'

Peter nodded. 'I've seen a soup kitchen in Tallinn.'

'Estonia? I should start calling you Heineken. You're reaching the parts other detectives cannot reach.'

'Don't quit the day job, mate.'

'You'll find them in most cities in northern Europe, though they were kicked out of Amsterdam and denied charitable status a few years ago. They're less visible here in the south, but there is no denying their reach has extended. They're a young Church – and I don't just mean in how long they have been in existence. Their membership is predominantly under thirty-five. They have a strong presence on university campuses.'

'Sounds like they're planning for the future. Grab all the lost souls now so there's fewer left for your mob.'

There was a silence for moment. All he could hear was the other man's breathing.

Peter didn't know whether Donatti was annoyed at his lack of faith, but he was almost certainly choosing his words carefully.

He always did.

'The competition for souls is not won or lost at any single point in time. People change their beliefs as they go through life, much as their needs change. Look at yourself, you are a prime example, Peter, an altar boy who wouldn't be seen dead setting foot inside a church now unless it is to be crucified by a madman. There will always be those few lost and broken souls who find hope in a fringe Church because they seem to offer what they need most at that time in their lives, but they eventually find their way, seeing through the charlatans. Far from having to fight for the faithful, we benefit rather than suffer because of movements like One World.'

'You're equating them to a gateway drug? Does that make your lot the hard stuff?'

'Something must have really damaged your soul, my friend, because your mind is a dark, dark place.'

'I blame my days as an altar boy.'

'That's probably it,' Donatti agreed. 'What you need to remember is all of these pseudo-faiths and new religions have some sort of USP.'

'USP?'

'Unique selling point. They're providing what they see as a safe place for the people we are accused of turning our back on.'

He didn't need to ask who that might be. 'OK, slightly more blunt question: have you heard or seen anything that might suggest they would be involved in anything dubious, immoral, or illegal?'

'They have accumulated a vast wealth in a relatively short space of time. Far more than you would expect them to raise through donations. Does that help?'

'It certainly makes you wonder. So how do they do that? Mysterious benefactors? A lottery win?'

'No idea, I'm afraid. But I suspect our forensic accountants will have taken a look at their tax returns. And we're always interested in how other Churches thrive financially.'

'That sounds almost like corporate espionage.'

'Oh no, they are public record. If you want to leave it with me, I'll see what I can find out for you.'

'Sounds like a plan. I'll owe you one.'

'You say that now . . .' Donatti said, letting it trail off, the rest unsaid.

Peter Ash knew he'd just written the Vatican man a blank cheque.

He reached for the coffee, but it had grown cold. He drank it anyway, because it couldn't have tasted any worse.

THIRTY-TWO

The quality of the road changed beneath the limo's wheels, bringing Frankie out of her doze. She was angry at herself for slipping, but it was only natural, given the last few days. She'd been aware they were still moving, though she'd lost track of the songs. The ride, up until now, had been smooth as silk but now they were travelling on a rutted surface the suspension was being made to work.

She tried to peer out through the glass even though she knew it was pointless.

The limo jounced and juddered along what must have been a dirt road.

She couldn't be sure if the light coming in from the outside world was dimmer because they were in the cover of tall trees, or if they'd been travelling so long the sun had already begun its gradual decline towards dusk.

They seemed to be travelling on a relatively straight road, at least.

She assumed that Galileo could more than handle the interference the trees offered.

Because if things went tits up she was going to need that phone.

She was beginning to have reservations about coming out here alone. The fact the driver had been so eager for her to leave her stuff behind, then proceeded to dump it in the boot where she couldn't see if anyone took it out again didn't help things, either. And neither did the fact the tinted glass rendered her essentially blind. Both combined to leave Frankie feeling more helpless than she would have liked.

She wasn't a massive fan of the screen that separated her from the driver, either.

She'd been hoping to use the time one-on-one to ask about One World.

The car slowed. She heard the raw blare of its horn announcing their arrival to people within the compound as it drew gently to a halt. The music continued to fill the back of the car with what was now relentlessly chirpy eighties pop. The engine idled for a few seconds, before the car moved forward again. She assumed it was some sort of safety barrier or gate. Not great.

Frankie could just make out the blur of movement through the dark glass but it could have been anything out there.

Leaning forward, she scrolled through the playlist, looking at the duration of the individual tracks and guessing they'd been travelling closer to three hours, which was a lot longer than Tomas had suggested. As far as she could tell there hadn't been any bottlenecks of delays, so he'd lied.

She heard the gravel crunch beneath the wheels for a couple of minutes, and then the music died as the engine was turned off.

She tried the door. The child locks were still engaged.

She heard the driver's door open and close, then a moment later Tomas was opening hers and telling Frankie, 'Here we are.'

She slid out, glad to be able to stretch her legs. The air was crisp and cold. Colder than back in the city by a good few degrees.

She took her first look at her new surroundings.

The compound appeared to comprise of a number of single-storey wooden buildings. None of them looked particularly luxurious. Each had a large number painted on the short side. Frankie's first thought was that it was some sort of repurposed army barracks. She heard the slight thrum of a generator behind one of the buildings. There were trees. Lots of them. Twenty, thirty, and some even forty metres high, looking over the compound like something out of a grim little fairy tale.

'This way,' Tomas said, leading her towards one of the larger cabins. He didn't turn to see if she was following.

'My stuff,' she said, but he showed no sign of slowing.

'Don't worry about it. I'll get it later and bring it through to your cabin. Someone's waiting to meet you.'

Frankie didn't like it.

But she had no choice.

She hurried after him as he entered what appeared to be some kind of office. A middle-aged woman looked up from the screen she'd been working on. Her face was creased with the kind of concentration only computer-illiterates suffer in the face of technology. The creases melted into a smile when she saw Frankie.

She stood up and held out a hand, 'Well, hello there. You must be Ceska? John spoke so warmly about you. I can see why. My, aren't you just lovely?'

'Thank you,' Frankie said.

'He was very impressed with you. He said you had the right stuff. Lots of great ideas. He really thinks you could make a difference here.'

Frankie inclined her head, like she was shy and embarrassed by her kind words. It felt like something a younger her would have done. 'I was just helping out,' she said, by way of explanation. 'Paying back an act of kindness.'

'Oh, it was far more than that, my dear. I've heard so much about you. Believe me, John wouldn't have invited you here if he didn't see something special in you. Now, why don't we get you cleaned up and into some fresh clothes? I've laid some stuff out for you.'

'That's OK, I've got my own clothes.'

'Of course you do, but while you're here, we like everyone to dress the same way. It's just a little thing, but some who find their way to us are in desperate circumstances, while others by comparison are almost rich. This way it makes everyone equal and saves any embarrassment.'

She couldn't really argue against that, and found herself being ushered through another door at the rear of the office.

'What about my stuff?'

'Don't worry,' the woman assured her. 'I'll make sure that Tomas brings it in. You won't need it for a while, anyway.'

'Thanks,' she said, knowing it was the only response she could give.

The door led through to a wood-panelled shower room. There was a small table with a pair of black jeans, a T-shirt, sweatshirt, socks, and a pair of basic trainers ready for her to change into.

There was an assortment of plain underwear in a wicker basket beside them.

'Why don't you freshen up after the drive?' She reached through to turn on the showerhead, a not so subtle hint. 'There's toiletries and deodorant, too. Take your time. You can leave your dirty clothes on the floor, I'll see that they are washed and ironed, and put with your other stuff.'

For one awful moment Frankie thought that she intended to stay with her while she undressed, the smile still plastered on her face. 'Sorry,' she said, eventually. 'I'll leave you to it.'

There was no lock on the inside of the door.

Frankie moved the small wooden table up against it. It wouldn't stop anyone getting in if they were determined to get in, but it'd stop her from being taken by surprise.

THIRTY-THREE

The red cursor on the screen stopped eventually. It was a remote spot deep inside a dense forested region. Laura pulled up some satellite images of that precise location.

Her first instinct was that the coordinates she'd fed into the system must have been wrong, because it didn't look like there was anything there at all.

Her second was that the tracker had been discovered and abandoned, meaning Frankie was on her own.

It wasn't until she enhanced the image, narrowing her focus down and down, that she finally made out the corner of what looked like a long rooftop. There were others clustered in around it, all of them obscured by the dense trees. Finally she saw a stretch of track that ran through the forest like a thin black stream, and part of what was obviously a vehicle.

The compound, whatever else it consisted of, lay at least sixty kilometres from where the body had been found. Too far for the flames to be a threat, and too far for the girl to have run, but close enough that she couldn't dismiss a possible connection, especially with a car parked up outside the largest of the buildings.

She scrolled across the image, looking for more structures within the forest. She couldn't see any, but that didn't mean they weren't there.

She knew full well that if it was Peter Ash jumping to these kind of half-arsed connections she'd have been shaking her head and telling him to rein in his imagination.

She looked at the satellite image again.

Was she seeing things that weren't there?

She had zero evidence that said the burned girl's death had anything to do with One World, and a compound that was probably forty-five minutes' drive down some pretty treacherous single-track roads filled with switchbacks and choke points, from where she'd been found. That was a long way. It didn't fit with the idea that she'd made a run for it and been hunted down. You didn't run sixty kilometres through rough woodland. It would have taken days.

But that didn't mean she'd died there, Laura thought to herself. She could have been killed a lot closer to home and dumped somewhere far enough away that people wouldn't make the obvious connection.

No.

She was sure Frankie was in the right place for both her cousin's disappearance and for the burned girl's murder. It was just putting the two together that worried her.

She reached for the phone to call Peter and bring him up to speed when an alert pinged from her computer.

The crawler's initial sweep was complete.

She took a deep breath before switching windows to the program she'd left running in the background.

She saw several thousand hits, which would take some narrowing down, but that didn't matter because she had the name to run against the broader results, and there weren't going to be hundreds of Maria Bartoks in Europe. Of course, that was assuming the girl had used her real name. If she hadn't, it would take a lot more legwork to sift through them. She wasn't going to think like that.

It didn't take long for Laura to find the name Bartok on the screen. She delved into the result, drawing out the data behind the hit, and spent a couple of minutes verifying it. Her heart started beating just a little faster as she read. It was an arrest report for one Maria Bartok, who had been brought in for vagrancy in Stockholm.

The report itself was in Swedish, but the date wasn't. Numbers were universal. She was looking at something which proved Maria Bartok was alive three weeks ago. Meaning she couldn't be the body in the woods.

Laura stood up and called across the Operations Room, 'Anyone speak Swedish?'

A hand went up. 'Badly, if that counts. It's basically a prettier Danish,' Magnus Edgarsson, one of the team that had been based in Copenhagen said, with a grin. He was a big, burly guy with a shaved head. The kind of man you wouldn't want to meet in a dark alley, as her mum used to say. Thankfully he was one of the good guys. He got up and walked across to her terminal. The fabric of his shirt strained just a little as he leaned forward, his biceps almost too much for the material. 'What can I do for you?'

'A little translation help.'

'It'll cost you.'

'Of course it will. What do you need?'

'Coffee,' he said with a grin.

'You check this out, I'll make a coffee run.'

'Do you need me to write it down for you, or is it OK to just read it to you'

'Reading it's fine. It might be nothing.'

'OK, then I'll do the work in advance and we can go and get the coffee together. It's a police report. Maria Bartok, arrested for vagrancy, no documentation. She claimed to have come from Estonia, but there was some doubt about that. She claims not to know how long she's been in the country and there's no point of entry paperwork. The arresting officer, Kristoff Andersson, suspected she may be involved in prostitution – which of course isn't illegal in Sweden from the perspective of the girls selling themselves, only from the point of the buyer, or a pimp if she's being put to work. He didn't have the evidence, but issued her with a warning. He told her about a group home that could help her if she was at risk, and warned her what the impact of a criminal arrest could be for her. Certainly it would cause problems for any long-term residency permit.'

'He seems like a good guy. He's tagged a note on the file that he believed she was frightened and possibly acting under duress, which is often the case. He asked her if she needed a way out. He's written here that she said there was no need, she was leaving the country anyway.'

'I don't suppose it gives us any idea where she was heading?'

'I'm afraid not. Was that worth the price of a coffee?'

'Maybe.'

'What were you hoping to find?'

'Honestly? Maria Bartok.'

'Could she have gone home?'

'Back to Russia? Unlikely. I think she's running. You run away from somewhere or towards somewhere, you don't tend to run back to whatever you ran away from.'

'Unless it's really bad where you end up.'

'Not a fan of Stockholm?'

The big Dane grinned. 'When God made the Nordic countries he gave us the beauty and the brains. He made the Swedes dull.'

'Don't let Frankie hear you say that.'

'She's only half-Swedish, she doesn't count. Her other half is exciting.'

'Good save.'

'But, if she's not going back, she's going forward. The obvious choice is Denmark. Over the bridge, though I think they still check IDs now, after the refugee crisis, which could make it more difficult if she doesn't have papers.'

'Maybe. But that doesn't really help. Still, at least I know that she left Estonia alive, which is more than I knew an hour ago.'

Magnus raised an eyebrow. 'Why would she have?'

'She was mixed up with sex-traffickers.'

'Fuck. So Andersson was right?'

'On the money.'

'You could try face-recognition software,' he suggested. 'Run her through the system. We've got all sorts of toys here.'

'I would if I had a photograph.'

'Ah, well, finally I can offer you some good news,' he said. 'But it might cost a cinnamon bun on top of the coffee.'

'OK, I'm game, but only because you're pretty and I don't believe for a minute you'll actually eat it. Meaning I get to.'

He laughed at that.

'Bottom of the page. There's a link to her mugshot when she was booked in.'

THIRTY-FOUR

The trainers were a size too big, the T-shirt a size too small, but the jeans and sweatshirt were a good enough fit. She left the spray running in the shower considerably longer than she was under it, letting the small room steam up. She enjoyed the water. It felt good to be clean.

A couple of seconds after she killed the spray there was a soft knock at the door. 'Everything OK in there?'

'I'm fine,' she promised. 'The trainers are too big. I don't suppose you've got a size smaller?'

'Of course we have, honey,' the woman said.

A couple of minutes later she returned with a different pair and opened the door without knocking.

'Here we go. And goodness me, I just realized I never introduced myself. Where is my head at? I'm Elsa.'

'Thanks,' Frankie said, taking the trainers from her. 'It's just that I'll like to run in the mornings. Gets the blood pumping, clears the cobwebs out of the head. It's been a while since I've been able to just stretch my legs and really run, you know, without it being with my sack on my back, running because someone's chasing me.'

'I can understand that,' Elsa said. 'We've all got our versions of your story. They're different of course, but they're the same, too. You enjoy your run tomorrow. The woods are great for it. But it's probably best not to go too far. It's easy to get turned around and end up getting lost. These woods are vast. I think they go a couple of hundred kilometres in one direction. We'd need a search party if you wound up getting lost.' She smiled at that. 'I've an old track-suit you can borrow. That's got to be better than running in jeans.'

'You're very kind. Thank you.'

'No problem, honestly. We're all one big family here. I'll put it in your room later. And talking of your room, let me show you where you'll be sleeping, then I'll take you to join the others. They're all looking forward to meeting you.'

Elsa led Frankie across the compound to the building with number three painted on its end. It was wood rather than brick, which made sense given the abundance of building materials the forest offered. There were three small windows, slightly higher than her eyeline, and she was tall.

Tomas's car was nowhere to be seen. As much as she wanted to, Frankie decided not to say anything. Maybe he'd been good to his word and put her bag in cabin three before he quit? And maybe she'd spot winged bacon over the Baltic.

If the backpack was still in the boot of the limo that was going to make the next week a lot more isolated and dangerous than she'd bargained for.

'Here we are, home sweet home,' Elsa said, pushing open the door.

Inside was pretty basic: a single bed, a desk, a chair, and a single-door cupboard. It was more like a student dorm or a nun's cell than a holiday chalet, emphasis on the 'cell'.

'It's a shared bathroom, but it's only you and three other girls so it shouldn't be too much of a hardship.'

Frankie gave her a smile. 'It's better than the last doorway I called my own,' she said. 'This is luxury.'

'I can imagine.'

Repeat a lie often enough and you begin to believe it; that's what the psychologists say. It's one of the reasons they drill undercover officers over and over to make sure they've got their stories straight. It's not just that they need to know their stuff, it's that they need to believe it. And Frankie was starting to convince herself she'd actually been rescued from a life on the streets, not just a few nights in a shop doorway – even if she did go through a trial by urination.

'You must see a lot of people coming through here.' Frankie tried to make it sound natural. She looked around, walked across to the bed and tested the mattress springs.

'Oh, I see girls coming through here all the time, honey. We've got new groups nearly every week.'

'Only girls?'

'Girls, young women, I never know where one age is supposed to end and another begin. It's not like when I was young, we all called each other girls. Heck, we still do.'

'No, sorry, I meant are there no men?'

'Well, sometimes we get a few, but they're usually people like Tomas, volunteers who help take the girls on to the next stage of their journey within One World.'

There was something odd about the way she said that, but again, Frankie resisted the temptation to push. It needed to be done gently. Gain trust. Did it mean the men went to a different camp, or that they only 'saved' young and vulnerable girls from the street? The second made sense if this cult really was some sort of cover for the sex trade and the compound was a staging post in a human railway. She thought about Irma here, on her own, thinking these people were going to save her somehow, and felt sick to the core.

'How many other girls are here at the moment?'

'Twelve. They're a nice group, but then John has an eye for the right kind of girls.'

'Do you ever have people that just don't fit in?'

'Oh, it happens, but not often. Rather than let them upset things here, we have to let them go.' Elsa obviously saw something in her face and assumed it was worry for her own situation, so offered a reassuring smile and said, 'We get Tomas to take them back to the city, we even buy them a train ticket so they can go back home if that's what they want. There's never any hard feelings, at least not on our side. But you don't need to worry about that, I know you're going to fit in just fine.'

'I just don't want to disappoint anyone.'

'Oh, honey, you won't disappoint anyone. John will look after you if you're feeling a bit lost. He's a good man.'

Frankie wasn't sure that she wanted looking after. Being invisible was always better, but that wasn't what she'd come here for. So if she needed to be whatever John wanted her to be, then that's what she'd be.

'You know, I was thinking,' Frankie said, 'I don't really know what actually happens out here.'

'Oh, all in good time, honey,' again with the honey, it was folksy, too friendly, and was already beginning to choke in her craw. Frankie smiled and nodded. 'We've just got you settled. Now we've got to go and meet your new friends. Maybe you'll stay here for the whole week with us, or maybe you'll be given the chance to move on somewhere else. That's what this camp is all about, finding out what your particular talents might be and how One World can help you.'

THIRTY-FIVE

'Y ou'll be glad to know you're not the only one getting twitchy about Karl Tamm's arrest,' Mirjam Rebane said. 'There are doubts about the underwear they found in Tamm's room, too.'

'Are you saying it doesn't belong to Annja Rosen?' Peter could hear the sound of traffic in the background as well as the echo of his own voice feeding back to him down the telephone. She was on the handsfree, most likely driving.

'It's definitely hers. We've got a DNA match on that.'

'So what's the problem?'

'There's no trace of Tamm's.'

'Is that so surprising?'

'The guy's a sexual predator. Last time he was brought in he'd jerked off into the vic's panties.'

'Maybe your guys brought him in too quickly? He didn't have time to get his jollies?'

'It's possible, but not likely. It's only a matter of time before someone cross-references the emergency logs.'

'Anyone spoken to Kask yet?'

'He's MIA. No one has seen him all day. He's not answering his radio or his phone. It's only a matter of time before someone goes knocking on his door.'

'Then maybe we should get there first.'

It didn't take her long to come to a decision. 'It doesn't count as a date,' she said, and he realized that if they were counting dinner and coffee, then they were moving into third-date territory and barked out a short, highly inappropriate, laugh. 'Has anyone ever told you you've got the filthiest laugh, Peter Ash?'

'That would be a yes,' he said.

'OK, where are you?'

'Back at the hotel.'

'Wait in the lobby. I'll come and pick you up. Give me fifteen to get to you.'

'Are you sure?'

'About it not counting as a date? Positive.' He could hear her smiling.

'Well, you can't blame a lad for trying.'

'Oh, and I got confirmation, Kask's part of One World. He attends their church in the city.'

'Shit. But it's what we expected. I just really hoped I was wrong.'

'Me too,' she said. 'Because it makes it a lot more difficult.'

'I did a little digging last night,' Peter told her. 'They're an incredibly wealthy organization with interests all across Europe. Everyone seems to love them. They do all of this great work for the homeless, hands on, like the soup kitchen down at the docks here. Anything we do that paints them in a bad light is going to affect the lives of real people who have no one else to help them.

'Which is shitty,' she agreed, 'but the law is the law, and there's a dead girl who needs us to bring her justice. It doesn't matter if it's a new religion or the oldest. If there's corruption at the heart of it we've got a duty to root it out for the greater good.'

'Absofuckinglutely, Detective Rebane. We're soulmates. Just a shame there's only the two of us, because we could really use some manpower here.'

'There are four of us,' she said and it took him a moment to realize she meant they had Frankie on the inside and Laura back in Bonn. Four wasn't exactly the magic number, but it doubled their resources.

'Somehow we've got to prove there's a connection between One World and your dead girl in the forest.'

'If it's there we'll find it. But there's something else we need to talk about.'

'You're going to ruin my good mood, aren't you?'

She made a face, and he knew she was about to do just that.

'Spit it out,' Peter said.

'Kask isn't the only member of One World serving in our police force. OK, get your sexy arse downstairs, young man, I'm only a few minutes away.'

She ended the call. Peter Ash grabbed his jacket, checking that he had his wallet, and slipped his phone into his pocket.

He really wanted to put questions to Kask, look him in the eye and do that human lie-detector thing, but even if there was just cause the fact that Kask was in the wind pretty much put paid to that. That last comment though really had been the sting in the tail. Anything he did with Kask was going to get back to One World and whoever was pulling its strings. There was no way it wasn't, with however many faithful hidden away within the force. It wasn't like there was a check box on the application that said *please disclose any crackpot faith you have sworn allegiance to.*

The question was, just how corrupt were the others? Would they give Kask the protection he needed to get away with murder?

By the time he reached the front entrance she was already parked outside.

'You took your time.'

'The lift took for ever.'

'Ever thought of taking the stairs?'

'From all the way up there?' He pointed to a window up on the ninth floor. 'I may look like a paragon of health, but like it or not I'm not as young as I used to be. And I wouldn't have taken nine flights of stairs back then, either.' He grinned. What he wasn't saying was that he was far from recovered from the tortures Stefan Karius put him through six months ago, but that wasn't for public consumption.

'So we're off to the monster's lair?'

'Yes indeed.'

'How far are we talking?'

'Twenty minutes from here, maybe a little longer in this kind of traffic.'

She lied. But then, there was no accounting for the fact she drove like a madwoman. Mirjam Rebane put the car through some serious abuse, taking corners like Mika Häkkinen. It was more than just familiarity with the route. It was a rat run. 'Eleven minutes,' she said as the car came to a sudden stop outside an apartment block. She checked her watch. 'Ten and thirty-two seconds. Even better.'

'I think I lost at least one of my nine lives back there. Heart failure.' She laughed at that. He realized he liked making her laugh. 'OK, which one is Kask's?'

'Third floor, 302. I double-checked before I left the station.'

'That's a risk. Does your search record raise any kind of flags with IT? Back home I'm pretty sure someone looking for a cop's home address is going to trip all sorts of alarms.'

She reached across and opened the glove box, pulling out a small black leather notebook. 'Names and addresses of every officer in the city, which department they're with. The only thing it doesn't have is their social security numbers, but you can get those just by phoning the tax office. We're an open society. So, in answer to your question, no trail.'

'There's something to be said for old-school pen and paper,' he said.

'Shall we?'

'Let's go and ruin his day.'

They clambered out of the car. Mirjam used the button on the keyfob to lock the doors behind them.

There was no lift in the small block so they had no choice but to take the stairs. Peter did his best to hide the wince as they turned the last corner.

They were too late.

A neighbour, an elderly woman with a small pug clutched tight to her, stood on the landing waiting for them.

She said something.

Peter listened to Mirjam and the old woman exchange words. He had no idea what they were saying. All talked out, the neighbour retreated into her own apartment.

'We missed him by half an hour.'

'Shit.'

'He had a holdall. She said he was rude, which was unlike him. He told her to mind her own business when she asked if he was going anywhere nice.'

'Do we call it in? Get people hunting for him?'

'That's tipping our hand.'

'It is. But every minute he runs is a mile he gets further away.'

'Up to a point. I've got an idea.'

'Do you want to share?'

'Let's just say Laura for now.'

The old woman emerged again, holding something. She pushed it into Mirjam's hand.

Mirjam uncurled her fingers to show him the spare key.

'Can you smell gas?' Peter said.

She tilted her head like she was considering it for a moment.

'Why, I do believe I can,' she said.

'Then we better get inside and make sure there isn't a leak.'

'It's the decent thing to do,' she agreed. 'Public safety.'

'You read my mind.'

'It's not difficult,' she said, with a grin and slipped the key into the lock and opened the door.

THIRTY-SIX

Maria Bartok looked young.

Mid-teens.

The report put her at twenty-three, which was a lie.

She was a pretty girl, even in the stark glare of the mugshot that never made people look good, but it was painfully obvious she was tired. Her face was washed out.

Living on the streets would do that.

It was a big step forward. She knew she owed Magnus more than just coffee. Maria Bartok was alive. While that meant they were no closer to identifying the burned body in the woods, it also meant they were following a live lead. Presuming she could get Peter in the same room as Maria that changed everything.

But it was still a huge ask.

Three weeks was a long time for a girl like Maria Bartok to disappear.

The chances of facial recognition – no matter how advanced the software they were running in Division – being able to track down her current whereabouts was beyond slim and into the realm of science fiction. It wasn't as though they could run an endless scan through the system playing mix and match with the traffic cameras and CCTV until they found her on a street corner somewhere. It wasn't TV.

Even so, having a picture of the young woman made her feel more real, and that made Laura all the more determined to find her.

The crawler she'd created could work with pictures too, but it could only handle very small chunks of data effectively, meaning it needed separate searches and narrow time frames or it would just get hung up in an endlessly incomplete subroutine.

But she didn't need a huge window.

She had more precise parameters this time. According to the arresting officer Maria was leaving Sweden, which limited the points of exit – she wasn't going up over the mountains and through the Arctic, for instance. Major ports, Gothenburg, Stockholm, Malmö, were good places to start. And Magnus was right, the Öresund Bridge was the obvious way out, which meant Denmark was her most logical destination, even if it wasn't her final one.

Laura set a search in motion, looking to compare the facial features of the girl in the mugshot to any arrests carried out in Copenhagen in the last six months. The temptation was to scour the entire database for Denmark arrests, but prostitution was predominantly a big-city problem.

Of course there was nothing to say she'd actually left Sweden, so Laura ran identical searches in the three major port cities. Just because Maria Bartok had told the cops she was leaving the country, didn't make that the gospel truth.

Once the searches had been put into action she printed off a copy of the girl's photograph and pinned it to the soundproofing walls that created her office.

It would be good to have a reminder that they were looking for a real girl. Someone's daughter. No matter what her reason was for leaving Russia and then Estonia, she was running away from something before she was running away from One World, rather than to somewhere.

There was a real difference.

She settled back down in front of her screen and started to compose an email to Peter, bringing him up to speed with what she had found.

She attached the girl's photograph and was about to hit send when she received a ping on one of her searches.

Rather than an error report, the search had found a match. And it was current. Maria Bartok was still in Sweden. And what was more, she was in custody – not in a prison cell or the custody suite of a police station, which was why it hadn't shown on her first searches – she was currently sitting in the Marsta detention centre close to Stockholm's Arlanda Airport.

She was due to be deported the following day.

The Swedes were sending her back to Russia.

Once she was outside the EU, the chance of getting to her and any meaningful answers about what had happened to her were negligible – which wouldn't help Frankie's search for her cousin.

She was going to have to set the wheels in motion immediately.

First, she needed to get the Swedes to delay the deportation, which was easier said than done.

Eurocrimes had no real clout with a country's immigration service – unless Maria was suspected of a pretty major crime, and even then there was no guarantee that would be enough.

She needed to get hold of Peter Ash.

She punched up his number.

He didn't answer.

Eventually she heard his answerphone message.

'Call me. I mean right now. Stop listening to this message. Call.'

She didn't need to say who it was.

THIRTY-SEVEN

'OK, what are we actually looking for? This is your show,' Peter said.

'Anything that gives us an idea of what Kask's really like when he's not playing cop. Something that gives us a clue where he might run to.'

'Works for me.'

'Glad you approve,' Mirjam said.

He wasn't sure what sort of links to One World they'd turn up, but Kask had left in a hurry. That meant he hadn't had time to clean the place. It wasn't going to be sanitized, so treating it like a crime scene and hoping they got lucky seemed like the best course of action.

'Well, let's play cops and robbers, shall we?'

Peter's phone rang. He muted it in his pocket without looking at the caller ID.

He'd call back when they were out of Kask's place.

The living room was spotless. Anally so, it was like a scene from that old Julia Roberts movie, *Sleeping with the Enemy*. All of the labels were lined up kind of thing. Everything most certainly had its place.

The bedroom on the other hand was almost schizophrenic in the level of mess it presented. Kask had upended drawers and tipped them out onto the bed, throwing everything he needed into his bag. Everything else he'd left where it landed.

The bedside cabinets held little in the way of interest, but Peter spotted what looked like a collector's coin in a small perspex case. It had the One World logo embossed on it. Beneath the coin he found a selection of literature about the Church, including something that called itself *The Pursuit of Happiness*, which looked like some kind of guidebook for how to live your life as a better person. He skimmed the pages. It looked like a mix of Jungian and Freudian theory garbled through some sort of plainspeak filter.

'Anything?' Mirjam said, looking around the door.

He held up the book. 'The unholy Bible.'

'Any sign of a passport?'

'Not in here. Any luck your end?'

She made a face.

'In which case, I vote we bug out before your colleagues turn up and start getting the wrong idea.'

He nodded, pocketing both the book and the coin. 'OK, here's what I'm thinking. You're a member of a cultish group with places all over Europe. You're up to your neck in the shit and you know you've got to get out of town. Where do you go?'

'To your people,' Mirjam agreed. It was the only option that made sense.

'So he's looking for sanctuary.'

'Somewhere beyond the reach of the Estonian cops. He's got a head start, hence the lack of passport here.'

'Agreed,' she said. 'Which means we're shit out of luck.'

'Or we're not.'

'Laura?'

'Laura,' he agreed. 'I'll get her to flag his passport. Hell, she could probably revoke it if she put her mind to it. That'll slow him down at least.'

They closed the door carefully and slipped the key through the neighbour's mailbox before they headed into the fresh air.

'OK, so, you get on to Laura, I'll get you back to the hotel,'

Mirjam said as they got back in the car. As she started up the engine, he saw a marked police car coming around the corner behind them and pulling into the vacant spot they left outside Maksim Kask's apartment block.

'A little too close for comfort,' she said, looking in the rear-view mirror.

'Could have been worse,' he said.

It felt like they'd struck out. He wasn't really sure where they went from here, but he really didn't feel like saying goodbye to Mirjam Rebane just yet.

It was a more leisurely drive this time, taking all of seventeen minutes.

They didn't talk much. They'd been close and Kask had slipped between their fingers. That took a little bit of getting over. In Peter's experience alcohol always helped with that.

They pulled up outside the portico, the doorman coming out to open the passenger door for him.

'I'm going to be cheeky now,' he said. 'But right now there's not much we can do, and I'm dying for a drink. Want to join me?'

'I thought I was going to have to hit you over the head with a brick or something,' she said, and killed the engine, taking the keys out. She tossed the keys to the doorman as they walked up the red carpet to the foyer.

'What can I get you?' Peter asked.

'Room service,' Mirjam said, walking straight across the foyer to the row of elevators.

They barely got into the room.

Breathing hard, she pushed him up against the wall. He reached for her even as she clawed at his shirt. The door still hadn't closed. He kicked it closed with a booted foot before he tried to kiss her properly. He wanted it to be good. Right. He cupped his hands around her cheeks, angling her lips up to face him, but she had no interest in tenderness.

Which was a problem, because nothing was going to kill the mood more than him wincing in pain as she worked her hands over his ribs.

It was all he could do not to cry out as she slammed him up against the wall again as he tried to steer her over to the bed.

She was having none of it.

This was all on her terms.

She tore his shirt open and worked her lips down his chest, biting at his nipple as she pulled his T-shirt up over his head.

'It'll be easier if you just give in,' she said.

And he didn't doubt it for a moment.

Mirjam Rebane knew what she wanted and wasn't afraid to tell him.

She was vocal.

Demanding.

And it was good.

Better than good.

For a while at least Peter Ash forgot himself. It had been a long time since he'd managed to get outside his own head. He didn't even care as she lingered over his scars, feeling her way across those old hurts. She ran her hands across his skin. Insistent. Urgent.

And then she was struggling with his buckle and working the buttons of his jeans while she was still fully dressed.

'I feel at a bit of a disadvantage here,' he said.

'And you're loving every minute of it,' she said.

It was hard to argue.

They lay in the aftermath of sex, the sheets tangled around their legs, their doppelgängers sweated into the cotton.

Peter's clothes were strewn all across the floor. Most of Mirjam's were at the foot of the bed.

He saw his phone on the red carpet, the message alert light in the corner flashing, and realized he'd forgotten about the call he'd ignored in Kask's apartment.

He walked naked across the room.

One missed call.

Laura.

He didn't bother checking the message, he hit redial.

She answered on the first ring.

'You took your bloody time.'

'I got tied up,' which earned a snigger from the woman in his bed.

'Well, get yourself untied and pack your bag. I need you on a plane in two hours. I've found Maria Bartok.'

'Where?'

'Stockholm. She's due to be deported in the morning. I tried to sweet-talk immigration, tell them we needed to speak to her, but no joy. She's on that plane whether you get to her or not. So, get that perky little behind of yours dressed and get to the airport.' Laura killed the call, leaving Peter standing there naked, phone in hand.

'So much for pillow talk,' Mirjam said.

'How far is it to the airport?'

'Twenty minutes.'

'Then I've got an hour to kill. I could go again.'

THIRTY-EIGHT

A ll the heads turned to face her as Frankie was led into the room.

It was a weird feeling walking into a room where every other woman was dressed in exactly the same ill-fitting clothes as she was. They sat around a large circular table. She noticed that all of the women had a coffee mug in front of them, One World logo facing out towards her. Weirder still was the fact that every single one of them looked at her like she was going to be their new best friend.

'This is Ceska,' Elsa said. 'Her English is great. I'm sure you'll all make her feel welcome.'

A couple of the girls pushed their chairs out and started towards her, arms open in welcome. Instinctively, she wanted to recoil from the touchy-feely nonsense, but she knew that was a big part in any of these new faiths, so she leaned into it, offering them hugs one after the other. It was very European. It was the kind of thing that made her skin crawl, and always marked her as a little less European than a lot of her counterparts. A few of the hugs were more enthusiastic than the others, just like the smiles.

They were still smiling when Elsa left them to it.

'I'm Alex,' one of the smilers said. 'Can I get you a coffee?'

'Now you're speaking my language, Alex,' Frankie said, accepting the final hug.

She was ushered into one of the spare seats at the table.

It didn't take long to work out some spoke better English than others.

'So, where are you all from?' she asked, steering the conversation away from her. She'd figured it was an easy question.

It was greeted by silence.

Alex put a coffee down in front of her.

'We are all from One World,' she said, sweetly enough, even if there was a bit of strange echo to it.

'I meant—' she started, but Alex interrupted her.

'I know what you meant, and I told you we are all from One World.' She turned to the other girls. 'Don't worry, this isn't a test. Ceska's one of us.'

'Test?'

'When we arrive here, one of the first things we're told is that we've to forget everything that happened to us before we came here, good and bad. It's like we are born again into this life. Here we are all from One World. It is one of the fundamental lessons of The Shepherd. We cannot truly move on to the next level until we accept this. One World is our only family. One World provides everything we need, both spiritually and physically.'

Frankie had heard a watered-down version of the same mantra from Tasha back at the soup kitchen, but out here in the middle of nowhere it had a slightly more sinister edge to it. She wanted to ask how long they'd been there, and maybe mention Irma at some point, but not now. Instead, she asked, 'Will there be lessons? I think I'm too old to go back to school.'

'You'll be just fine,' Alex promised. 'After all, you've got all of us to look after you. As far as pressing needs, that's the bathroom through there,' she said, pointing to the door at one end of the room. 'There's a kitchen through there,' a different door. Frankie nodded. Alex didn't say what was behind door number three. She guessed it was some sort of interview room.

'How many staff are there?'

Alex shrugged. 'There aren't any staff. There are only the faithful. Different people keep coming and going. There's Elsa of course, we see her more than most of the others. She's nice.' Alex reeled off the name of half a dozen others – Frankie noticed they were all men. 'And there's John, of course. The Shepherd. We thought he would have brought you himself, but they told us this morning that he's not coming until tomorrow.'

There seemed to be some genuine sadness at the news. Frankie noticed that the eyes of a couple of the girls lit up at the mention of his name. He was obviously the king of this little cult.

The girls around the table were undoubtedly sheep, so it was apt.

'Isn't he lovely,' one of them said. They were the first words out of the girl's mouth since Frankie had entered the room. She hadn't said so much as hello, even as they were exchanging hugs.

He was charismatic, that was different.

Dangerous men had charisma.

Hitler had charisma, for fuck's sake, she thought.

It was interesting listening to them talk about him. Because of their disconnect with the past, none of them seemed willing to admit they'd encountered John before they arrived at the compound, despite the fact he'd almost certainly hand-picked them, just like he had Frankie. And like Frankie a couple of them had a little more about themselves than the average frightened runaway. Alex, for one. She possessed slightly more self-awareness and confidence than the others. But even for her there was nothing before One World. The Shepherd existed as part of the now. There was nothing before it.

'How long have you been here?' Frankie asked, after a while, hoping it was safe ground given the diversity of the group. Their answers surprised her, given their level of adoration for John and their commitment to their new lives.

'Some of us came yesterday,' Alex said. 'A couple were already here when we arrived.'

'And everyone feels good? I mean it feels like a home? I don't even remember what home feels like.'

'It feels like this,' Alex said. 'Alina's finding it a little harder than the rest of us, but she'll get there.' She nodded to the smallest girl, who couldn't have been more than fifteen or sixteen, which gave Frankie a serious case of the creeps. The girl seemed to shrink behind her neighbour, not wanting Frankie to look at her.

Just like with the soup kitchen, all the women around the table had a similar look about them. The resemblance between Alina and another girl in the circle, Tania, however, was so striking they must have been sisters. Surely?

Her hunch was confirmed a moment later.

'Hi, Alina,' Frankie said, smiling.

The girl didn't answer her.

'I'm sorry, my sister doesn't speak a lot of English.' Tania spoke up for her.

'Ah, that can't be easy.' She didn't want to think about what could have put two sisters on the streets.

'It isn't. We've been told we're only allowed to speak English here. It is the language of the world. If we don't, we won't be able to stay here. And we want to be here. We all do. We want to be part of One World.'

She wasn't going to get much out of them when they were all together. The trick was going to be getting to them when they were alone. No one was going to admit to any doubts or fears in front of the rest.

She looked at the faces around the table.

Her new family.

Even just the thought of it, the enforced bond, was all a bit Mansonesque for her taste. That or *Children of the Corn*. She wasn't sure which.

Frankie was still trying to weigh her new sisters up and get a feel for which was likely to talk when the third door opened.

Everyone around the table fell silent.

'You must be Ceska,' said the man standing in the doorway. He looked like a preppy Harvard reject with slicked-back hair and pebble glasses. He had a grey stubble that gave his slightly chubby face some definition. 'My name is Charles. Why don't you come through so we can get to know each other?'

THIRTY-NINE

Maksim Kask knew he needed to disappear.

The problem was he didn't believe in magic.

He'd done everything The Shepherd had asked of him. He had been true. But somehow his plan had been flawed. He couldn't stay here. Not when they were already looking for him. He couldn't understand what he'd missed. But they were already beginning to unpick things.

He had thought about staying and trying to brazen it out. He was a decorated cop. He was respected. Tamm was filth. Tamm was the kind of filth that masturbated into dead girls' panties.

But it wasn't the police he was afraid of.

It was The Shepherd.

If he believed Kask was a weak link, or he posed a risk of betrayal, then Kask would suffer the same fate as the girl.

So he needed to go. To get as far away as he could and hope to disappear.

He needed to find sanctuary.

That was the only way The Shepherd would ever believe he wasn't a risk: if he returned home to the bosom of the family.

It had been a good plan.

Maybe not foolproof, but solid.

And Karl Tamm deserved to be behind bars. He was filth.

He couldn't understand why everyone was so fucking interested in Irma Lutz. She was nothing. A nobody. Why had it flagged all the way up to Eurocrimes?

He'd been so unlucky.

He was a good man.

He didn't deserve this shit.

He didn't deserve them rooting around, asking questions, under-mining all the years of good service he'd given the force. But they were gunning for him. He knew it. He could feel the noose closing around his neck. He didn't know who was playing executioner, but he'd find out, and if he had to, he'd kill them. Fair payback for ruining his life. But for now, he had to leave that life behind.

His police radio squawked into life, reminding him that the car had a GPS transponder built into it. He was running with a bright flash-ing sign above his head. He needed to dump the car and move on.

Fast.

He looked at the clock on the dashboard, trying to decide how much time he realistically had. Enough to risk the airport and a flight out of the country? Maybe. But more realistically not. He had to assume they had people in place waiting for his passport to flag up so they could swoop down on him. And even if they didn't, Eurocrimes were involved. Touch down anywhere within the twenty-eight member states and they'd have people waiting for him at the other end.

He was fucked.

He hadn't thought this through enough.

He wouldn't be able to run for ever.

So then what?

He pulled over to the side of the road, still in the outskirts of Tallinn, and not a million miles from where he'd dumped Annja Rosen's body.

He needed to make a call.

'You're calling to tell me that you've taken care of everything?' the voice at the other end said.

'Yes.'

'You're lying to me, Max. I always know when you are lying.'

'People are looking for me. I don't know if they know, or just suspect, but I'm in a bad place here.'

'Can you ride it out?'

'I don't think so. I need to get out. And quickly.'

There was a moment's pause, thinking time. 'Go to the airport. Leave your car in the long-stay car park. Make your way to the Departures drop-off point, and I'll arrange for you to be collected. Someone will be there within the hour.'

'Thank you,' he said, feeling a sudden wave of relief.

'Don't thank me. I'm not doing it for you.' The line went dead.

For the first time in what felt like for ever he didn't have to think. Someone else was doing that for him.

He gunned the car back into life and pulled away.

When he turned on the radio the impossibly bright, impossibly perky voice promised him it was going to be a lovely day, lovely day, a lovely day.

FORTY

'It really is lovely to finally meet you, Ceska,' Charles said, as he ushered her into the small office. It was as spartan as the rest of the place. Very minimal, very functional. There was a plain desk and a plainer bookcase which contained several copies of the same few titles.

She detected an edge of French, or perhaps Belgian, to his accent, but his English was good.

'I hear that you've been working with Tasha, helping out in the soup kitchen?'

'You make it sound like a lot more than it was. I did a couple of shifts to thank her for her kindness the night before.'

'I heard about that incident. Most unsavoury. People can be such filth.'

She nodded. 'This, here, everything seems to be happening very quickly.'

'That's because you impressed John. He saw something in you, Ceska, and John is never wrong. He believes you have the potential to make a real difference to the work we do. Believe him, because he has a gift. When he says we need someone like you, then you are exactly the person we need to carry on our mission.'

'I don't even know what you do. How crazy is that? I'm here, and I don't know how I fit in, or how I can fit in.'

'You have to trust us, Ceska. You are good with people, I can tell that myself, already. It's instinctive with you. A lot of the girls who come here are very badly broken and need putting back together again, but every now and then John brings home someone like you, someone who can help us help the others. We teach a lesson here, about communication, how there are dynamics to it. I would ask you if you've ever tried to talk to someone in the depths of their anger – you know how hard it is to have a rational discussion with them. Their reality is distorted by rage. There is no communication, not really, no matter how much you like or love one another. Some of these lessons can take years to learn, but you are a natural. And that alone is a gift beyond measure. There are many things we can give you here, a world of opportunities we can provide, if you are receptive?'

Frankie nodded. 'I just want to be a better person,' she said.

'And so you shall, my dear, but first things first, we need to talk, just you and me, to share and understand. I want you to trust me, to unburden yourself, so that we can get down to the real you. Do you trust me?'

Not in the slightest.

'Yes.'

'We need to get to the heart of what is troubling you – and before you tell me you're fine, everyone carries a burden of troubles, things that stop us from being the best version of ourselves we can be. It's not a test, not something you can pass or fail.'

'OK. So what is it?'

'Just a chat really, a conversation. We work on our communication to go deeper. We build a bond of trust. You will feel better for it, I promise. You got on well with Tasha, didn't you?'

She nodded. 'Without her I might still be on the streets.'

His smile widened. 'That's the way that so many people who come through these doors feel. Tasha has a special empathy, a way of doing or saying the right thing at the right time. She makes a difference.'

'She does.'

'And all we want is for you to make a difference.'

'I'll do my best,' she said.

Now his smile was almost condescending, at least the part that made it as far as his eyes. 'It's not about best or worst, Ceska. It's about being yourself. Only you can be that, and there's only one real you. So I'm going to ask you some questions that should help us strip away the face you present to the world, the tough, street-smart kid who doesn't need anyone or anything, and get to meet the real Ceska. How does that sound?'

Fucking terrifying, she thought.

'Good,' she said. 'Let's get to know me, shall we?'

'I'm excited to meet the real you, Ceska. So, first, I'd like to ask you what made you run?'

She'd rehearsed this story so many times she believed the lie, so she repeated the story she'd told Tasha on that first morning, but he shook his head. 'No. That's not it,' Charles said.

She didn't know what to say.

How could he know?

She'd been flawless in the lie, every last detail.

'It is,' she insisted.

'No, it isn't. Not really. You need to go deeper. Why did you run, really? What was it that made you finally say enough? What was the breaking point?'

He was asking for her secrets, she realized.

She resisted the impulse to look around the room, and assumed this conversation was being recorded, a spy camera somewhere capturing her confession.

So, she decided to give him what he wanted.

'Can I really trust you, Charlie?'

'Of course you can, Ceska. We're a family now.'

She nodded, and proceeded to lie some more. 'He used to come into my room at night.'

'Who did?'

'My father. He used to come into my room.'

'Why?'

'You know why.'

'No. I don't. Your truth isn't mine. Only you know why, and if we're going to unburden you, to clean your soul, then you need to share it with me. Why?'

'Because I was his special little girl, that's what he used to say.'

'No,' Charles said again, stopping her short. 'No really, why?'

'Because he lied and told me he was protecting me. That he would always protect me.'

'No, really, why?'

'Because he was a sick man,' she said.

Charles nodded. 'Yes, he was. He was a sick man. But that's his truth, not yours. So, dig deeper. Why did he come into your room? Really?'

'Because I wanted him to,' she said, and Charles's smile turned predatory. He nodded, like she'd just unlocked a world of truths that would keep him in secrets worth using against her for ever.

'So what was different? Why did you run, really?'

'Because he stopped coming into my room,' Frankie said.

'And there is the truth, Ceska. How does it feel to finally know your darkest heart?'

'I don't like it,' she said.

'Few of us ever do, my dear, but you've taken the first step to cleansing your soul so that you can be the real you. You've recognized the darkness within you. That you *wanted* what happened to you. Now, we are going to do this every day while you are with us. It needn't be long, but each day we will try to understand another aspect of what has caused you to hide the real you, and to understand how you have reached this point in your life.'

'OK.'

'Don't worry, honestly. You'll come to enjoy it. There is

something liberating about freeing yourself of these lies you've woven around yourself.'

'Do you do it? I mean does someone sit with you and ask you the same questions?'

'Of course. I am on a search for answers. We all are. Everyone here is looking for their own personal truth. We can only hope that one day The Shepherd guides us to it.'

'He sounds like a good man.'

'He is. He created One World to help others who can't help themselves. He built this place with his bare hands. He has written his wisdom down as tenets we might follow. Everything he does and thinks is to make our lives better. We have some rules, of course we do, but rather than give you a long list of what you can't do, I think it's better to remove the word no from our vocabulary and look for the positive in everything. So, instead I'd rather focus on what we can do, and how our actions affect others here and why that's important.'

'Like the fact we only speak English here?'

'That's only while you're here. It helps create a bond so everyone feels as though they are part of the same thing. If some speak Estonian, some Russian, some English, French, Ukrainian, or whatever, then it's only natural that native speakers will group together. They have a shared language. That's a commonality. Something that is just theirs. It brings them together. But if we all share a single language then at least while we're here we become closer.'

'That makes sense,' Frankie said.

'We will look out for each other. We care for each other. We protect each other. We nurture each other. I know sometimes it's all a bit overwhelming, and maybe even a bit strange, but if you think of it like this, you came to us as a caterpillar, and this place, this is your cocoon, when you leave here you get to fly as a beautiful butterfly, reborn into the real you. The best you. Anything that had happened to you before you came here is gone. Lost. It bears no relevance on who you become.'

'Maybe I'm a moth?'

'Oh no, my dear, you're no such thing. The world has hurt you, but we are here to help your metamorphosis. We won't allow you to be damned by your past. Family doesn't abandon family.'

She could see what he was doing. It wasn't subtle, or particularly clever. He was appealing to the lost soul, making promises of belonging that it inevitably craved. And it might have worked on her if she was truly lost. If she didn't let herself think about it too deeply. Most people wanted to belong to something, it was part of the human condition, even if it was as basic as belonging to a tribe, a lover, a clan, some group that shared some kindred spirit. Belonging to something was underrated. It was also the first step in a much more insidious process. This was about breaking people down, making them malleable and open to coercion. In cruder terms it was about brainwashing, though nothing was as simple as that. The brain couldn't be erased like some chalkboard. But what they could do was create the perfect little One World soldier.

'So, how do you feel? Any questions? Concerns?'

She thought about asking for her backpack, but knew that ran counter to everything he'd just said. The stuff in that bag was the past. Asking for it when he'd just told her to let go of it was tantamount to admitting she didn't have the right stuff after all.

'Not yet,' she said, instead.

'Good. Well, if you do, Elsa's always around to help or you can come and find me. My door's always open. And of course I'll see you tomorrow for our session.'

'Sounds good.'

'Why don't we go and join the others?'

He reached across to the bookcase, plucking a copy of one of the titles off the top shelf. 'This will give you a better idea of what we do around the world. Sometimes it's good to get the big picture. It helps you know how important you are even if you feel like you're the tiniest cog. I know you're aware we work with the homeless, but that really is only the tip of the iceberg. We are involved in much more than that around the world. So much more. And I'm sure that somewhere in here we'll find something perfectly suited to your gifts, Ceska. Because you are one of us.'

He offered her the book.

She saw the now familiar One World logo embossed on the cover.

FORTY-ONE

K ask parked as far from the terminal as possible, and used the free shuttle bus for the final stage of the journey. He checked his watch as he walked through the terminal building surrounded by the heartbreak and hope of travellers going away and coming home. He still had twenty minutes until he was due to be picked up.

He sidestepped a fat American who seemed to be arguing with himself. Seeing the small white airbuds in his ears, Kask assumed he was on the phone. It wasn't so many years ago seeing someone talking to themselves in public was a sure sign of a mind unhinging, now it was commonplace. The world was changing and leaving people like him behind.

He hadn't been told who was coming to pick him up, but he assumed his contact would be bringing false documentation, that or diplomatic credentials which would allow him to travel with immunity, such was the power of The Shepherd in this new world.

He made his way to the departures board. There was a small cafe directly across from it, offering a range of deluxe Illy coffees and lots of drinks that were anything but coffee despite the caffeine. He ordered and took one of the spare seats, watching the faces go by.

The coffee came. He was too stressed to drink it. It sat on the small table beside him, untouched.

Kask found himself staring at everyone who stopped to look at the departures board, wondering: *Are you the one?*

He watched them struggle with their hand baggage and trying to get their liquids into those small plastic bags to clear security. It was a pointless little check really, but it was as much about pacifying the public as it was about making the air safe. They formed their lines and put their laptops and other electronics in the trays and went through the body scanners. It was too much like watching sheep. Instead, Kask turned his attention back to the row of glass doors that led back out to the real world.

He saw a long black limo glide to a stop.

He recognized the driver, Tomas – he'd met him several times at the compound. It was The Shepherd's personal car. That made him twitchy. He waited in his seat until Tomas walked through the doors to stand beneath the departures board. His arrival was timed to the second.

He saw Kask stand.

'Mr Kask?' Tomas said, closing the distance between them. 'The car is waiting. I can take your bag.'

They walked back out to the waiting limo. Tomas opened the rear door. 'You'll be more comfortable in the back,' he assured Kask. He opened the boot and put the holdall inside.

Kask did as he was told. He was very much at Tomas's mercy.

Even if it felt like he was a dead man walking.

No. He couldn't think like that.

He'd done everything John had asked of him.

He was worthy.

He was being rewarded.

As the door slammed closed, sealing him away from the world outside, he realized just how isolated the interior was from the real world. He couldn't see anything beyond vague shapes through the glass. There was no light. It could have been the middle of the night or the bright heart of day, both imposters were treated just the same by the glass.

Tomas clambered into the driver's seat and a moment later they pulled away from the drop-off point.

'Where are we going?'

'Somewhere safe. My job is to get you out of harm's way.'

Which sounded good, but the bottom of Lake Harku was out of harm's way, too. It just depended who was being harmed.

'Will John be there?'

'I'm going to pick him up now. He is not best pleased that I am taking you to his door, but given the urgency of your situation he understands it cannot be helped.'

'I appreciate it. Truly.'

'We could not risk your colleagues discovering your involvement in the movement. If they were to unearth the truth about the girl you killed it would be bad for all concerned. John is nothing if not a practical man.'

'You knew . . .?'

'Of course. John would not put me at risk without apprising me of the situation. I agreed to bring you in because we are one family.'

'One World,' Kask echoed.

'It will take us a little while to reach him. There is whiskey in the decanter, cigars in the humidor. I know it is difficult, but I suggest you just relax and enjoy the ride.'

A glass screen closed between Tomas and Kask.

He felt safe for the first time in hours.

But then, he trusted John implicitly.

The man was the beating heart of One World.

He was special.

Different.

And that difference was intimidating, even to a man steeped in violence like Kask. It was hard not to be afraid of John, even as you were in awe of him.

They drove for more than an hour, which took them well out of Tallinn. They could have been anywhere within a hundred-kilometre radius of the city.

The car slowed, then stopped.

'I'll only be a moment.' Tomas's disembodied voice crackled through the speaker. A moment later he heard a door open and close.

He felt his heart beat just a little faster.

It was part fear, part anticipation.

The door opposite him opened, and for a moment he caught a glimpse of a very modern building, all glass and steel, that looked more like an office than a home. It was bathed in blue light.

John slid in beside him.

Tomas closed the door behind him.

'Hello, Maksim,' John said. There was genuine warmth in his smile, which allayed Kask's initial fear. 'I trust you are well?'

'I am now,' he said. 'I need to thank you—'

'No,' John said. 'There is no need to give thanks. You did everything that was asked of you. We are one family.'

'One World,' Kask completed.

The limo pulled away.

'Now we need to focus on keeping you safe. We need to be sure you are beyond the reach of your crime. We will need to give you a new identity.'

He knew it was the only solution to his problem. Maksim Kask had to die for Maksim Kask to go on living.

'I was worried for a moment.'

'Why?'

'I thought I had failed somehow . . .'

'But you assured us you took care of the problem. You have not failed us, brother. You have sacrificed yourself. That kind of commitment deserves reward, not punishment.'

'But—'

'No more, Maksim. You need to trust me. There are still so many ways you will be able to serve us, even if that is not here. You have special talents, brother. We cannot – and will not – allow them to go to waste.'

'Thank you.'

'I told you, gratitude is neither expected or needed. Now, I think the best use of your talents while we make arrangements for your extraction will be to evaluate some of our newest recruits. I want you to test their limits. We need to know that they are ready to serve the family.'

'We're going to the compound?'

'Indeed.'

It had been a long time since he'd been to the compound, but his first visit was seared into his memory. He had been told that it would prove his commitment to the family, and that he was deserving of his place.

The things they had asked him to do . . .

There had been a moment when he had questioned his faith, unsure that he wanted to be part of their family, but as he'd looked down at the girl something inside him had awoken. In that moment he had changed. The Shepherd called it his awakening. It was as though a different man had emerged from the compound. A man capable of so much more than the one who had first set foot in the place.

'In many ways it is unchanged. We have many such places across Europe, each devoted to different aspects of One World. This one, we use to identify people's skill sets and how they might best be put to work. There are others where people with special abilities are given the opportunity to show their worth.'

Kask nodded. It made sense. It was a business. Not just a faith.

It grew by identifying skill sets and potential and recognizing how to develop them.

'What do you want me to do there?'

'I was thinking that you might run a course.'

'What kind of course?'

The Shepherd's smile was cold. 'I would have thought that was obvious. You have a rare talent, Maksim. Even I was not aware you possessed this gift. It changes things. It changes your value. Yes, some aspects were executed well whilst others went wrong. But that is where we can look to improve. The ability to take a life, to be the reaper of the group, that is rare. You are special, my friend. I always knew you were. I just did not know how special.'

The words were so matter-of-fact, he could just as easily have been asking him if he could play killer riffs on the bass or shoot some serious curls on his surfboard.

The Shepherd was asking him to teach others how to kill.

Kask rubbed at the dark stubble beginning to show through his chin. He hadn't thought about killing Annja Rosen. It hadn't been a planned and thought-out execution. It had been necessity and, to a huge extent, fear. It had been about protecting something he loved: his family.

What The Shepherd was asking him to do here, that was different.

It was premeditated.

It wasn't defensive.

How could he talk to others about what it felt like to look someone in the eye as you strangled the life out of them, and talk them through the practicalities of getting away with murder?

It felt . . . insane.

'I don't know if I can—' he started to protest, but John silenced him.

'The best educators suffer failures and learn from them. Believe me when I say death will become easier now. That first time you take a life, that is by far the hardest. I am proud of you, brother. You have surpassed even my wildest hope for you. You are one of the best of us. And believe me when I say this, you can.'

FORTY-TWO

The lights went out without warning, leaving her in pitch darkness.

Frankie had been in her room for an hour. They had all retreated to their own spaces.

The segregation made it impossible to talk to the girls alone. They were only ever together as a group, and as a group it was much more unlikely they'd share. There was method here. None of it was random. It was well thought out, and chilling to the core.

After her confession session with Charles she'd watched a propaganda film about the work that One World did and how it intended to reach out into the African nations to do more good works and win the hearts and minds through charity, opening up the people there to the words of The Shepherd.

At first, it was easy to see the good, the way the message focused on the hungry and the food banks and the message of hope, but there was a second layer to the message of the film, a sort of missionary zeal to it, that was uncomfortable. She couldn't say exactly what it was about the film or its message that set her teeth on edge, but it was obvious the intent of the short piece went beyond the spreading of the word. It was a blueprint for building a cult entwined around The Shepherd's identity.

Alone on her bed, she'd spent the last hour reading the book that Charles had given her. There was nothing in it but cheap psychology and more propaganda about all the good work One World did. The message was crude. Charles had told them to think about it, and in the morning they'd be asked what they could do.

Frankie could think of plenty she could do, but she wasn't about to offer any of her unique talents up to One World.

She took the toothbrush and towel that had been left for her and went through to the shared bathroom.

From somewhere along the narrow corridor she heard the muffled sound of sobbing.

She knew she shouldn't risk getting involved, because getting involved wouldn't bring her closer to Irma, but she wasn't about to walk away. She paused by the next door, listening. Behind the door, the crying stopped, as though the girl knew someone was listening.

A floorboard creaked, and a moment later the next door opened. 'It's Alina,' Alex said, emerging from the room. She was already in her nightwear. 'She's homesick. I have tried to tell her this is a better place, but she's young. She doesn't understand. If she doesn't settle then I'm worried she won't be able to stay with us.'

'What about her sister? Why not room them together. Make it as easy for her as possible.'

'Tania's in a different building. Charles thinks that Alina's been using her as a crutch; that their relationship is detrimental to Alina's development. We are all one family,' she said, then waited for Frankie to respond.

'One World,' she said eventually, but with a lot less enthusiasm than the other girl had expected.

'She needs to learn that we are *all* sisters. There are bonds stronger than blood.'

'So, she's left to break her heart alone in the dark,' Frankie said. 'If she's our family, then we should share her pain, shouldn't we? Sit with her in the darkness until she is calm and finally sleeps. If we share her pain, then we forge a bond that cannot be broken.' She knew she sounded too together, too OK, all things considered, but she couldn't listen to a kid in pain and not try and do something about it. What was Alex going to do? Turn her in to Charles because she didn't sound broken enough?

'Knock yourself out,' Alex said, sliding past her to enter the bathroom.

Frankie taped softly on the door. 'Alina? It's me, Ceska. Can I come in?'

There was no reply.

Maybe the poor kid had managed to cry herself to sleep.

She waited at the doorway for a moment, then heard another muffled sob.

'I'm going to come in,' she said, then opened the door before Alina could say no.

She was sat up in bed, wiping her hands across her eyes. She looked so incredibly small in the dim light, sitting cross-legged in pyjamas that were far too large for her. The effect made her look even smaller. Frankie smiled softly and sat at the edge of the bed. She couldn't have been more than twelve or thirteen, she thought, reappraising her original guess, which was so much worse. She didn't belong in a place like this.

'I think this is a scary place,' she said, doing her best to keep her English simple so the girl could understand.

'I want to go home.'

'I bet there are times when we all want that,' Frankie said, but the girl just shrugged. What she really wanted to do was reach out, take her hand, and promise that she'd do everything she could to get her home. But she had no way of knowing if their rooms were bugged. A little kindness could ruin any chance she had of finding out what had happened to her cousin. And even if the rooms weren't bugged, there was every chance Alina herself would say something, by accident or design, that would just as easily betray her best intentions. So she didn't. Instead she asked, 'Did you see anything in the film that you thought looked like fun?' Another shrug. 'What about the animals? Do you like animals? I like animals. I like dogs. We used to have a dog when I was growing up. He was a scruffy little soul called Buster. He had the curliest coat, it was always tangled so I had to brush him every day.' There had been a brief clip of One World volunteers working on some kind of nature reserve somewhere in Africa. Nothing about the location or the work they were doing there had been remotely specific, but they were smiling as they washed the elephants, and Frankie gambled that that was the kind of thing that a young girl would like.

That earned a slight smile in the shadows. 'I like dogs.'

'Did you ever have one?'

'We're not allowed to talk about before . . . is this a test?'

It was heartbreaking that even now the girl thought they were trying to trick her into failing whatever tests they set up for them all.

'It's not a test, I promise. I was just thinking that maybe One World have some sort of animal shelter where you could help out. Would you like that?'

The girl nodded and reached for her copy of the book, flipping through it. She stopped every few pages. Even in the poor light she seemed content to just look at the pictures.

It was like a little sprinkle of magic, a few kind words and a fond memory, and the whole atmosphere of the room lifted.

Frankie couldn't help but think she was doing the worst of One World's job for them.

And she hated herself just a little bit for it.

Frankie returned to her room.

Alex sat on her bed, waiting.

As Frankie came through the door she cupped her hand to her ear and cocked her head. 'Silence? I guess you got through to her?' She smiled.

Frankie shrugged. 'I just talked to her.'

'What do you promise her? Cookies and milk if she was a good girl?'

'I didn't lie to her. I just asked her if she saw anything in that little movie they showed us that she liked. And we talked about animals for a bit. She's just a kid. I told her that maybe there was a chance she could work with animals if she had an affinity for them. It gave her something good to think about. It gave her a glimpse of a good future, not the past.' She shrugged as if she thought it was nothing, but Alex seemed to think otherwise.

'Maybe they're right about you. Maybe you really do have a gift. Because she's been crying for two days straight and you've got to her in a few minutes. You're the child-whisperer.'

'Ha, I don't know about that. It just seemed like the obvious thing to do.'

'Not to anyone else, which means it wasn't obvious. So if you've got nothing to suggest in the morning when they ask you how you can help people, I'd say that. You've got a gift with kids. You're a natural.'

'What about you?'

'Me? I've got a never-ending list of talents, but I'm not sure sucking a softball through a straw counts.'

'You're really quick to put yourself down.'

'I know me.'

Frankie shook her head. 'They saw something in you or you wouldn't be here. That's how it works.'

'Seriously, I doubt they'll have any need for the things I'm good at. But I am very good at them. Or so I've been told.'

She slid off the bed and Frankie was sure Alex gave her a wink before she slipped out of the room, closing the door softly behind her.

The girls in this place came from all walks of life, from privileged to desperate and every stop in between. Life hadn't been kind to any of them or they wouldn't have ended up here, looking to save themselves or be saved by something bigger.

She knew exactly how Alex had survived.

Frankie perched herself on the desk, feet on the chair, and lifted the edge of the curtain a fraction to look outside.

There wasn't much to see. In the next building along another curtain twitched, offering a tantalizing glimpse of light before it fell back. It was almost certainly Alina's sister, Tania, worrying about her.

She heard the sound of an approaching car, then saw the headlights cut across the night as it came up the dirt track. It took a lot longer for it to reach the turning circle in front of the cabins than she'd have expected, meaning the real road was a lot further away than she would have guessed.

Frankie watched it pull up outside Elsa's office.

When he finally stepped into a puddle of light from one of the few spotlights illuminating the compound, she realized the driver was Tomas, the driver who had brought her here.

He opened the rear passenger door.

She saw John.

The second door opened, and another man climbed out of the car. She didn't recognize him.

She watched them a little while longer, but it was impossible to see what passed between them.

The stranger deferred to John, she saw that much. He let him walk ahead, he nodded as he spoke.

She watched them enter the building. The chances were good that her bag was still in the back of that car, and with it her lifeline back to Laura. But could she risk trying to get out there to retrieve it?

It was a big risk, but at what point did risk outweigh reward?

She dug her fingernails into her palm, focusing on the sharp stab of pain.

Going out there was stupid.

Going out there wouldn't help find Irma.

What could she do?

Realistically?

Sleep.

FORTY-THREE

There had been no sentimental farewells. Mirjam dropped him off at the airport with twenty minutes to spare before the gates closed.

Laura had managed to arrange an interview with Maria Bartok three hours before her deportation back to Moscow was scheduled. Ten-minute sit down. It wasn't much, but it was a lot more than he had any right to expect, given a couple of hours ago he'd had her down as the body on the mortician's slab.

He'd come straight from the airport, leaving his carry-on with reception as he took up a seat in the empty waiting room. It didn't take long before a uniformed customs agent came through to collect him.

'Mr Ash?' a man in uniform said. 'Lennart Pettersson.' He held out a hand.

Peter shook it. He offered the Swede his badge.

'I've not seen one like that before.'

'I'm special,' he said, chuckling.

'That's what my mother used to say, too. I understand you're here to see Maria?' He nodded. 'Are you able to tell me what this is all about?'

'That depends upon whether it will affect whether I get to speak to her.'

'I'm just curious, to be honest. She doesn't strike me as a particularly remarkable young lady, and as you say, you are special.' He handed Peter's ID back.

'Honestly? We think she might be able to help us with the people who brought her out of Russia.'

'How so?'

'We believe she was brought into Sweden as part of some

sex-trafficking operation. Organized cross-border crime. Traffickers bringing young girls into the EU.'

'And you really think she's going to help you? She is being sent back to Russia. You cannot offer her salvation. What do you have to bargain with?'

'My charm? I know, it wears thin really fast. Right now, I suspect fear is my best hope. She's being sent back to where they picked her up. They're going to know she's back, they know she's been in custody, they're going to think she's talked. Or at least they can't risk the fact she might have. The only safety I can offer her is taking them off the streets.'

'Which you can't do in Russia.'

'I'm not going to lie to her.'

'But you're not going to put her right if she jumps to the wrong conclusion, are you? That's the sin of omission.'

'I'll take it up with my Father Confessor later. Right now, she's all I've got, and I'm trying to make a difference for another girl who I think is a prisoner of the same people.'

'Then let's get on with it. I don't need to remind you that this is voluntary. If Maria decides at any time that she wants to end the meeting then we end it.'

'Understood,' Peter said.

Pettersson led him through a series of corridors to one of three interrogation rooms. He keyed in a four-digit code which let them through a security door.

Just a few metres along the corridor he stopped and opened another door, into Interrogation Room Two, and stood aside.

Peter looked through the door to see a waif-like girl sitting on one side of the table. He felt like he knew her life story in that second. She was vulnerable, frightened, and still showing the physical marks of abuse that had finally brought her to this place of relative safety. His heart broke for the kid, and that's all she was, but for ten minutes he couldn't look at her as a human being, he had to look at her as a cop, and that meant turning his back on every instinct for compassion and vengeance, and just focusing on asking the right questions.

He knew there wasn't a single thing he could offer her that would make her life better.

'Maria,' Pettersson said. 'This is Peter Ash.' The girl looked up, wondering what fresh hell had just been brought to her door. 'He's with a group called Eurocrimes Division. He's a police officer. I've had a chat with him, and he just wants to ask you a few questions. We can stop this interview any time you feel uncomfortable. You don't have to answer any of his questions, but maybe it'll help another girl like you if you do. Is that OK?'

The girl nodded.

'OK then, I'll leave you to it. How about I go and make you both a nice cup of coffee?'

Peter nodded. 'Sounds good.'

He waited until the door closed behind him before he took a seat on the other side of the table.

'Hi, Maria. I don't know how much Mr Pettersson has told you—'

'Lenny. We call him Lenny.'

Peter nodded. 'I'm going to speak quite frankly, Maria. I'm not going to sugar-coat things or use pretty words, because that won't help either of us. I spoke to someone who knew you in Tallinn. She seemed to think that you'd been brought into the country by traffickers and were being forced into prostitution. Is that right?'

'Who did you speak to?' the girl said. She lifted her face to look him in the eye for the first time. Through the dark patches he saw a surprising defiance.

'She wouldn't give me her real name.'

'But she was happy to give you mine.'

'We had found a body in the woods outside of the compound you ran away from. She thought it might be yours.'

'That's not how it was.'

'Then talk me through it, Maria. Tell me what happened to you. Help me understand.'

He needed to keep her talking. Ten minutes wasn't long. But it was a lot less if half of it was lost to silences.

She looked at him like he was crazy. 'It wasn't what they promised. It wasn't a new life. They wanted me to fuck men for them.'

He looked at her again, properly this time, and realized that dressed the right way she could have passed for maybe fourteen or fifteen, which was another nail in his heart.

'They promised me a better life. I believed them. I wanted to believe them.'

'I know it's got to be hard talking about this stuff, but I really need you to help me understand.'

'I'm trying,' Maria Bartok said. 'I remember hearing someone . . . we weren't supposed to be listening. I was in the kitchen, they were in the chapel, I heard them say they needed one of the girls to get close to someone. A man. I don't know who he was, I never heard his name. They were going to use one of us to get to him.'

'Get to him how?'

'Blackmail. They needed him to do something. It was part of the grand plan. That's not what they called it. They had another word for it, but I didn't understand it.'

'OK,' Peter said. It was a pretty short list of people you'd bribe with compromising photos, or video footage. The KGB might have gone, in theory, but the FSB and SVR weren't averse to using the same kompromat tactics. It went all the way back to the Stalin era. The earliest stuff often included doctored photos, planted drugs, grainy film footage of the target in bed with prostitutes, all fairly primitive entrapment techniques by modern standards. Now, of course, it was a lot more sophisticated, even if it was still more often than not sexual in nature. It was about cybercrime.

The door opened. Lennart returning with their drinks.

He set them down on the table, all smiles.

'They had someone . . . a policeman.'

Peter already knew the answer to the question, but he wanted to hear it from her lips anyway. 'Do you know his name?'

She shook her head. 'Sorry. I just know they were going to use him to help get me close to the man. I had to run. I couldn't do it.'

'OK, Maria, that's fine. You're not in trouble here. I'm looking for the people who smuggled you out of Russia. Not you.'

For the first time since he sat down at the table with her, Maria Bartok's expression changed completely. Peter saw the confusion in her eyes. 'I wasn't smuggled,' she said. 'It was an organized trip. I came over to work with a charity. They had my passport and everything. The Church I was involved with arranged it all. One World.'

Peter Ash saw the look on the Lennart Pettersson's face change when the girl said the words One World.

His first thought, like a punch to the gut, was that the man had some sort of connection to the cult. He refused to think of it as a faith. The more he learned, the more disgusted he became with the so-called Church.

He knew he was being stupid, seeing things in the shadows when there was nothing but the normal darkness of man there.

'They were good to me while I was in Russia,' Maria Bartok explained. 'They looked after me when no one else was interested. They gave me something to do with my life. They gave me meaning.'

He nodded, but really he was just trying to encourage her to open up. His questions were always going to be the same blunt traumas. He needed her to find her way through this, to open up.

'At first I used to help in a home for the elderly, people without other family to care for them. I volunteered. I liked it there. We used to sing and tell stories and they seemed to enjoy it. It wasn't very glamorous, but it meant something. It was making a difference. One World funded the home. They had a couple of volunteers on the staff who helped out, and they explained that One World ran a series of missions, and that we could sign up to work in other countries, helping other branches of the Church deliver kindness to the less fortunate all over the world, like their name suggested. Most of us had never left St Petersburg, let alone travelled to somewhere like London or Rome. It was exciting. We were getting to do something good with our lives and experience something incredible.'

'Which must have felt terribly exciting. When did they tell you where you were going?'

'They didn't,' she said. 'It was always talk of all these incredible-sounding places like Vienna and Prague, Dubrovnik and Madrid.' She shook her head, like she still couldn't imagine a world where these countries and the adventure they must have represented to the young girl from St Petersburg existed. She picked up the coffee that Lenny had put in front of her.

'So you got away from them in Tallinn?'

She took a sip at the coffee, nodding. 'There was this place in the forest. They call it the compound. It's like an army barracks. We had travelled for hours and hours. It was the middle of the night when we got there. We didn't even know which country we were in.'

'What about your passports?'

'We travelled as a group. The Church coordinators sorted

everything out for us, including the visas. None of us had even owned a passport before. You have to understand we weren't the kind of kids who got to explore the world on our gap years.'

'Tell me about the compound.'

'It was a long way from the road. Very remote. At night the sky was pitch black. You could see thousands of stars. There was no reflection from the world, just the night sky. It was beautiful.'

Which wasn't what he'd asked, and he was conscious of the time getting away from him.

'How did you get away?'

'One of the other girls, not one that had arrived with us, another one that had come in from some other branch of the Church, had gone missing. She'd run off into the forest and the whole place was going crazy. They tore the woodland apart trying to find her. There was something about that moment that changed everything for me. It's hard to explain if you haven't lived through it, but I hadn't thought of us as being prisoners until then. They went after her with *dogs*. They'd told us they were going to introduce us to our husbands. I remember that. I remember thinking it was a joke, you know, like hey, here's your camp buddy, you look after each other.'

'But it wasn't a joke?' Peter pushed gently.

'I don't know. I don't think so. But I knew I only had this small window when everyone else was looking the other way. So I got dressed. I was going to run, until I saw the car and realized they'd left the keys in the ignition. I drove for a couple of kilometres. Not as far as I wanted. I didn't get clear of the trees. The weather was awful. A snow storm. I hit something. Maybe a moose. The car died. I didn't have a choice. I couldn't just sit there. I could hear voices, and the dogs barking, but they were getting further away. I stood there in the snow, freezing, terrified. I wanted to run but I couldn't make my legs move. I kept thinking they'd know, they'd have to know that I'd run, and they'd hunt me down with the dogs.

'Then I heard the gunshot and my legs started working. They killed her. They must have killed her. The dogs went crazy. All I could hear was this frenzied barking. I knew I had to run and keep on running and not stop, not even when it got light. So I did that. Even when my legs buckled from exhaustion and I was on my knees, heaving for the next breath, somehow I found the strength to push myself back to my feet and run on.

'And when I thought I couldn't go on, I saw it, this old VW Camper Van that looked like it had been dumped at the side of the road. I climbed inside. It was damp and reeked, but I'd slept in a lot worse places before that, and after. I got lucky, the snow really came down. We're talking thirty centimetres in a few hours. It buried my scent and my tracks. I slept the night in the van, then walked to the main highway. I saw a couple of cars I'd seen at the compound, at one point. I figured they were looking for me, so I hid off the side of the road. I was able to hitch a ride into Tallinn, but even there in the big city I knew I wasn't safe. I had to keep moving. I had to get away. Somewhere they weren't.'

He looked at the clock. His ten minutes were up, but if Lenny wasn't dragging her out of there to wait in line to be deported he wasn't going to tell him to do his job.

'Did you know the girl? The one who ran first?'

She shook her head.

'She was assigned to a different building. They arrived a few hours after we did. It was the middle of the night. When we arrived, they took us to a communal area and we got to know the girls who were already there, but with it being so late, I think they were going to do that in the morning.'

'And you definitely heard gunshots.'

She nodded. 'Just the one. You know the sound when you hear it. I grew up around that sound.' She didn't explain in any more detail than that.

Peter didn't push it.

'And this was six months ago?'

Maria Bartok nodded.

Meaning the body in the woods was going to remain nameless, at least for now.

'Can I ask you one last question, Maria? Do you know what was going to happen to you when you left the camp?'

'I heard someone talk about Germany, one group was going to Berlin, but we were meant to be going to London.'

So One World were looking to develop compromising intelligence on someone in London. It was a big city, ten million strong. That was a lot of people with the potential to be blackmailed. He wasn't really narrowing things down here.

'Does the name Irma Lutz mean anything to you?'

'No. Should it?'

'She's missing. We think she might have joined One World and been taken out to the compound.'

'I hope you find her.' She looked over at Lenny, who still stood in the doorway, and told him, 'I'm tired, Lenny. I'd like to go get my things before the plane leaves. Is that OK?'

'Of course,' the guard said.

Peter Ash pulled his badge, and from behind it one of the crisp new Eurocrimes Division business cards they'd given him before he left Bonn. He gave it to the girl. 'If you think of *anything* that might help me find Irma, please, call me.'

'Sure,' she said slipping it into the pocket of her jeans. 'But I don't remember much. I wasn't there that long. I wish I could help you.'

FORTY-FOUR

The detention centre wasn't far from the airport buildings, but the shuttle bus didn't run back to the terminals so he had to wait for a taxi.

Lenny had given him another coffee, this one in a plastic mug, and left him to wait on the pavement outside. It was just easier, the guard explained, not a punishment. The driver would need clearance to get through the gates. It made sense. It might not be a prison by name, but it was in practice.

He didn't object. He needed to fill Laura in, anyway.

'Any joy?' she asked as soon as the line went active.

'Some. Maybe not how we figured it. Maria escaped from the place in the forest. She wasn't there long. She took advantage of another breakout. She basically confirmed they were expected to have sex with men, but I got the impression it wasn't straight prostitution, which kinda surprised me.'

'How so?'

'You know the old KGB technique of kompromat? Same deal. They're using these girls to get close to people they want to manipulate. She was being groomed. They were going to get her close to someone pretty influential in London. She didn't know the target.'

'So not just money?'

'I don't think so. But I'm just joining the mental dots here.'

'You think that's what's happened to Irma? That she's been used to blackmail someone?'

'If it is, I don't want to think about what they'd do to her when her usefulness was over,' Peter said. 'The name didn't mean anything to Maria though.'

'Did she tell you how they got her out of Russia?'

'She did. A Church trip, arranged by One World.'

'So they travelled on legit passports? They should be in the system somewhere then.'

'None of the girls had their passports. The church kept them.'

'Only girls?' she interrupted.

'That's what she said. And none of them had passports before the trip was planned. One World sorted everything out for them. She heard mention of some going to Germany, she guessed the others were going elsewhere. One thing I did catch, but it may just be me jumping at shadows, the guard seemed to get a little jumpy when she mentioned One World.'

'You didn't get to speak to her alone?'

'Most of the time, yes. It was just bad luck. He came in with coffee just as she mentioned them.'

'You want me to run his name through the system?'

'Honestly, not sure I see the point. It doesn't matter if he's supped from the poisoned teat. It's not him sending her away. And unless he's delivering her gift-wrapped to The Shepherd himself, then the only thing that it's going to achieve is drawing attention to the fact we found her.'

'So what now?'

'I'm going to check into a hotel. I haven't slept in thirty-six hours, and quite honestly, I'm fucked. I'll catch a plane back to Tallinn later. I want to be on site for Frankie. I just have this shitty feeling something bad's going to happen and I'm going to be nowhere near. And yes, before you say anything, I know that's guilt over Mitch and nothing to do with Frankie, but I can't help the way I feel.'

'No. I get it. I'll be happier with you there, too. She seems to be bedded in. She'll reach out if she needs us.'

Peter killed the call and slipped the old phone back into his pocket.

He saw the taxi approach from some distance away. It slowed to a stop beside him.

'Ash?' the driver asked out of a rolled-down window.

'Only after someone sets fire to me.'

'Funny man. Where to?'

'A good, cheap hotel.'

'A really funny man.'

'Do your best.'

A few minutes later he was on his way to a small soundproofed room with a view of the second runway and silent behemoths thundering along the tarmac towards the sky. He wasn't bothered about booking a flight. First, sleep, after that everything else.

It felt like a wasted trip.

Just about everything Maria Bartok had told him he already knew, or could have guessed, with the exception of the whole Church trip thing at the beginning. That was his win here. And it was precious little. But a win was a win. Wasn't that how it worked?

FORTY-FIVE

A sh woke from a dream, covered in a sheen of sweat.

The details were lost in a fog of panic and confusion, but one part of it was fever-fresh in his mind because he'd lived through it time and time again: he had been back in that church, strung up on the crucifix while the flames surged up all around him. The searing heat was incredible. It burned and blistered his bare skin.

In this version of hell someone had come to save him, but it wasn't the Vatican man Donatti. No, he knew the face of his saviour. It was his old friend and partner, Mitch Greer. The gunshot had cut across the roar of the flames. He could see the bullet. It flew in slow motion. He'd tried to warn Mitch, to scream, but the only sound that emerged from his dream-mouth was the mad cackle of flames. He couldn't stop it. Not in the dream. Not in real life. Peter watched him fall. The blood pooled around, but like acid it bubbled and curled back toward Mitch's corpse, eating away his face until there was nothing there, not even bone. There was no saving either of them.

Peter leaned forward, sweating and gasping for breath that he just couldn't catch.

Panic gripped him.

For a moment he had no idea where he was; the contours of the dark room were utterly strange to him. The darkness felt wrong, too. Too dark. Too absolute.

He realized then it was the blackout blind he'd pulled down to shut out the daylight. There was a dim crack of light coming in around the blind. He had no idea whether it was the same day, or if he'd slept through.

A check of his phone showed that it was almost ten. The chink of sunlight meant it had to be morning.

He had one missed call.

He checked the log. It was an unknown number. He'd missed the call by three minutes, meaning it had somehow been subsumed into his dream, probably as the cackle of flames from his screaming mouth. There was a voicemail waiting.

He turned on the bedside light and rubbed the sleep out of his eyes before he listened to the message.

In an instant he was wide awake.

'Mr Ash? This is Maria Bartok. I don't have very long. I don't know if I will get the chance to call you again. I've just seen something on the news that I thought you should know about. There was a girl in the camp called Cristiana, a pretty girl with blonde hair and very blue eyes. She wasn't Russian. Romanian maybe, but I could be wrong. I don't think I ever knew her last name. I've just seen her on television with a German politician. I think he was trying to keep the cameras away from her, but I'm sure that it was her. It was her eyes that convinced me. I don't know if that helps, but I hope you find the girl you are looking for. Maybe Cristiana will be able to tell you something?' There was a hesitation. A long lull. He thought she'd hung up but the silence just went on until she said, 'I'll have this phone with me, unless someone takes it. If you hear about any of the other girls . . . please tell me they are safe. I have to go now.'

She didn't say goodbye.

The line went dead and the automated voicemail voice told him the date and time of the call he'd just listened to.

Peter tried to call her straight back but her phone went straight to voicemail.

'Maria, if you ever hear this, I just wanted to say thank you. I'm going to try and bring these girls home. You have my word.'

It took him a moment of reaching about to find the remote control on the nightstand. He hit the red button to wake up the wall-mounted screen and flicked through each of the channels until he discovered an English-language news station. He didn't recognize the logo in the top corner.

If this was the right channel the story had already moved on. This one was focused on some devastating climate-change news and an old clip where the American President claimed he had better instincts for science than some of the world's best minds because they were agenda-driven and he just had a big science brain. This kind of dumbing-down and the whole Gove bullshit about how we didn't need experts was sending the world back to an age of unreason. It was crazy. Years of advances and understanding willingly cast aside because we didn't want to feel inferior to experts in their field. Maybe the world really had gone to hell when they switched on the Large Hadron Collider after all?

The beauty of the twenty-four-hour news cycle was that there wasn't enough stuff happening to fill it, so the story was always going to cycle around again, even if he had to wait an hour for the new round to begin.

There was a little capsule coffee machine on the desk instead of a good old-fashioned kettle. He filled the water tank and looked on the capsule case for the strongest hit of caffeine, then dropped back onto the bed to watch reports about last night's Champions League games, full of the usual last-minute heroics and failures that seemed to beset English teams abroad. The Spurs result was just depressing.

A special feature on the trial of a Catholic priest came on, and he saw his old friend Ernesto Donatti promising that the Vatican would get to the truth, that their thoughts were with the victims in these tragic circumstances, and that the paedophile priest would be removed from all duties while the investigation was underway, though of course he avoided those actual words. Donatti was good on screen. He was natural, said the right things with the right kind of gravitas that you believed it might actually be different this time. And maybe it would be, because the very last thing he promised was a root-and-branch investigation into the clergy with the new Pope's determination to root out all sickness from the Church.

'Good luck with that,' Peter told the screen a little bitterly, remembering all too vividly those few flashes of nightmare that were hung over from his torture at the hands of Stefan Karius.

He figured he'd got enough time to take a shower while the financial report was on.

He held off on booking the flight back over to Estonia.

Call it instinct. Years on the job. Call it a hunch. Superstition. Call it whatever the fuck you wanted, there was nothing to be gained by doing anything until he knew what Maria Bartok had seen.

If there was another girl who'd come through the compound and made it all the way to her final destination, building that kompromat against someone powerful enough to be considered day-time news then maybe there were answers after all.

It took another twenty minutes before the item was repeated, by which time he'd showered and dressed and was on his second capsule coffee trying to wake himself up.

It was one of those who's-dating-who fluff pieces.

'*Gerhart Schnieder, the rising star of German politics, and hotly tipped to take up the mantle of Chancellor in the coming elections, was seen leaving a top Berlin nightspot last night in the company of a mystery blonde who most definitely wasn't the forty-two-year-old father of three's wife. Schnieder was spotted by eagle-eyed locals coming out of the infamous Berghain nightclub. So who is this mystery woman? Has Schnieder been stepping out? What's the story, morning glory?*' the presenter said, obviously enjoying the whiff of scandal far too much.

Peter Ash couldn't help but wonder what kind of man took delight in the collapse of a family. But that was us, wasn't it, we build them up, we put our trust and faith in them, and then we delight in knocking them down, thinking that'll teach them for getting ideas above their station. We're fucked. Royally. '*We apologise for the rather poor quality of the clip, which was captured on a cell phone by a fellow partygoer.*'

Peter leaned forward, even though the screen was as big as the wall. Schnieder had grown to prominence in recent years on the back of a tidal wave of nationalist fervour. He was very much the people's choice: charming, charismatic, good-looking. His face had graced the front pages of Europe's newspapers. He was very much Germany's answer to France's Emmanuel Macron. But his real popularity had come through social media and an understanding of the power of the modern media.

But it was the girl at his side Peter Ash was fascinated by: Cristiana.

He watched Schnieder's body language as he tried to hide the girl behind him as soon as he realized he was being filmed.

First instinct, that was because he was trying to protect her from the inevitable scrutiny of the world. Second, more thoughtful assumption, was shame. He was hiding her to protect himself. There was no valour in it. He was embarrassed by the girl at his side.

Peter struggled with ageing people sometimes, especially as the kids these days seemed to be in such a rush to become adults, but there was something about Cristiana. An innocence of youth that was deceptive. For all the make-up and poise she could just as easily have been sixteen as twenty-six.

And that disturbed him.

The next image on the screen was of Schnieder with a woman closer to his own age, elegant, strong. She had a young daughter on her hip. They stood on the steps of what Ash assumed was their family home.

The dutiful wife standing by her man. The reminder of the family they had together held in her arms.

At least that was what it was meant to look like.

It wasn't hard to see the cracks in the veneer.

Reaching for his phone, he called through to Division.

'Law, I need you to scrub some footage from this morning, the nightclub thing with Gerhart Schnieder. It's the girl I'm interested in. I need a name. Anything you can find on her.'

'I didn't have you pegged as a *Hello!* reader, Pete.'

'Funny girl. Maria Bartok rang me this morning. I was asleep. She left a voicemail. She'd been waiting for her transport when she saw a clip on the news and recognized one of the girls from the compound.'

'The girl with Schnieder.'

'The girl with Schnieder. I'm guessing it's not going to be hard to find. She called her Cristiana. No last name. Maybe Romanian. Definitely not Russian. I need you to work your magic, Law.'

'We've got good facial-recognition software, so it's possible, but no promises. And if I track her down, are you coming to Berlin?'

'What do you reckon?'

'I'd say you were right before, go back to Tallinn. Be close to Frankie in case she needs you. The girl could just as easily be a wild-goose chase. Sit tight. I'll see what I can find out. Go and have some lunch.'

'I haven't had breakfast yet.'

'It's nearly twelve. Go. Eat. I'll call you in an hour.'

'I'm going to. I just figured this was a conversation for four walls only. Because if it's not just about One World, if it's about a high-ranking German politician, a man who could become one of the most important people in Europe, and they're developing kompromat on him, fuck, Law. I don't want to think about the damage stuff like this could do if it played out in a worst-case scenario.'

'And we'd thought this was only about girls being trafficked into the West as sex-workers.'

'I really don't like these people,' Peter said. 'Because on the one side they're trying to blackmail him, meaning he's the kind of man we need more of in the world, but is weak and they're going to use him, or on the other, they're rewarding him for some service to their cult. And what sort of person wants a kid as a reward?'

FORTY-SIX

I t was barely light when Frankie woke.

It was impossible to tell the time beyond broad strokes like morning, day, evening, and night.

She listened for sounds of movement from the other rooms before she got out of bed. The old tracksuit and trainers that Elsa had left were on the chair beside her bed. Gathering them into her arms, Frankie slipped out of the room and padded barefoot to the bathroom to wash and dress, then went outside.

The air was cold. The morning sun hadn't risen high enough to penetrate the canopy of evergreens that covered much of the camp.

The cabins had been built under the natural shelter, meaning little of the sky was clear. It went both ways. If she could see little of the sky from down here, it was going to be hard to see much of the buildings from the air. The right kind of colouration would make it virtually impossible unless it was being looked for actively.

The Shepherd had chosen his bolthole well.

Frankie stretched, leaning against the cabin wall to work her muscles and loosen them up before she set off in an easy lope. She'd barely covered fifty metres before a voice yelled for her to stop.

There was real anger in the shout.

Frankie slowed and turned, her hands raised like she was surrendering.

She saw a young man in a One World tracksuit.

He carried a rifle. It wasn't pointed at her, but that wasn't a particularly comforting distinction.

She stood very still.

'Where do you think you are going?' he said, closing the distance between her.

'For a run. Elsa said it would be OK.'

'Elsa doesn't have the authority to say that.'

'She lent me her old tracksuit and a pair of trainers.'

'Do you have trouble understanding English? I told you Elsa does not have the authority. Now, go back to your room. I will deal with Elsa later. Your name?'

She almost got it wrong. After a beat she said, 'Ceska.'

'Well, Ceska, let this be a lesson to you. If you had come to me to ask permission to run this morning, I might have told you that it was all right. But I can't have you running around in the woods on your own. For your own safety. It's hunting season out there. It's not just that you might fall, or how much trouble we'd have finding you if you had an accident, there are people out there hunting bears and stag right now. Without the right fluorescents you could get shot.'

'I wasn't going into the woods, I just wanted to stretch my legs. Along the road and back. I'm just feeling a little cooped up, you know?'

He thought about it for a second. 'Go on then,' he said, like he was grudgingly doing her the biggest favour he could. 'The track is pretty straight so I'll be able to see you all the way from here. It's more than 10k to the crossroads, that's a long way there and back, so don't go getting any ideas.' A smile had found its way onto his face, like he was enjoying his own beneficence.

'Thank you,' she said. She picked a spot out in the distance. 'Just to that cluster of trees and back,' she pointed. Shouldn't be more than half an hour.

He nodded.

She didn't wait in case he changed his mind. She set off at a steady pace, jogging across the hard-packed dirt towards the track that led out of the compound.

She could feel his eyes on her.

She didn't look back.

She stretched her legs, savouring the cold bite of the air in her lungs. It was the first time she'd found the opportunity to run in a week. Normally she ran every day. It didn't take her long to hit a steady rhythm. It was good to be free with her thoughts. But she needed to be smart. She was being watched. And she'd supposedly been living rough for weeks if not months. There was no way a street rat was going to be able to just run and run, even if she could, so after a while Frankie slowed up and half-walked a stretch, then bent over, resting her hands on her knees as if struggling to breathe.

She glanced back in the direction she had come.

The guard was still watching her.

She straightened up slowly and carried on a little, much slower this time, carefully pacing one step in front of the other, barely moving faster than walking pace.

Ahead of her the track bent slightly, and if she kept on she'd eventually move out of sight, mainly because of the trees that shrouded the coming stretch of track. The branches dragged low enough to scrape the roof of a decent-sized car.

She ran beneath the canopy of trees. The ground underfoot was damp and covered with a layer of decaying leaves, which made it treacherous. Her footing felt uncertain. She slowed a little more, which was the smart thing to do, anyway.

As Frankie rounded the bend she saw that the road was blocked by a large metal gate.

To either side of it a high chain-link fence stretched away through the trees, ringing the compound.

She wasn't getting away even if she wanted to.

The fence looked new, as did the gate. She assumed they'd been added in the last six months.

As Frankie approached the gate the security camera mounted on one of the gateposts turned slowly in her direction. She squatted down, pretending to heave into the vegetation and the side of the track. The camera watched her.

This was anything but the simple teaching camp in the woods it claimed to be. Guards with guns, mounted cameras, high fences – almost certainly electrified. It was a prison camp. The only reason not to let her run was that they were afraid of her finding something.

But what?

She turned around and made her way back, taking the return run even slower.

The guard had a broad smile on face when she finally reached him.

IN THE DARKNESS . . .

W*hen the man returned, he asked. 'Do you have the answer?'*
'Not yet,' she said, 'But I am getting closer.'
The iron lid slammed closed.
No food. No water.
She wanted to weep.
She wasn't lying. She was getting close.
But close wasn't good enough.
She sank down to the ground as she heard the door close once more, stinging tears welling up in her eyes.
She would never escape the hole.
She would die here, a failure.
She was going to disappoint John. That was worse than failure.
In her mind she desperately tried to imagine the architecture of the software that protected the system. It was hard to do as

everything was theoretical, but she knew code, and she knew the kind of protections a government department would fall back on. They were predictable. That was their weakness.

But this was different. It was easier to conjure up fresh lines of code, narrowing her options down to smaller, simpler exploits, feeling out for the weakness that would eventually spring the trap – because she had been involved in developing it.

There had to be a way, no matter how good she was. There had to be a solution.

That was the test.

She had spent months testing it, challenging the system to be sure it would withstand any sort of attack. That was why the Riigikogu had paid her school a lot of money; because she was the best.

But in the darkness she heard the gentle voice mock, 'You aren't good enough, are you?' even though he wasn't there.

She thought through the programs and worms she'd used to test it, the viruses and trojan horses and everything else. It wasn't that the system was unbreakable. No system was. She had tested an American electoral machine and opened the source code up in less than four minutes, remotely. Every system had its weaknesses and exploits.

She had found one here, in this code, too, but also been able to demonstrate how it could be secured, meaning she'd patched the exploit she needed now.

She tried to think, but there was only confusion and that voice.

'Not good enough, are you?'

A sense of panic threatened to overwhelm her.

How could there be someone else in there with her?

She was losing her sense of self.

There was the code.

There was her.

And there was the voice.

All around her.

Inside her.

She scrambled to her feet, holding out her arms to try to find whoever had spoken, but there was no one in the hole with her.

She stumbled, kicking over the bucket and spilling her day's filth across the floor where she was going to have to sleep later.

She slumped to her knees.

'Not good enough. Not good enough.'

She knew there was no one else in there with her.

She knew the voice, too. It wasn't the gentle giant who had trapped her in this hellhole.

It was a teacher. Someone from long ago. From her past.

'Leave me alone,' she begged. 'I can't remember you. We are one family now. There is no past.'

She felt like she was losing her mind.

FORTY-SEVEN

Tracking down the raw footage wasn't a challenge.

Rather than waiting for it to appear on screen, Laura had just run a Twitter search against Schnieder's name and had turned up hundreds of hits. There was plenty of German-language chatter about the mystery girl, too.

Getting a decent image of Cristiana was simple enough.

The spin doctors were already trying to fix Schnieder's tarnished image with staged photos of him exchanging a kiss with his doting wife as he left for work. The message was obvious, this thing was nothing, a nothing story, their marriage was stable, they were very much in love.

And that was enough to convince Laura that it was a lie.

She'd seen far too many shots like this dating all the way back to Profumo by way of Archer and Johnson. It was a sham. The cracks were there, showing in the wife's body language, and the way she looked at him when she thought the camera wasn't on her.

This was the sort of thing that opened a crack in his reputation. It didn't bring about the fall all by itself, but it wasn't meant to. It was like claiming Cameron stuck his dick in a dead pig's mouth. It didn't need to be true. It was never meant to sound true. All you wanted when you made a claim like that was for the guy be remembered for making a statement denying putting his dick in a dead pig's mouth. The denial ended his influence on the world stage.

She almost felt sorry for Schnieder.

Or would have if he wasn't a miserable cheating bastard.

Division's facial-recognition software searched for a match in the background.

It was a long shot.

The girl was glamorous and well groomed in the image she'd extracted, but it didn't matter if the only photos they had in their databases were of her fresh off the streets in a starkly lit mugshot or a staged, no-smile passport photograph – a face was a face. The points of similarity in the bone structure and set of the features didn't change just because of a bit of make-up.

Ideally, they would have had eyes on the ground, someone to walk the street outside the nightclub, check buildings in the vicinity for CCTV and try to tap into them and work a path either forwards or backwards to work out where the girl came from and went to. Lots of security footage self-held on self-contained systems still, sandboxed from the outside world. It was safer that way. It was also a pain in the arse for Laura.

That was where old-fashioned police work, canvassing the scene, walking the beat, paid off. Which, of course, was why Peter Ash was in a hurry to get to Berlin instead of Tallinn. He was like a magpie chasing the next shiny thing sometimes.

She needed coffee to help her think.

She was surprised to find Magnus at the machine, the news playing silently on the TV behind him. He saw her and made a second cup.

The report about Gerhart Schnieder's indiscretion came on again.

'Have you seen this?' the big Dane asked, shaking his head. 'Might as well subtitle it Man With World At His Feet Fucks Up Again.'

'Not exactly newsworthy though, is it?'

'Everything is grist to the machine, Laura. Everything. It sees all. Knows all. And in the end destroys all.'

'That's a bleak outlook on life.'

He grinned. 'I come from a place where it is dark more than half the year. Life is bleak.'

'Do they know who the girl is?'

'Not as far as I know, though as you'd expect Twitter is going wild over it. There's a mob of them out there hunting like they're all suddenly paparazzi.'

'Because places like *Hello!* will pay a small fortune to get at her first.'

'Someone knows who she is. My money's on the bodyguard, because they didn't just drive away from there, did they? And he's a high-profile guy, we're talking government car, government-sanctioned affair. They just didn't expect to get caught on camera, because some people are just idiots.'

'What makes you think that?'

Magnus walked to the screen just as the image froze on Cristiana's striking face. 'You see this guy?' He pointed at a man in a suit a couple of steps to the side of Schnieder. 'See the bulge in the jacket, that's his gun. Plain, serviceable suit. Secret Service bodyguard.'

The image on the screen changed too quickly for her to see the bulge properly, but she trusted the Dane's eye.

She turned back to face him, only to see that he was flashing a pearly white smile.

'What's so funny?'

'I'm cheating. I've met him. His name's Jakob. Schnieder came here when this building was opened.'

'Cheating or not, you've a decent memory for faces.'

'Do you think he's the kind of guy who'd tattle to the press for a quick payday?'

'There's not a payoff big enough.'

'That's my thinking, too. So, just random bad luck, or someone else tipped them off and made sure there was at least grainy cell-phone footage to end Schnieder's career.'

'Makes you wonder who he's pissed off, doesn't it?'

FORTY-EIGHT

'Enjoy your run?' The young guard laughed as she approached. His rifle was slung over his shoulder now. He was very much at ease. Enjoying himself.

'I think I'm going to puke,' she said. 'I'm so out of shape it's not funny.'

'Well, if you feel like stretching your legs tonight, I'll go with you. I know a decent track through the forest. Much more interesting route. And I can make sure that you don't get lost.'

A little voice inside her head damn near shrieked out its steer-clear warning, but he was exactly what she needed right now. She needed to gain his trust. Even if that meant putting herself directly in harm's way.

Not that she expected him to tell her what had happened to Irma, or who the body in the forest was. That would be too easy. But get him onside, get him to trust her, and maybe, just maybe, he'd let his guard down and she'd see or hear something she shouldn't.

She offered him a smile she hoped was just the right shade of cheeky to work, and said, 'My mother warned me about going into the woods with men like you.'

'Did she now?'

'Lucky for you I've never done anything my mother told me.'

He burst out laughing at that and shook his head.

'In that case, I'll see you back here at six thirty, assuming you're up to it.'

'Always. But right now, the shower block is calling. I stink.' Frankie turned her back on him and walked over to her cabin, knowing full well he didn't take his eyes off her.

There were sounds of movement coming from a couple of the other rooms in the block. People were beginning to wake. It wouldn't be long before there was a queue for the bathroom and the shower was out of hot water, so she bounced up the short flight of wooden steps and went inside, making sure she was the first in.

By the time she emerged, wrapped in a towel, a couple of the other girls were waiting in the corridor.

'Sorry,' she said.

'It's what sisters do,' one of them said. 'They hog all the hot water so the sleepy heads have to take a cold shower.' But she said it with a chuckle. Frankie was surprised at how quickly she'd shucked off the outsider status; maybe it was because she'd sat with Alina? Well, for whatever reason, she was one of them now.

One family.

One World.

Back in her room she dressed in the ill-fitting uniform of the sect, and worked the muscles in her legs. In truth, she'd barely broken a sweat.

There was a tentative tap on her door.

'Come in,' she called. 'I'm decent.'

The door open. The girl behind it made no move to enter. 'Hi, Ceska,' she said. It was Tania, Alina's sister. 'I heard you looked after Alina last night. Thank you. I don't know what you said to her, but she's happier than I've seen her in a while.'

'We just had a chat. Honestly, it was no big deal. I did what anyone would do.'

'But you did it, not anyone, and it is a big deal. To me anyway. If there's anything I can do, anything, you only have to ask. Promise me you'll ask.'

'I promise,' Frankie said, and the other girl slipped back out of her room and closed the door behind her.

Half an hour later they were all gathering round for breakfast and this time everyone wanted to talk to her.

How things could change in twenty-four hours. There was a genuine warmth around the table now. The chatter continued throughout their shared eating time, as they drank their juices and black coffees and breakfast teas. The meal itself was a step up from the soup-kitchen fare, with eggs, cooked meats, fresh breads, cheeses, and plenty of fruit. There was choice. It might not be fine dining, but it was considerably better than the girls around the table had been eating before they found One World.

It was easy enough to say forget the experiences that brought you to the compound, but much harder to do. Suffering was ingrained. Hardship carved scars into the soul. Some of this stuff couldn't be forgotten. What they really meant was don't talk about it. Don't share the hells that caused you to run, because now you've stopped running. One World wanted this place to be some sort of oasis, a safe place. Somewhere the bad stuff didn't happen.

When the remnants of breakfast were being cleared away, Charles entered. He rubbed his hands together briskly as he looked around the faces, like he was trying to warm himself up.

'Good morning, everyone. I do hope you had a good night and are fully rested. I've got a treat for you this morning. I didn't want to say anything last night because I wasn't sure what time The Shepherd would walk amongst us, but John arrived while you were all asleep, so very soon he'll be coming through to talk to us all.'

There were smiles on the faces of most of the girls, hungry to experience his coercive charisma again, like a drug they'd been off too long.

'Before that though, I need to speak with each of you individu-
ally. Remember, I asked you to think about whatever special skills
or talents you might have to offer? I know it will take a little longer
one on one, but we've got time and this way everyone is free to
talk.' Plenty of nods around the table. 'Another thing I want you to
think about when you give your testimonies is if you've seen any
special talents in the others, anything they might be too shy to say
about themselves, or might not even know. Sometimes it takes the
eyes of loved ones to help us see the best in ourselves.'

There were a few more nods, like he was imparting great wisdom
and they were eager to soak it up.

She didn't like his choice of words as much as anything; words
like 'testimonies' carried a duality, first as their truths, but more
often in her world as their confessions.

Three or four of the girls glanced around, Alex and Tania looked
in Frankie's direction. It was instinctive, and she could happily have
done without the attention.

FORTY-NINE

Laura didn't know if she would be able to do it.

And if she could that didn't mean she should.

The risk was that she'd get hauled upstairs and made to
explain her actions. It was one thing to pull this kind of shit when
they'd been back in River House and no one was looking over their
shoulders, but now they'd taken up residence in the custom-built
Division office that had them all under one roof it was so much
more difficult not to think of themselves as part of a much bigger
team.

Would Akardi, their ODA, buy the justification that the endgame
was more important than playing by the rules?

Probably not.

But better to be slapped on the wrist for doing something that
worked than told you can't do it in the first place, right?

She took her capsule coffee back to her desk.

She knew what she needed to do.

The key, she hoped, that would keep her safe from serious breach recriminations, was her prying was retrospective. She wasn't digging into future itinerary, nothing that could be useful for a potential terrorist threat.

It was the finest of fine lines.

'Here goes my glittering career,' she muttered, not realizing she'd said the words out loud.

In a matter of moments she was lost in her work.

She'd expected it to be considerably harder to get at this stuff than it actually was. In a couple of minutes she'd proved the theory, at least.

What she needed was there: all ministerial cars had GPS monitors installed, logging all routes the cars covered. The idea was that in the event of a kidnapping using the vehicle or theft of the car, the security services would have immediate access to up-to-the-second location data.

It wasn't so much different from what she'd done with Frankie, looking back over her movements since she went active in Tallinn. The difference here was that she was spying on a Government minister, and her neck was very much on the line.

But it was better than trying to trawl through disparate CCTV feeds from around Berlin hoping to pick the vehicle up in one of them and follow it to wherever Schnieder dropped off Cristiana, so it was worth it.

The ease with which she found details from the car was disturbing. How easy could it be to find details of designated drivers, including their personal information and tracking them back to a point of weakness? How vulnerable, really, were profile politicians like Schnieder?

And how did she raise this without putting herself in the shit?

She was used to being the smartest person in the room; that wasn't such a big deal when the other people in the room were Peter and Mitch, but this was different. There were plenty of people in this room who were a lot smarter than she was. That was going to take some getting used to.

Tracking down Schnieder's car allowed her to see the route it had taken both before and after his dalliance at the nightclub. She tracked the glowing trail as it progressed along a detailed street map of the city with the names of buildings and businesses easily highlighted by fingertip contact on the touch screen. More submenus, all equally as easy to access, brought up ownership details, tax details, and other salient facts about the goings on in the various buildings.

She followed the car's route from the depot to the door, with its time-stamped arrival within the minute of Schnieder's filmed exit. It was precision. She assumed a cross-reference with Schnieder's minder's phone would show the summons a few minutes before the politician had decided to leave. It was all there.

The car stopped once between the nightclub and Schnieder's home address. A touch revealed the name of the building: Hotel Q! on Knesebeckstraße. The car then drove on. It was deceptive. It was only when Laura went back to examine the time logs that she realized Schnieder's car had been parked outside the hotel for an hour.

A lot could happen in a hotel in an hour.

The hotel room wasn't going to be booked in Schnieder's name, not if he was trying to keep their liaison on the down-low. It gave her another angle to follow, if nothing else, even if Schnieder had used a fake name when he booked that couldn't be traced back to the girl or One World in any way.

After dropping Schnieder off, the car continued on to the assigned driver's home address, no extra stops.

She thought about that for a moment.

There was a pattern, always. It maintained safety. First, Schnieder, Cristiana, and the bodyguard got into that car. First stop they drop off the woman, second the minister, with the bodyguard securing the politician's house before handing over to the night shift and heading to his own home. He wouldn't sleep at Schnieder's house, there was a team stationed outside the politician's place, maintaining his privacy.

Of course, he should have secured the hotel as well.

It was procedure. Even if the politician was having an affair. The man had to keep the principal alive.

FIFTY

Kask felt safe.

There was a familiarity to it, though there were a few startling differences from the last time he'd set foot within the compound.

The building had been refurbished and redecorated, the generator had been upgraded, but the biggest change was the perimeter fence. It was difficult to tell if it was there to keep the family in or the inquisitive out. The Shepherd hadn't shared that wisdom with him. Yet. He would if he felt the time was right. John wasn't above confiding in those he trusted. And Kask had surely earned that trust by now.

He had slept in one of the staff bedrooms, with instructions to remain unseen. It was strange to be alone with his thoughts, especially after John had asked him to teach the others how to kill. That wasn't who he was, surely? No matter what the other man said there was a difference between necessity and cold-blooded rational killing. He had been forced to end Annja Rosen's life for the greater good of the family. He had taken no pleasure from it. He wasn't a monster. Had there been any other way, surely he would have taken it?

Surely?

In the darkest hours of the night it was hard to be sure of anything any more.

Tomas arrived with a breakfast tray, which he set down on the bed. Before Kask could ask about John or what he was supposed to do, the driver told him, 'You stay here until you are collected. The girls will be moved first. You are not to be seen.'

So he ate his breakfast alone and waited.

It took another hour before Tomas returned to tell him to follow him outside. 'Keep away from where the girls have gathered,' he said, indicating a separate part of the compound. Kask nodded, eager to do as he was told. If The Shepherd wanted his presence to be a secret then who was he to question him? He was nobody.

It was a pleasant place, the fresh air agreed with him. There were certainly worse places he could be forced to live as an exile. He could even imagine taking charge of the compound, overseeing security. That was how the family worked, after all. It relied upon each of them offering their unique skill set to the collective. He had certain skills as a policeman none of the others possessed. He decided that if John asked he would make himself available. It was the least he could do.

To pass a little more time, Kask decided to walk around the compound. He made sure he stayed out of sight of the buildings so as not to go against Tomas's instructions, and walked into the trees thinking it might be useful to familiarize himself with the improvements that had been made to the old place.

It was better than sitting brooding.

And he knew how The Shepherd liked to test his followers. There were countless challenges designed to stretch the individual and challenge their commitment to One World. Who was he to say that this wasn't just another test for him?

The Shepherd would never stop testing him, he knew. Some might be physical, simple tests of endurance, while others came down to sheer force of will. He remembered the first time he had sat across from John, the other man taking his hand and telling him how incredibly proud he was that Kask had gone far beyond their expectations, and first suggested how he could best serve them.

What that experience taught him was that he had needed the other man's approval desperately.

There was a lesson in that, too.

'What do you think you are doing?' a voice behind him said. Polite but firm. Kask turned. He saw a young man, an assault rifle in his hands, watching him closely.

He hadn't even heard the kid creeping up on him.

He was becoming careless.

These were basic lessons.

'Remembering,' Kask said. 'I came in last night with John.'

The younger man relaxed a little at The Shepherd's name. Kask figured he wasn't sure how he was meant to act, but hearing John's name was as good as The Shepherd himself vouching for Kask. No one wanted to get on The Shepherd's wrong side, so by naming him Kask had given himself liberty here. He sympathized for the man, because really his only option was to treat Kask as an intruder, but who in their right mind wanted to risk offending The Shepherd's guest?

'Why don't we go and find Elsa? She can vouch for me. Sound good?'

The man nodded.

He lowered his gun a fraction. Kask was calm. He was trained. He knew he would be able to disarm the young man if he had to. It could even be a part of his continuing education; a test for him to fail. It would certainly send a message in terms of security. But now wasn't the time for lessons, that was just his own vanity speaking to him. He was a guest in the compound.

Kask took one last look towards the skirt of the woods.

He knew it was still there.

Did they still use it?

It was hard to believe they wouldn't; it was a torment that had broken the best of them and destroyed the worst.

Without it, men like Kask would be a shadow of the souls they were now, for better or for worse.

Was it that place, that darkness, that pain, that had sown the seed that finally bore fruit in the death of Annja Rosen?

He felt the cold shiver of remembered fear whisper not-so-sweet seductions in his ear. He felt it calling to him, but knew he would rather die than return to that place. That darkness.

Maksim Kask's heartbeat raced. His mouth dried. His tongue cleaved against the palette. His lips clung to his gums. A sheen of sweat broke on his forehead despite the crisp chill to the morning air.

He looked away from the woods that hid the hole and all of the secrets that damned place had stolen from broken souls.

He would not go back there.

He had survived it once.

That was a miracle in itself.

No.

He needed to believe that they would keep him safe.

They were one family.

One World.

FIFTY-ONE

'Change of plan,' Laura said. 'As much as my heart says Frankie, my head says Berlin.'

Peter Ash had spent the last two hours trying to relax in the lounge bar of his hotel. He was already checked out, and it wasn't as if he had a lot of baggage to pack, so he was ready to go. And highly caffeinated. He ditched the potboiler he'd stolen from the shelf of abandoned books, some stupid first-contact alien thing by Ronan Frost.

'Details?'

'I've tracked your mystery Cristiana down. But there's a clock ticking on her. She's booked into a place in Berlin called Hotel Q! and yeah, the exclamation mark is theirs, not mine.'

'And she's still there?'

'As of right now, yes. But since the news broke putting her face in the frame, she could bug out at any time. This is our window. Miss it and there's every chance she could disappear.'

He nodded. He didn't ask how she knew that. He was already moving, bag over his shoulder, heading out towards the terminal building to check the flight numbers to see which of the five terminals had flights departing for Berlin.

He talked as he walked.

'Come on then, Law, you know you're dying to tell me how you found her.'

'Detective work, pretty boy. It's what the best of us do while the rest of you run around like headless chickens. I tracked his ministerial car. It's not rocket science.'

'Sounds like it to me.'

'That's because you live in the dark ages.'

The mini-departure board at the end of the concourse walkway gave him two choices, Berlin Tegel, Terminal 5, or Berlin Schönefeld, Terminal 2. The only problem was a four-hour wait for the next flight out either way.

'Not knowing what name the room was booked under made it

more interesting. If people knew the kind of overreach we've got going on in this place, Pete, they'd shit a brick.'

'Meaning?'

'We've got backdoors built into all sorts of public-building CCTV cameras, for one. And plenty of private ones.'

'Jesus, that's a gross invasion.'

'Thank fear and rising global terrorism for that, we've got all sorts of extrajudicial powers we wouldn't have dreamed about even twenty years ago.'

'The world is going to hell.'

'Going?'

He laughed at that – a short bitter bark of a laugh. 'Point taken.'

'I watched the thirty-second footage of them coming into reception to collect her room key. And they still use keys,' she said. 'Good old-fashioned keys with big brass fobs with the room number embossed on them. She walked straight up to reception, Schnieder two steps behind her, and asked for her room key. The receptionist put it on the counter number-side up. I got lucky. Room 612.'

'Nice.'

'She was very much in charge, you can tell by the body language. She led him. She knew where she was going.'

'And it's definitely her?'

'No doubt at all. The room was booked under the name Cristiana Albu, but the charges are being billed to a company called 1W.'

'One World,' Peter said, as a tannoy announcement came for a last call for passengers going somewhere a lot warmer than here.

'On the money.'

'The noose is tightening.'

'Or we're just going crazy, which is always a fun thought.'

'All roads lead to One World,' he said. 'You know it and I know it. And I've not forgotten how this started as a supposed cover story to get me into Estonia. When I get home you and I are going to have words about all this, because I get the feeling you set me up here.'

'Guilty as charged,' Laura said. 'Now get a move on. With luck you'll be in and out of Berlin in a matter of hours, and back in Tallinn before morning.'

'Speaking of?'

'There's been no sign of movement since yesterday, and she's made no attempt to get in touch.'

'So all's good.'

'All's good.'

He didn't want to think about the fact that it wasn't actually reassuring; without eyes on her they had no way of knowing if Frankie was fine. But that's what losing Mitch had done to him. It had his mind living in the dark places.

'OK, so Tegel or Schönefeld?'

'Tegel, leaving in twenty minutes.'

'That's not an option? I'm looking at the departures board right now, next flight out is four hours away.'

'Terminal 5. Gate 9. I put a hold on it. Just show your badge at the door, they're waiting for you.'

'Priority treatment?'

'We've got some clout, my friend. Strings that can be pulled that I didn't even know existed.'

'So, what you're saying is you could get to like Bonn?'

'There are definite advantages to being here,' she said, and the way she said it he figured she wasn't talking tech.

FIFTY-TWO

The room was dark.

A silver light flickered from the projector.

On the screen a fairly slick production showed a very one-sided history of One World, glorifying the early years. It was the usual evangelized nonsense about revelations and hardships, and how The Shepherd found his truth.

This canonized the guy. Seriously. It was like he was some sort of secular saint. And every time his face came on the screen there was an audible sigh. He was adored. It was creepy as hell. Even just saying his name seemed to have an almost orgasmic effect on the girls.

It was pure cult behaviour dressed in the trappings of organized religion.

And Frankie wasn't learning very much watching this bullshit.

According to the scriptures on offer The Shepherd was a regular superhero. There wasn't anything he couldn't do, be it daredevil exploring, curing the sick and the lame, inventing lifesaving techniques to feed the starving in Africa, or other nonsense that wouldn't hold up to any actual study, but they ate it up.

The testimony of one girl, pulled from a burning building in the midst of an earthquake in Caracas, was particularly heart-breaking bullshit with the youngster talking about the fire searing her skin and the agony of it, and how John had reached her, and with nothing but his hands and his faith had healed her, soothing her burning skin and gradually taking the pain away. She had lost her mother and father in that building but had found a new family in One World and would for ever think of John as her true father. She touched her cheek where there should have been scars, and looking directly at the camera in that moment said, 'He is a miracle-worker.'

One by one, the girls were called through to give their testimonies to Charles.

Frankie was the last to be summoned.

One obvious thing she noticed was that all of the girls had gone into the room with him looking unsure, their nervousness obvious, but they were full of smiles and obvious contentment when they emerged. Like magic. So whatever was said in there, no one was unhappy about it. She wondered what they were being promised, and what Irma had been promised when she'd walked into that same room six months ago?

'No need to look so nervous, Ceska,' Charles said as she sat down across from him. She wasn't feeling nervous, but maybe it was his opening gambit for each of them, a little 'hey don't worry we're all one big family, we wouldn't hurt you' to put them at their ease?

'I'm fine,' she said.

He nodded slightly, the gesture barely perceptible. 'I'm glad to hear it. Tell me, Ceska, how do you think you are settling in here with the girls?'

'Fine. Everyone is friendly. I feel,' she chose her next words carefully, weighing the emphasis as she said, 'like I belong.'

Charles's smile was broader now, the nod more pronounced. 'Good. That's really gratifying to hear, Ceska, because everyone loves you. They've been talking about you all morning.'

'They have?'

'I've asked everyone the same question, which of the other girls do you most admire, and why. And yours was the name on their lips.'

'Me? Why?'

'Because you made a difference. You didn't turn your back on young Alina's pain. You sat with her. You talked to her. You helped her. You made a difference. That's a rare thing, Ceska, believe me. Most go through this life not making a difference to the world in any way. Those who do, like you, they are special.'

Frankie shrugged. 'I just talked to her. Listened.'

'Well, you must have listened very well, and found the right words to bring her comfort.'

'Really, all I did was try to get her to find something to look forward to rather than worrying about the past. I remembered what you said about the chains of the past weighing us down, and how it's a new life here, we get to leave the bad stuff behind.'

'It's for the best, but we don't force it upon people. It's not like we can stand over them with cattle prods and shock them every time they think about their childhood.' He smiled as he said it, but there was something utterly unconvincing about that smile. He was a hollow man. 'So, now I will ask you what I've asked everyone else, what do you think you can offer One World?'

She looked him in the eye. 'I'm a hard worker. I want to help people. The first time I felt any sort of contentment was working in the soup kitchen with Tasha. Maybe I could do something like that? Help feed the homeless?'

'Oh, I think you have far more in you than that, and that belief was there even before I spoke with the others. I think you could be a mentor to the younger girls. In fact, in time, I wouldn't be surprised if you were chosen to replace me.'

'Replace you?'

'We all serve One World as best we can. It is our calling. When I am called to help elsewhere someone will be needed here. That is just the way of things. We open ourselves up to opportunity by not saying no. My hope is that over the next few days you start to see what opportunities wait for you here. There will be challenges, of course, but I am sure you will overcome them if you want it badly enough.'

'Well, I'd be lying if I didn't admit that sounds intriguing.'

'It is supposed to,' Charles said. 'I truly hope you feel the same way in a few days' time. Now, that is only half of why I wanted to talk to you, my dear. My second question was about your fellow family and the talents you feel they might have. I am very interested to hear what you have to say.'

She didn't have to think about it. 'Tania.'

'Tania? Interesting. I had rather expected you to choose her sister, Alina, after your time together.'

'Alina is easy. She loves animals. She had her heart set on working with elephants in Africa, but would be just as happy working with stray dogs in a shelter.'

'And I'm sure that we'll be able to find her something like that, in time. As you say, she is very young. There may be other things we'd like her to do first. So Tania?'

'Number one, she's ferociously protective of her sister.'

She saw his brow furrow. 'And how is that of use to One World?'

'You don't see it? We are one family,' she replied.

'Ah,' he said.

She didn't need to spell it out any further.

He understood, grasped exactly what she meant. To be ferociously protective of a sister makes her ferociously protective of all sisters. It was a simple enough concept, but sharing it made Frankie uncomfortable, as though she was betraying the girl to One World. She knew how cults worked. They looked for ways to manipulate. And she'd just given them one when it came to Tania.

For some out there it was worse than bad, or hard, or any other basic adjective, it was a case of being willing to sell their soul in exchange for a hot meal and a bed for the night. The homeless she'd found in Tallinn had help given freely. It was different. There was no demand of anything in return. At least not for most of them. It felt actually, honestly, altruistic. And that was One World, too.

It would be easy to focus on the good they did to the exclusion of the ugly things she suspected they were behind, but that wasn't why she was here giving her testimony to Charles. She was here to find her cousin, Irma. Or at the worst, God forbid, find out what had happened to her. She wasn't here to buy into the stuff they were selling. The burning-building rescues, the laying-on of hands, the whole Shepherd thing, was just make-believe. Propaganda. One thing that was becoming increasingly obvious to Frankie was how easy it would be for someone who was vulnerable and needing to find some sort of belonging to fall for this bullshit he was peddling. Not only fall for it, cling to it.

'There will be a place for all of the girls, but I suspect many more opportunities will open up for you, Ceska. You are different.'

She wondered if he'd said the same thing to Irma when she'd sat before him. Maybe he said it to all of them, just like his line about looking nervous.

He could offer a place for everyone, but that didn't mean animal sanctuaries and food kitchens. Not everyone they brought in off the street was getting a happy ending here.

There was a burned body in the woods that stood testimony to that – if they could prove the links.

But, for the first time, Frankie wondered if that lost girl was the only one that had been buried in the forest, or if there were others buried out there?

FIFTY-THREE

John was already in the main room when Frankie left the office.

He didn't look like the messiah.

Indeed, he didn't look like much of anything. He was attractive without being beautiful. He was tall, but without dominating. It wasn't until he opened his mouth that what made him special became obvious.

He chatted easily with the girls over a cup of coffee, all smiles and kind words, and they loved him. It was like watching schoolgirls leaning in all 'Summer Nights' as the dreamboat told his story of summer dreams, ripped at the seams, uh huh, uh huh.

All she could do was pretend she was as fascinated as they were.

'Ceska,' he said when he saw her, all smiles and that full-bore charm. He reached out a hand, calling her over. She could feel his heat through her sweatshirt as he put his hand on her arm. 'It makes my heart soar to look at you, dear girl. I hear you are making friends?'

'No,' she said, and for the silence between heartbeats the room was utterly silent. She smiled. 'I'm making a family.'

'That's our Ceska,' Charles said, moving to stand beside her. 'She's a star.' There was a look that passed between the two men that Frankie almost missed. Another one of their not-so subtle tests, no doubt.

'I knew there was something special about this young lady the moment I set eyes on her. It's her soul colours. They are so vibrant. You can see them coming off her in waves. I've never seen an aura so strong.' Which sounded like hocus-pocus voodoo bullshit as far as Frankie was concerned, but no doubt it was part of the teachings of The Shepherd that somehow explained how people could overturn cars to save crash victims like Tasha and heal the burns of others. After all, hadn't one of the first miracles of Jesus been healing? It was a good precedent if you were going to convince your faithful you were worthy of devotion. 'I'm looking forward to telling Tasha how right she was to call me. She's an incredible judge of a soul. One of the best I've ever met. We bless the day you walked into our lives, Ceska. You have made us all so much richer.'

'I'm not sure what I'm supposed to say to that. Thank you?'

He smiled his benevolently condescending smile. 'Well, what I'm hoping you'll say is that you've found your home and want to commit to One World,' he said, smoothly.

She'd known this moment was coming, but hadn't expected it so soon, and not in front of the others. She needed to get this right. She chewed on the inside of her lower lip, then let the smile touch her eyes. She couldn't believe they were so eager to claim her. Part of her wondered all over again if it wasn't too easy, that they'd somehow rumbled her and were setting her up to fail.

And then what?

Chase her through the woods, dogs on her heels, put a bullet in her chest and leave her to rot?

She couldn't think about that.

She needed them to buy her devotion to the cause.

What worried her was she knew precious little about them, less – it felt like, at least – than she'd known before Tasha found her. How far could she actually go before she learned anything of worth that would help her find her cousin? Or help Peter tie the body in the woods to One World and bring this house of false gods tumbling down around The Shepherd?

'I feel at home here.' She looked away from The Shepherd and shared a secret smile with Alina across the table. 'I've got some really great new sisters.'

John nodded. 'They are the best people,' he said, like somehow he'd always known they were, and that it wasn't their weaknesses that drew these lost girls to him. 'Now, no doubt Charles told you that you would face a series of challenges?'

'He did, though he was vague as to their nature.'

'There is nothing to be frightened of. They are merely designed to test your commitment to our life. Normally, with new followers we wouldn't even consider the possibility of them facing the first of the challenges until after the end of their induction, having listened to at least a fortnight of testimony and coming to learn their true soul. But you are different, Ceska. You are extraordinary, an old soul, and it behoves us to treat you differently.'

'Honestly,' she said. 'There's no need. I don't want to be treated differently from my sisters. We walk this road together.'

'Consider it a fast track. We recognize your gift. I brought someone with me last night. Like you, he has special talents. I hope, if you decide that you are ready in a day or two, that he will be the perfect man to help you reach the next stage of your journey with us. He was one of the best to pass through this place. Like you, a truly incredible soul. Every challenge he faced, he overcame. I think you will bond well with him. I see a lot of you in him.'

She nodded. 'I will try to prove myself worthy of your faith.'

'Of that, my dear heart, I have no doubt.'

Frankie took her seat with the other girls.

She listened to The Shepherd talk about the talents they each possessed, coaching them in vaguely spiritual terms that were borrowed from cheap pop psychology. Bits of Freud, pieces of Jung and Kant and a few others thrown in for good measure. He was such an obvious bullshit merchant it was frightening to realize just how gullible these girls were. But all that meant was they were desperate, didn't it? They really were lost girls, like Peter Pan's boys. Frankie had always had a different take on that J.M. Barrie story: in her head Peter was the Angel of Death who appeared to children in the moments after their deaths to help them cross to the other side. That was why they didn't grow up.

What was interesting was how John could talk for so long about their futures and their new family here without it ever feeling like he was repeating the sermons of those propaganda films. He was a gifted speaker. His voice wasn't just velvet, it was fascinating. He knew how to use it to manipulate the listener, like the best politicians, educators, and life coaches – he was like a living TED Talk.

And what was truly impressive was how he managed to make and maintain eye contact with everyone in the room, making them all feel included and engaged as he talked. He encouraged questions, and seamlessly returned to the main thread of the sermon without losing his train of thought.

He was word-perfect.

His charisma went beyond anything natural; he was a performer. An entertainer.

When at last he'd finished, John was rewarded with a rush of applause – a rapture. Frankie looked at her sisters, wondering if any of them had ever given such a frantic-to-please response in their lives?

She matched them.

It wasn't hard to get swept away by their enthusiasm if she didn't think about why she was applauding.

Afterwards, John took the girls aside in small groups for more intimate conversations. He leaned in close. He leaned back and spread his arms. He was so expressive with his body, talking with all of it, hands and heart and voice, Frankie thought, watching him.

In the middle of it all, she noticed a stranger enter the room. He made an effort not to draw attention to himself, simply taking a seat on the periphery and waiting.

Frankie watched him watching the girls.

She assumed he was the man John mentioned, her would-be mentor.

Seeing him, John excused himself from the last of his conversations and moved away from the cluster of girls surrounding him. He caught Frankie's eye and waved her over, beckoning the newcomer to join them.

'Ceska,' he said. 'I'd like you to meet someone. This is Maksim Kask. He's a much-valued member of our family, and like yourself possesses unique talents that make me believe he will prove to be a wonderful partner and mentor for you. Max, this is Ceska, the girl I told you about.'

FIFTY-FOUR

P eter Ash walked through the reception.
   He saw a couple with huge hard-body suitcases head for the lifts, and followed them.

He didn't make eye contact with anyone.

He wasn't about to risk being challenged, because the last thing he wanted to do was show his identification and make a whole big thing about why he was there.

The couple paid no attention to him; to the extent that they didn't even ask what floor he wanted, which was rude, but again he wasn't going to make a big thing out of it. The husband pushed the button for the ninth floor. Peter said, 'Six, please.'

The woman smiled back as her husband punched the button for a second stop. She didn't say anything. Maybe it was just the language barrier rather than plain rudeness, Peter thought. It didn't really matter, he was out of there before the silence became uncomfortable.

Room 612.

He needed to think. He couldn't just barge in. Schnieder wasn't an enemy he wanted to make, even if his stock was falling thanks to the end of the whole perfect family guy reputation he'd built up being shattered by that mortal weakness of many a man, a pretty young girl.

What it came down to was just how far in-deep Schnieder was with One World.

And if Maria Bartok was right and the girls were being used to build compromising intelligence on the rich and powerful, what One World intended to use that stuff for.

He doubted very much Cristiana would have all the answers, or even any of them, but she was his best bet by far when it came to digging for the truth. Even if she wasn't a willing ally.

Corruption in the heart of government made for a decent story for someone, and despite the best efforts of the US to discredit journalists and brand anything bad as fake news, there were still a lot of very good reporters out there who would give their lives in pursuit of the right story. That was how important the truth was. It was just a case of putting the story in front of the right person if he couldn't chase it himself.

Peter knocked on the door and waited.

He heard movement on the other side, then a woman's voice called, 'Just a second.'

When she opened, still on the steel chain, he saw a fringe of blonde hair, the side of her face and the shoulder of a thick terry-cloth robe. 'Can I help you?'

'I hope so,' he said, 'Though, actually, I'm here to offer you my help.'

On the flight from Stockholm he'd skim-read the book he had retrieved from Kask's apartment, and gleaned as much as he could of the secrecy around One World and how it all worked. He produced the coin – which he knew now wasn't a coin at all, but rather a medal that had been presented to Kask in honour of his services to One World – still in its plastic case, and made sure she could see it as he told her, 'We are all one family.'

'We are all One World,' she replied with the fervour of a cult devotee, and took a step back to let him step inside.

Peter slipped the coin back into his pocket and looked around the room.

It was more luxurious than his own budget would have stretched to, by some distance.

Being in a cult obviously has its advantages, he thought.

The bed had been freshly made. Nothing seemed immediately out of place or suspicious. A small suitcase was on the stand beside the wardrobe. He could see clothes that would have cost him a year's salary hanging on the rack inside.

'Have I disappointed The Shepherd?' she asked, knotting her fingers nervously.

'I need you to talk me through what happened last night.'

'I did everything I was told to do, I swear.'

'The Shepherd knows that, Cristiana. This is not about your failings. You are a valued part of our family. We are concerned that you were observed, and what that watcher intends to do, and if it impacts upon our plans. For that reason I need you to talk me through everything you remember, every detail, there can be no room for error, no possibility of any misunderstanding.'

'Of course.' She sat down in the armchair. He realized she was waiting for him to tell her he was ready, so he took his phone out of his pocket and set it to record. It was a gamble, but he figured a sect like One World habitually recorded the words of the faithful to use against them if the need ever arose. The benefit of the recorder was that it would make her more careful with her words, taking the time to get everything right.

She nodded. 'Where do you want me to start?'

'How about we take it from the time you checked into the hotel?'

She nodded again and started to walk him step by step through what had happened since she'd first collected the key for room 612.

It didn't take long for him to be sure Schnieder had no idea there was a connection to One World. He wasn't one of them. A meeting had been set up, and he'd been set up in turn, flattered by her attention. It was crude stuff, not great tradecraft, but then simple was often the most effective when it came to this kind of thing. He was in a pressure-point. Trouble at home. Stress in the public eye. That adulation as one of the new bright hopes. All of it was enough to steer him towards breaking. She had simply been in the right place at the right time, because he was vulnerable. That, of course, had always been The Shepherd's plan. The poor bastard hadn't got a clue. 'Being photographed hadn't been part of the plan,' she said. 'I tried to stay out of the shot. Gerhart even tried to shield me, but they got my face and suddenly there was a story and I was in the middle of it.'

Peter waved her apology away. 'Everything is as it was meant to be,' he said, trying to sound vague and portentous, as he imagined a real One Worlder who'd drunk the Kool-Aid would sound.

Her eyes widened in surprise. 'It was arranged, wasn't it? You are behind the film?' Peter said nothing, letting her fill in the silences. 'Why? He was eating out of my hand. He would have given me the world if I'd asked for it.'

'You brought him back here?' he said, ignoring her questions because he didn't have the answers and trying to make stuff up was only going to trip him up.

'He walked me to the room, but didn't stay.'

'You didn't try to persuade him?'

'He's in love with his wife.'

'That has never stopped a horny man before,' Peter said.

'I was told to let him go as soon as he wanted to.'

'You did the right thing. He needs to see you as an ally not the enemy. You are his friend as his world comes down. You didn't see anyone in the club you recognized? Anyone you didn't expect to see?'

'Like who?' She hesitated for a moment, as though unsure she could actually say what she was thinking.

'It's not a test,' he said.

'You mean someone who knew me from before?'

Ash said nothing.

The less he said for the moment, the better.

'But I don't understand how anyone could? I don't look the same as I did before I joined the family.' She shook her head, struggling to process it. 'I've never been to Germany before. No one would know me here.'

'What about from the compound? From before you were chosen?'

'The compound? I don't understand.'

'Not all of the girls who were there with you remained with the family.'

'You think one of them might be here?'

Peter Ash shrugged as if to say it's possible. 'Have you stayed in touch with anyone?'

She thought about it. Then shook her head. 'Not really. There are a couple of girls who moved on to the place in Stockholm when I left, but we haven't stayed in touch. It isn't encouraged.'

'No. Of course not. And you're not in trouble. I promise you. But can you recall the whereabouts of any of the others? Take your time.'

She shrugged. 'No.' And then she seemed to have a revelation, and looked up at him, eyes hopeful, like she'd cracked it. 'Apart from Irma, of course.'

'Irma?' Peter felt the fine hairs prickle on the back of his neck.

He tried not to let his excitement show.

The girl inclined her head slightly, trying to judge if this was another test.

'The computer whizz-kid. She always thought she was smarter than the rest of us. Though to be fair, she was.'

Peter nodded, he needed to be so careful here, a blank slate. Let her talk. Let her fill the silences. Don't push.

'She's in the place on Lossi Plats, isn't she?'

He said nothing.

'I'm assuming that she's still there?'

He waited.

Silence was powerful.

She looked at him, desperate for approval.

He said nothing.

Finally she asked, 'You don't think it's Danika, do you?'

'Danika? Why would you think of her?'

'She ran away.'

'She did,' he said, thinking of the burned body in the woods. 'Why?'

'It was her name,' Cristiana said. 'We couldn't help it. We teased her . . . like you'd tease your sister . . . but she couldn't take it.'

'Is that what made her run?'

'A Russian girl called Danika Putin? Can you imagine having to live with that?'

'Sometimes it is better to leave your past behind,' he said.

'We are one family,' Cristiana said.

'Poor kid,' Peter Ash said, shaking his head.

FIFTY-FIVE

Frankie knew the name. Of course she did. How could she not? Maksim Kask? How many Maksim Kasks could there be in Estonia?

Right now her fake name was all that was between her and a world of hurt.

Maksim Kask.

The same policeman who had given up investigating Irma's disappearance.

The same policeman who had 'lost' the incriminating statement by Annja Rosen.

'Nice to meet you,' she said, fixing a smile on her face. There was a moment, a flicker behind his eyes, and for a moment she feared it was recognition. But it shifted quickly into . . . what? Hunger? Lust?

'And you, Ceska,' he said. He didn't offer his hand. There was no contact between them. 'Tell me, what do you hope to do for One World?'

'Ceska has a gift,' John said. 'She sees potential in others and helps them unlock it.'

'Ah, then she seems like she would be good here, perhaps running the compound to help the new intake of girls? That would free Charles up for other duties,' Kask said.

'You have read my mind, Max. That's exactly what I've been thinking. But Charles isn't quite ready yet. Soon, I think. But these things are not to be rushed. And, to be fair, neither is Ceska here. There is still so much for her to learn.'

'Always,' Kask said. 'If we stop learning we die.'

John nodded at that.

'There is always so much we can do to push ourselves, to grow. I thought that you would be perfect together.'

'I only wish to serve the family,' Kask said. 'If that is your wish, then I will dedicate myself to her preparation.'

John said nothing for a moment, considering something. Frankie got the distinct impression a plan was slowly forming in his mind. After a few seconds he said, 'We could always take her back to the city with us.'

'Is that wise? I thought we were going to be staying here for a while?' Kask said. There was a trace of worry in his voice. A glance passed between the two men. It was obvious Kask wasn't happy with this turn of events. Frankie wondered what kind of crap was waiting for him back there.

'I will meditate on it. Regardless, we won't leave the compound until tomorrow. Take the time to get to know Ceska. For now, I believe you are the man to help her reach her full potential.'

Kask gave the slightest of shrugs.

'Maksim here was one of our very brightest stars back in the day. He was a revelation. Indeed I haven't been so excited about a recruit since him until your arrival, my dear.'

'Sounds like I've got some big boots to fill,' Frankie said.

'I do hope there's not a but coming,' John said, giving her his brightest and widest smile.

'Not at all. I'm a competitive soul.'

John smiled. 'We'll talk again later.' And he turned his attention back to the other girls, needing no more than a few seconds to make them feel every bit as important as Frankie and Kask, even though they weren't being singled out for any kind of special treatment.

It was a gift.

Just that thought made her smile, because in her own language 'gift' had a quite different meaning to English. Well, two quite different meanings, actually. One, gift, meant married. The other, poison. She couldn't think of anything more appropriate.

Kask offered her an uncertain smile, then excused himself.

It was obvious something was troubling him.

The biggest threat was that it was her. She'd never met him face to face, but that didn't mean he hadn't dug into her file when she'd started asking about Irma.

It was possible.

Distressingly so.

She needed time to think.

She remembered she'd promised to meet the young guard for a run.

She walked out of there thinking about her cousin.

Irma was a bright girl, a university student who was doing well by all accounts, a shining star of the department. That, surely, would have marked her out as special, too, wouldn't it? A different kind of special, but there were all sorts of opportunities to be special in a cult like One World.

She wasn't here. That much was obvious, anyway.

But at the moment Frankie had a more pressing concern: if she was going to be moving on, she needed to make sure the tracker came with her and that meant getting access to her things.

Without it, she was on her own.

FIFTY-SIX

'Pay dirt,' Peter Ash said as he left the lobby and stepped out into the busy Berlin street. He had his phone pressed to his ear.

Laura had picked up on the first ring; she'd been waiting for his check-in. He moved out of there, not looking back. He didn't know how long it would be before Cristiana's handler touched base and they began to realize he wasn't who he pretended to be, but then, he hadn't given her a name. He'd just let her make assumptions.

'Let's hear it, superstar.'

'Number one, we've got a new name. Money on she's the dead girl.'

'I'm listening.'

He paused for a heartbeat, looking forward to hearing her response. 'Danika Putin. Danni for short.'

'Putin? As in *Putin* Putin?'

'I'm assuming no relation.'

'You sure she wasn't taking the piss?'

'Nah, she thought that I was one of them. A test.'

'How did you pull that off?'

'Showed her the medal I'd taken from Kask's place. Then did some reading on the flight. Gave her the Vulcan salute and that sealed the deal. She wouldn't risk lying just in case I reported back to The Shepherd.'

'Makes sense.'

'She was there when Danni ran. She had no idea she didn't make it out.'

'Not just a pretty face after all.'

'I try to please.'

'OK, I'll run the name through the system, see if it hits. You said number one, that implies a number two?'

'She was there at the same time as Irma Lutz.'

'Jesus. You're sure?'

'I am.'

'Jesus,' she said again.

'Told you. Pay dirt. Seems she was quite the computer genius. Marked out as being something special. The last thing she heard, Irma was in a place on Lossi Plats. Mean anything to you?'

'Tallinn,' Laura said. 'Not far from the cafe where Annja worked, actually.'

'Bollocks. I really wish you hadn't said that. If we're even a minute fucking late I'm going to blame myself.'

'Better hope we're not a minute late then,' Laura said.

'OK, OK,' he said, thinking on his feet. He really didn't want to follow that train of thought for any longer than he had to. He'd be the one that carried the guilt and he already had enough ghosts to last a lifetime. *I'm getting her out of there alive.* 'We need to get word to Frankie.'

'I don't know, Pete. It's a risk. I ping her phone and she's not the one holding it, I blow her cover. She's out there alone. I'm not putting her in more danger unless I absolutely have to.'

'OK. We need to get eyes on her. I'll jump every bloody queue between here and Estonia if I have to.'

'Already sorted,' and he felt his phone vibrate in his hand as she sent his boarding pass through. 'Taxi will be with you in three, two, one . . .'

He saw the yellow sign on the roof of an E-Class Mercedes as it pulled to a stop in front of him.

'Sometimes you scare me, woman.'

'Only sometimes? Must try harder.'

FIFTY-SEVEN

Frankie didn't enjoy the run as much as she would have liked. She spent most of the time gritting her teeth and pretending it hurt. But she managed to get a better idea of the lay of the land, and scoped out a lot of the surrounding buildings she hadn't otherwise seen.

She caught several glimpses of the perimeter fence, which felt very much like a noose around her neck as she ran.

The guard, she suspected, was doing his best to control what she saw by following a route that gave as little away about the compound itself as possible. Even so, she noticed the dark silhouettes of other buildings further into the trees, though every time she tried to stretch her legs and run towards them he matched her stride and steered her away.

As best she could tell, all of the buildings in the main camp area were reserved for accommodation, catering, supply stores, and the assorted needs that came with keeping the compound functioning smoothly. But there was nothing that looked like a classroom or test centre, which made her think this was what those hidden buildings were for.

She wouldn't know until she got a look at them.

As they ran, Frankie was sure she caught a glimpse of a dark shape deep in the trees. A figure. Someone watching silently from the woods. Her running mate showed no sign of having seen it. She didn't mention it. Odds were it was nothing more than another guard, watching. Or maybe it was some sort of challenge she'd be tested on when they got back to the main building: did you see the watcher, where, describe him. She kept moving, keeping herself a couple of steps behind the guard. It gave her the chance to look around.

'I think you're holding back. You're a better runner than you're letting on,' he gasped between breaths when they completed another circuit.

Frankie did her best to make it look like she was struggling to catch her breath when he stopped with his hands on his thighs, but it was pretty obvious she was in considerably better shape than he was. She could comfortably manage another couple of circuits, maybe more, but he'd be lucky to get around a third one.

'I used to be,' she admitted, remembering the hours of pounding the pavements where she'd grown up in Sala. She used to run along the side of the huge lake in a 10k circuit, crossing the strip of country road to the silver mine that had been the lifeblood of the place once upon a time. She'd been running all of her life. She liked to do at least 5k a day. If she wasn't running she wasn't living. 'But it's been a while,' she lied.

'All I can say is I'm glad you're out of shape then, because trying to keep up with you like this is damn near killing me.' He gave a smirk, some cheesy line going through his head that disappeared in a coughing fit.

'I'll get you some water,' she said.

The administration building was the closest, a couple of hundred metres back. She'd noticed Elsa through one of the windows as they'd run past.

'It's OK,' he gasped.

'Don't be silly. The things some guys will do to try to impress a girl.'

'Rumbled,' he said, though it was clearly an effort for him to get the word out. He managed a cockeyed smile between ragged gasps.

'Come on,' she said.

Together they walked to a bench outside the cabin. He sat while she slipped inside.

Elsa looked up from her work.

'Everything OK, honey?'

'Need some water for pretty boy out there. He was showing off.'

The other woman laughed at that. 'You go look after him, I'll be right out.' She smirked, unable to pass up the opportunity to watch the young guard humbled by one of the girls.

'Ready for another go round?' Frankie asked when he finished up his drink.

'You're kidding, right? I'm ready for a beer.'

She grinned at him like he was just too precious for words.

'OK if I do another one without you then?'

'Knock yourself out. I'll just wait here. You know the way by now.'

She nodded.

Elsa gave her a smile. That was all the approval she needed. Frankie took off, and didn't look back. She kept her pace steady, again not stretching her legs even through the temptation was to really *run*. She had no idea who was watching her.

A few minutes later she reached the treeline and ran in. The shade was already giving way to darkness. She moved out of sight of the main building.

She was alone for the first time all day.

Even as the thought occurred to her she felt eyes on her. A cold shiver of dread ran down Frankie Varg's spine.

FIFTY-EIGHT

It was getting dark.

Darkness offered extra cover.

He'd been cooped up in planes for too much of the day. His entire body ached. He felt like he hadn't stretched his legs for more than an hour at most, and that his veins were plotting to get their own back on him with a little thrombosis just for shits and giggles. He savoured the cool crisp air. It was good to be outside, even if he wasn't dressed for it.

Laura had downloaded directions to the GPS unit in his tricked-out phone, allowing him to follow a track deep into the forest that brought him to within touching distance of the compound.

He'd walked five kilometres across rough ground, much of it through heavily forested terrain, meaning he wasn't going to be seen making his approach. He dragged his feet through mud and rotting leaves, each new step adding more mulch to his soles as he trudged on.

Eventually he reached the mesh fence which marked the compound's perimeter. It was at least three metres high. The wire coiled around it made him think that it was electrified. The One Worlders were serious about keeping people out. But then, what cult didn't value its privacy when it was busy brainwashing the faithful?

Unless of course it wasn't meant to keep people out, but rather keep them in.

He heard people coming towards him on the other side of the fence and retreated deeper into cover, hiding behind the thick bole of a tree. He made out two figures, running. They weren't moving particularly quickly. The first runner, male, obviously out of shape and not used to this kind of physical exercise, ran with his head down, oblivious to his surroundings. The other runner moved with more ease, head up, taking in everything around her.

She stared right at him.

He had no way of knowing if she'd seen him, but it was fucking fantastic to see her.

Frankie.

She looked good. Safe. He felt the weight lift from his bones in relief. He needed to make contact somehow, bring her up to speed with what he knew. But there was zero chance of him getting over that fence without getting fried. He'd already noticed the fresh yellow wood where overhanging branches had been sawn away, so that wasn't a workable option either.

But he couldn't pull her out, either.

Not that she'd have left without Irma. That was the problem when stuff got personal. You made mistakes. Errors of judgement you never would have made if you weren't sticking your neck out for family. Everything he did now risked blowing her cover.

He raised a hand, hoping she saw. But even if she did, would she realize it was him?

Blow this now and everyone from The Shepherd down would disappear with the wind, and that would screw any hope they had of finding justice for Annja and Danika and however many girls hadn't made it to the promised land, or bringing Irma home.

The fact that Kask, a fully paid-up member of the cult of crazy, was already on the run and wanted for murder must have had them spooked.

Frankie needed to come around again, alone. Though how she'd pull that off he had no idea. He settled down to wait, hoping it wouldn't be all night because what was a chill now would be bloody freezing after half an hour of standing still.

Twenty minutes later he was still waiting and debating whether to take a piss behind a tree when he saw movement.

He waited, trying to make sure that it was Frankie, and assuming it was, that she was alone.

He moved closer to the fence.

'Fancy seeing you here,' she said, her breathing steady and even, like she was out on an evening stroll rather than a third circuit through the woods.

'You lost your friend?'

'He couldn't keep up.'

'You won't be missed?'

'I figure we've got two minutes.'

She listened without interrupting while he told her what he'd learned on his travels, including the fact that Maria Bartok thought

One World were using KGB tactics to build dossiers of compromising material on people in places of power.

'We've got another problem,' she said, when he was done. 'Kask, the officer who buried the investigation into Irma's disappearance, is here.'

'Kask? Fuck.'

'I don't like the sound of that.'

'You shouldn't. Annja Rosen is dead. And Kask is in the frame for it.'

'Which explains why he doesn't want to go back into the city.'

'He hasn't made you?'

She shook her head. 'I almost feel sorry for Kask,' Frankie said. Seeing his look of confusion she added, 'He's locked in here with me.'

'When do you think they'll move you?'

'Soon,' she said. 'Maybe as early as the morning.'

'OK. Not ideal. But you've still got your tracker?'

'No. They confiscated my stuff when they brought me here. If I ask for it all back they'll either tell me I don't need anything from my old life or they'll get suspicious. Or both.'

Peter reached into his pocket a moment later and pushed his own phone through the links in the fence. 'Hide it. Law can find you. I'm not going to lose you, Frankie. I swear.'

She took it.

'Don't be so melodramatic, Peter. I've got this.'

'I trust you.'

'Of course you do.'

Voices carried from somewhere in the compound.

Frankie stepped away from the fence.

She glanced over her shoulder.

A moment later she was running through the trees, circling back towards the buildings.

FIFTY-NINE

'Time to go,' the voice whispered in the darkness. 'We're out of here in five minutes.'

Blearily, Frankie opened her eyes and struggled to focus through the darkness and fog of sleep. She had no idea what time it was. Too early. Four in the morning? Five? Before the sun brought the world to life, at least.

It was Elsa's voice but in her groggy state it took her a moment to work out who owned the voice in the darkness.

'OK,' she said, trying to summon some enthusiasm for moving. She hauled herself out of bed. Elsa put a holdall at the base of the bed.

'Pack your things. We'll meet you at the car.'

'What about my other stuff? The things I brought with me?' She said, even though she didn't need them. She needed to sound like the woman who came into the compound. No mistakes. Not at this stage.

'Do you really think you'll need them again, honey? Is there anything in there you can't live without?'

She shrugged, happy to give that stuff up now. It made it look like she was all-in, ready to leave the past behind. 'I guess not.'

'Well OK then. I'll make sure they're sent on to Tasha at some point. She can redistribute that stuff to kids in need. I can imagine there are plenty out there who would love a good sleeping bag like yours.'

Frankie nodded 'That's a good idea. When you've got nothing, anything will help.'

'I can remember,' the other woman said, and left her to get her stuff together.

Moving quickly Frankie stuffed her few belongings, including Elsa's old tracksuit and trainers, into the bag along with Peter's phone, which she folded into her underwear to keep it safe.

Tomas leaned against the hood of the now familiar black limo

with its child-locked doors. She nodded to him as she emerged from
the hut she'd called home for the last couple of days.

What little sky she could see through the trees was still blacker
than black, save for the single glimmer of the silver moon. The
floodlights were on full beam, lighting the compound up brighter
than sunshine.

Kask sat in the front passenger seat, the window wound down,
elbow on the door. The radio was on. She didn't recognize the song.

Tomas opened the rear door for her.

John was travelling with them.

'Sorry if I kept you waiting,' she said, ducking into her seat.

'Oh, don't concern yourself, Ceska, everything in its own time
and a time for everything, remember? We are exactly where we are
meant to be, the four of us, exactly when we are meant to be. That
is all that matters. If anything, it's me who should be apologizing
to you, waking you up at this ungodly hour. You are more than
welcome to sleep as we travel. We won't be offended, will we?'
The other men didn't answer him, because obviously the only words
that mattered here were his.

Kask closed his window as Tomas slid into the driver's seat and
started the engine.

A moment later the screen between the front and the back of the
car closed.

As soon as it settled into place, sealing her in with John, The
Shepherd said, 'Now, I don't want to alarm you, my dear, but as
we approach the property it will be necessary to blindfold you. The
house is a refuge. We don't allow any but a select few to know the
location; for the safety of others, you understand?'

She nodded. He was taking her to a safe house somewhere in
the city. Of course, Peter's tracker hidden in the bottom of her
holdall would blow that little secret wide open.

'The truth is that not everyone is as trusting or as accepting of
our family and what we are trying to do here as you are, sadly.
There are those that would do us harm.'

'We are all one family,' she replied, as if that was the answer to
everything.

'We are indeed.'

'Is this where I am going to be tested?'

'In a way, yes. Though perhaps not as you expect.'

'I'm excited to be part of this,' she said. She looked at John, the self-styled Shepherd, but didn't see the charismatic leader of men, she saw the Fork-Tongued Saviour of the exposé the man had tried to suppress by murdering the journalist who had infiltrated his sect. She couldn't remember his name. Bray? Laura had the book on her desk. Frankie was in no doubts as to the truth behind the allegations, no matter what the courts had failed to prove. John, The Shepherd, was capable of ordering a murder. Looking into his eyes now, she felt sure he was capable of doing the killing himself if it came right down to it. 'What can you tell me about my future?' she asked, careful to make sure everything was positive and laced with anticipation. 'I'm still not sure why you think I'm so special.'

'All in good time, my dear. You are no ordinary runaway. You're different. I can see into the hearts of people and see both the good and the bad in them. You have this same gift. I recognize it in you.'

Like hell you do.

'So you want me to help people? To be a counsellor? To talk to runaways and try to help them find a new place to belong?'

'No. Plenty of people can talk to lost children. No,' he said again, as though weighing up whether it was finally time to share what he actually saw in her or not. 'There are many who stand against us. Those, let us call them the Blind for they refuse to see, who undermine our abilities to help people. They mock and ridicule what they do not understand. And more than anything they seek to destroy us. We cannot allow that to happen. The Blind are fair game, Ceska. If we cannot make them see One World's vision we must protect ourselves from the harm they would do. I want you to be a Protector. I saw the way you looked after little Alina, I know your instincts are motherly, that you look to nurture and protect those you love. There is no one better equipped to protect her sisters than you, my dear girl.'

A Protector? That was some sketchy linguistic manipulation right there. Now she knew the kind of man Kask was, and what he'd done for the cult, killing to protect his so-called family, she realized that John intended to turn her into a weapon. A murderer like Kask. And Kask was meant to oversee her training.

She'd thought of plenty of things they might have been grooming her for, but turning her into an assassin?

'Of course. I love my sisters. We are one family,' she said, thinking it was the only right response she could give given the circumstances. 'I will do anything I can so that the family can continue to bring hope. I don't understand why anyone would want to stop what we do.' We. Deliberately inclusive, buying in to the group identity.

How long did it take before a lost girl truly felt that they were part of everything?

She needed to think very carefully about everything she said from now on. She couldn't appear too eager, too desperate to please. Not yet. But equally, she had to sound willing. It was a delicate dance. But if John wanted her to be a Protector, then that was exactly what she would be.

'People are frightened of what they don't understand, Ceska,' he said, as though that answered her question.

She nodded and settled back into the seat.

She allowed the gentle rhythm of the car to lull her into closing her eyes, opening them only now and again to see the window's tint change as though beneath brighter light: streetlights. They were back in the city somewhere, but she had no way of knowing where. She touched her foot against the bag, reassuring herself it was still there.

She couldn't shake the worry that without that phone it would be easy for The Shepherd and his pet murderer, Kask, to make her disappear. To make anyone disappear.

SIXTY

L aura woke to the sound of an unfamiliar alarm.

It took her a moment to realize where she was.

She rubbed the sleep from her eyes as she processed what was going on around her, then swung her feet off the cushioned seating block that until last night had served only as somewhere to pile the boxes that had been transferred from London ready to be processed before being put into storage.

She sat up.

The alarm that had woken her wasn't an alarm at all; it was Peter Ash's tracker on the move. Meaning Frankie was in motion. He'd debriefed her last night, obvious relief in his voice that Frankie was in good shape. She shared the sentiment. Her being out of contact had played on Laura's mind for days. If things went to hell she was going there with them. She'd kept Frankie's off-the-books investigation from Akardi, lying to his face more than once, and on top of that she'd sent Peter out into the middle of it, unsanctioned. As far as shit went she was in the brown stuff up to her neck. So this couldn't go to hell, it was as simple as that.

She grabbed her phone from where it rested on top of The Shepherd's smiling face. The Fork-Tongued Saviour wouldn't know what had hit him.

She speed-dialled Peter Ash on the burner he'd picked up after giving Frankie his modified phone.

By the time he picked up Frankie was already outside the perimeter of the compound and moving fast.

The one good thing about this was that he didn't need to keep her in his sights to follow as long as the phone was active.

'She's on the move,' Laura said.

He didn't sound as though he had been sleeping. But then it couldn't be that comfortable in a hire car out there in sub-zero conditions.

'About fucking time. I'm freezing my tits off out here, Law. Couldn't keep the engine running. Didn't want to draw any unwanted attention. Where is she?' Laura heard him start the engine. 'She's still on the track through the forest, but given her current speed, I'm thinking she'll hit the main road in less than two minutes.'

'OK.' She heard the car move away. 'I'm going to cheat, get ahead of them, assuming she's being taken into the city, so they can overtake me on the road. It's easier to follow them then. Any joy identifying the building Irma's in?'

'Nothing so far. None of the properties are showing as being owned or rented by One World or 1W or anyone associated with any of their trading names. But I'll find it if it kills me. There's a link to this Fork-Tongued Saviour,' she said, 'I'll bet my life on it.'

'Or Irma's,' he said.

'We're getting her out, Pete. No fuck-ups. We're bringing Frankie's cousin home.'

'Assuming she's in danger. She could be a willing little cultist.'

'Like Annja Rosen was a willing little cultist,' Laura said.

'Low blow, but point taken. But I don't want to have to choose between Frankie and Irma, Law. This goes one of two ways, and Frankie's always going to be my priority.'

'I understand where you're coming from, Pete, but Frankie wouldn't appreciate that. She's a field agent. She went in there knowing what the dangers were. She's not some innocent kid. She's a trained agent. If it's a choice between her and Irma, there's no choice at all. You get Irma out of there. We're not having another kid buried in the forest.'

'Let's just hope we don't have to make the call,' he said, which was his way of saying he was too tired to argue with her.

The problem was, given everything that he was carrying because of Mitch Greer's death, all of that guilt that had spent six months eating away at him while he was laid up, Laura didn't think for a minute that Peter Ash would do as he was told if it meant leaving his partner exposed.

'She's reached the main road. Taking the turn for the city. She should be coming up in your rear-view in a couple of minutes.'

SIXTY-ONE

The drive took more than an hour. Less than two. The car came to a halt.

'This is where I must ask you to indulge me, Ceska,' John said, taking a blindfold out of his inside pocket.

Frankie put her foot on top of her bag, making sure no one could take it away from her, while The Shepherd secured the blindfold in place. It covered her eyes, ears, and her nose, save for her nostrils. No light of any sort was getting through the cloth.

The car started moving again. She counted to four thousand three hundred and twenty-seven silently in her head before it stopped again. She reached down for her bag as she felt the door beside her open. A sudden draft of icy air coiled around her. She felt the frost prickle her face.

Someone took her arm and helped her out of the limo.

She could hear all sorts of sounds, faint traffic in the distance, bird song, even the wind itself carried its own distinctive susurrus. She tried to focus on what she knew. The air didn't possess the salty tang it had down by the docks, which eliminated a huge tract of land and buildings, but given the size of Tallinn that didn't narrow things down particularly.

She couldn't hear the engine of a second car, but that didn't mean Peter Ash wasn't close.

'Would you like me to take your bag?' a voice said. The door closed solidly behind her. Tomas.

'It's fine,' she assured him. 'I've got it.'

'Suit yourself.'

Two more doors opened and closed. She felt another hand on her arm, steering her away from the car.

She moved carefully, picking her feet up with exaggerated caution, listening for anything that might offer some kind of clue as to what she was walking into. She felt the two men walking behind her in silence.

'Wait a moment,' Tomas said after no more than a dozen cautious steps.

She heard what sounded like keys, a key fob, but the key didn't slide into the lock. It was some kind of electronic device, like a contactless credit card. The lock clicked open with a heavy sound. 'There's a step up ahead of you,' Tomas said without letting go of her arm. 'Careful.'

She edged her right foot forward until she felt the toe of her trainers touch something. One step up. Still leaning on Tomas. Then she stepped into warmer air.

Inside, they walked side by side for another half a dozen steps before they stopped again. She heard the door close behind them and the lock fall into place.

She felt hands at the back of her head and a moment later the blindfold came off, leaving her blinking at the stark electric light.

They stood in a hallway. There was a narrow stairs ahead of them, the carpet worn bare in the middle. There were two doors on either side of her, and in the narrowing corridor at the side of the stairs, a third door part in a shadow.

A hand on the small of her back guided Frankie towards the staircase.

She saw photographs lining the hallway. It took her a moment to realize that they were all pictures of John with celebrities and politicians, many she recognized as stars – if not superstars – of their fields. There were a lot of others she didn't recognize, but assumed they were equally important. No doubt they were the great and the good that The Shepherd had brought into the One World family, either by hook or by crook. The thing with photographs is they lied all too easily; every person in these pictures seemed thrilled to be standing beside the Shepherd. Most were black-tie and red-carpet events, not just random celebrity selfies. No doubt at functions that cost a small fortune to attend.

At the top of the stairs hung a larger picture of John, this time with a former American president, shaking hands and grinning within the Oval Office.

'He was much nicer in real life,' John said, resting a territorial hand on her shoulder. 'And, I have to admit, he has been a real help to the family in recent times.'

'How?' she asked before she could stop herself, and immediately regretted it.

John just gave her a wink.

'In more ways than you can imagine, but he's a private soul. He doesn't like the attention, so he likes to keep his work with us private. They all do. They are all very private people.'

Frankie glanced back at the rogues' gallery lining the stairs. She could think of a lot of adjectives to describe the publicity-craving, paparazzi-baiting men and women lining the walls, but private wasn't one of them. Several weren't the bright shining stars they had been. Actually, looking at the faces – and playing a slightly weird game of Six Degrees of Kevin Bacon – she realized several of them had been caught in a variety of scandals, often quite sordid affairs. There was one, she realized, that had been swept up by Operation Yewtree in the UK, with multiple counts of statutory rape against minors going through the High Court right now. One World's reach was *long*.

That changed the way she looked at these fading stars. Maybe they weren't supporters at all, at least not in the traditional sense. Maybe they were victims here. Peter had talked about them using girls to build compromising intelligence that could be used to blackmail people in positions of power, hadn't he?

Maybe that was how they made the lawsuits go away?

John led her into a bedroom. It was considerably larger and more luxurious than the one she'd slept in at the compound.

'Why don't you make yourself at home. You can leave your things here and, when you're ready, join us for breakfast in the room at the end of the landing.'

John held the door open for her.

She stepped inside and switched on the light.

'I trust you'll be comfortable in here.'

She nodded. 'I don't know how to thank you.'

John flashed that now familiar smile of his. The more you were exposed to it, the more you realized just how false it was. Practised. Like a second-hand-car salesman's faux bonhomie. 'No need to thank me, dear girl. You'll more than return our investment in you in the years to come. Now, why don't you have a shower and freshen up, we've got a long day ahead of us.'

Frankie waited for him to close the door, then listened for the creaks and groans of the floorboards as he walked down to the breakfast room.

She dropped her bag onto the bed, then went to open the blinds that covered the windows.

Her heart sank when she raised them only to find that there were shutters outside the window. She attempted to peer out through the narrow wooden slats, but couldn't see much beyond the dull grey sky heralding the dawn.

The window had been screwed shut.

She could only assume that through the window was a familiar landmark, something immediately recognizable that would give away the location of their safe house.

It also meant that if the shit hit the fan, the window wasn't an easy way out.

Likewise, the small window in the en-suite shower room was glazed with frosted glass that allowed daylight in but prevented her from seeing out. That, too, had been screwed shut.

An extractor fan started when she turned on the light.

She wondered if John had deliberately left her alone so that she could discover these things?

She turned out the lights and went to find the others.

SIXTY-TWO

Ash had listened to Laura's directions.

She steered him into the city and through the various ring roads on to side avenues that traversed them, cutting through the more businesslike offices to the decidedly more historical apartments that still dominated the heart of the Old Town. It quickly became obvious that Lossi Plats was his destination, right in the heart of the city. Meaning she was being taken to the same place Irma was being held. Which, at least, removed a difficult decision from the equation. He wasn't going to have to abandon Frankie in favour of exfiltrating Irma.

He realized he was still thinking in terms of Irma being a captive, but they had zero evidence to support that. She'd run off to join the cult willingly, she'd shown aptitude for whatever it was they did there and been selected for special treatment. That didn't make her a prisoner. Hell, he might have to drag her out of there kicking and screaming, truth be told.

But the fact that she'd cut herself off from her parents, causing them to reach out to Frankie because they thought their little girl had been brainwashed by a cult, yeah, that was more than enough to raise all kinds of concerns about One World, and the police work of Maksim Kask in particular. They'd got more lines of interconnectivity. But proving it beyond a shadow of doubt, satisfying the prosecutors that they'd be able to make the charges stick? That was another ball game entirely.

But, bring Kask in for murder while One World were harbouring him, that might, just might, blow the whole shit-show wide open.

He drove past the limousine where it was parked outside one of the old marble-fronted buildings.

There was no sign of anyone.

He pulled into a vacant parking space on the far side of the square, turning around to make sure that he was facing the black limo and the door it was parked outside.

He checked his watch. Given the slow start a lot of these people seemed to enjoy he didn't expect anyone turning up for work for at least another couple of hours.

'All quiet,' he said. 'Nothing was stirring, not even a mouse.'

'Did you expect anything else?'

'I dunno. To be honest, London is probably rammed with folks on flexitime trying to get an early start so they can survive the two-hour commute back home in time to actually go to bed before they have to do it again tomorrow. This is all very civilized.'

'Well, it is Sunday,' she said.

'Christ, is it? I had no fucking idea. I don't know whether I'm coming or going. Of course, it also means I didn't need to put ten euro in the meter to pay for parking.' She laughed at that. 'I'll just have to stick it on expenses. I'm assuming the cathedral has services later?'

'I'm sure it does. You might want to go and find some food. Frankie's ensconced now. If they move her, I'll let you know. And yes, I've got eyes on. You see the big yellow building behind you? German ambassador's residence. Surveillance cameras on the exterior. Very handy. So, I'll see her if they set foot outside the building.'

'Can I ask you something, Law?'

'Shoot.'

'What happens now? I can't storm the place if something goes wrong.'

'I was hoping you had a plan,' she said.

He couldn't tell if she was joking.

That troubled him.

He liked having a plan, it gave him something to ignore.

He wasn't going in blind. Not without some sort of signal from Frankie. He had to trust her. She must know he was out here. Right now, it was her show. He was just the support act.

Peter slid out of the car.

Everything ached.

Trying to move only served to remind him that he still wasn't fully recovered. He stretched his back out and worked the muscles of his neck. Laura was right, he needed to eat. But where would be open at this time on a Sunday morning?

As if reading his mind from back in Bonn, his phone vibrated in his pocket. Laura had sent through directions to a burger place that advertised twenty-four-hour service. It was a brisk ten-minute walk away.

The air was still chilly, but the buildings cut down the worst of the wind, starving it of the windchill. He deliberately walked past the building where Frankie was, though didn't slow as he scanned the facade.

Every window had been shuttered.

There was nothing to see.

Not so much as a chink of light crept out.

If it wasn't for the car parked outside, he would have assumed it was empty.

There was an almost sinister air about the place, he thought, deliberately not looking back over his shoulder. Which only made him want to go inside. Yeah, he was that kind of person.

Peter Ash was a meddling kid at heart.

By the time he returned, stomach full, the sound of his footsteps on the pavement provided a steady counterpoint against the hum of traffic building up in the streets close to the cathedral.

As far as he could tell there had been absolutely no change in the house – the windows were still shuttered, no sign of any lights, and the car was still parked up out front.

He settled back into the hire car and speed-dialled Laura.

'Did I miss anything?'

'Me?' she said sweetly.

'Apart from you, obviously.'

'Nothing. It's deathly quiet,' Laura said. 'I've got a tap on the only phone line into the place. No calls in or out, but that's not saying much. They could be using VoIP or any other service for all we know.'

'Got a name for the owner yet?'

'The entire block is owned by one John Shepherd, Canadian national.'

'Shepherd, as in The Shepherd?'

'The Fork-Tongued Saviour himself.'

'I guess fronting a cult pays well.'

'Like you wouldn't believe. He's got prime real estate in every city centre that One World operates in. That's over fifty cities. And it's all valuable land. Nothing that isn't central. John Shepherd is disgustingly rich, at least on paper. There isn't a single mortgage on any of the properties.'

Which fell in line with what Donatti had said about them amassing a not so small fortune.

'We're definitely in the wrong line of work.'

'Ever fancied starting your own religion? I reckon you'd be a natural,' Laura said.

'It's on my to-do list. So, background on this guy? Silver spoon in the mouth?'

'Far from it. Before he founded One World he was living on the streets. He's the definition of a self-made man.'

'Who would have thought helping other people could mean you could help yourself to millions?'

'Everyone from Billy Graham to Pat Robinson by way of Joel Osteen and Jerry Falwell,' Laura said.

'Good point. OK, so how does that help us? The tax man's already failed to bring One World down more than once.'

'And it's not like I can go kicking down the door because you think they're fiddling their taxes.'

'Ah, but Law, you beautiful human being, you might have given me an idea.'

SIXTY-THREE

Curiously, for all the supposed splendour of this place, what went on mirrored the compound surprisingly closely.

John left, taking Tomas with him. He gave no indication of where they were going.

The entire atmosphere shifted when he left her with Kask. Any pretence of friendliness the fallen detective mustered for John's benefit was gone the moment the door slammed, leaving them alone. He took pleasure in her discomfort. She bit back on the urge to argue with him, assuming that he was deliberately trying to goad her into a fight to prove she was unworthy. *Well, fuck that,* she thought, gritting her teeth, as Kask leaned in uncomfortably close, like he was trying to smell the lies in her pheromones.

He shook his head, like he couldn't believe how John could be so wrong, how disappointing she was. 'Why do you want to do this?' He asked the same question over and over again. Why, why, why?

'To help people,' she said the first time of asking. 'To help One World,' she said the second. 'Because we are one family,' she said the third time. And still he asked:

'Why?'

'Because we have enemies who would stop us.'

'Why?'

'Because of an act of kindness.'

'Why?'

'Because someone helped me when I needed it.'

'Why?'

'Because I want to help others.'

He shook his head, breaking the pattern. 'You can do that *anywhere*. There are a million places you can go to volunteer and soothe your conscience. So, no, really, why? Why One World?'

'Because they were the ones who helped me.'

'Why do you imagine One World wants your help?'

'Because John has seen something in me.'

'But *I* don't. So why shouldn't I just turn you out onto the streets where you belong?'

She stared him down.

'Because I'll give everything.'

'And if that isn't enough?'

'Then I'll still keep giving.'

'And what do you expect in return?'

'Nothing.'

It was relentless.

Question after question without a break, without a pause for her to muster her thoughts, pushing, pushing, always pushing, trying to dig down into her, to get to the core of who Ceska Volk was.

She wasn't allowed to eat or drink.

She hadn't had a thing since the slices of fresh fruit she'd shared with John. Not so much as a glass of water. It was emotionally draining, and in a strange way left her feeling worthless, as though nothing she said was good enough. And lying just made it more of a challenge, but she wasn't about to give Kask the satisfaction of breaking her.

So Frankie answered each challenge with stoic determination, daring him to bring it on.

And he did. Why had she run? Why had she stopped running? Why had she talked to the kid that was crying? And more personal stuff, digging into her past and her experiences, pushing her to describe the first time she had menstruated, the first time she had touched herself, the first time she had orgasmed, her secret perversions, how she liked to be touched, her failings, disappointments, and lies. Everything she had failed at, had dreamed of and lost. A lot of it seemed to be focused on loss. On dehumanizing her.

Eventually he said, 'That will do for today.' Kask dismissed her. 'Go back to your room until I summon you again.'

Frankie had no idea of how long she had been in the room with him answering his constant barrage of questions – and with the shutters keeping day and night out of the building with equal measure it could be lunch or dinner, or midnight just as easily. There were no clocks. Kask had worn a cheap wristwatch for the first ten minutes or so of questions, but the moment he caught her trying to look at it, he undid the strap and slipped it into his pocket. It was deliberate. Removing references to time messed with the clarity of your thoughts. It was subtle, but effective. A form of torture. Make time meaningless and there's no hope of an end. Everything just goes on and on.

Back in her room Frankie tried to peer up through the slats in the blinds to see if the sky was darkening, but after a while even that little smudge of grey became indistinguishable from the dirt on the glass.

She went through to the shower room and gulped down a glass of lukewarm water.

No doubt that bastard Kask would have taken that comfort away from her if he had realized it was there.

With nothing else to do, she lay back on the bed and tried to clear her mind, letting the exhaustion sweep over her.

It had been a brutal day, despite the fact she'd basically sat on a wooden chair all day, a bright bare lightbulb shining in her face while Kask played father confessor come inquisitor. That exhaustion seeped from her mind into her bones.

She expected him to come knocking at any minute to start it all over again.

No doubt he was eating, gathering his strength to go again. If she couldn't eat, at least she could sleep, even if it was only for a

few minutes before he came banging on the door or shrieking in
her face. She closed her eyes. But her mind refused to empty. She
saw Kask's twisted face behind her eyes. She heard his damned
voice and those endless questions cycling over and over. She couldn't
flush them from her thoughts for fear she'd somehow given herself
away and he'd caught her in a lie. If she didn't reset somehow she'd
break sooner rather than later. Mental anguish. She wasn't stupid.
Everyone had their limits. Again she felt the urge to lash out, to
drive her fist into his face as he asked another stupid, demeaning
question. She could have broken his nose and jaw, depressed his
cheekbones and fractured his skull before he'd finished with his
hard on from listening to her talk about masturbating. Fucking
pervert. But that would have been too easy. It was what he wanted.
How he won. He proved her unworthy. A failure. He was getting
under her skin.

She wasn't just playing the part of Ceska Volk, she was
becoming it.

And that was dangerous.

She managed to doze. It wasn't proper sleep, but in the silent
house it was restful. When she surfaced, she felt hunger gnawing
away at her belly. She wasn't about to go looking for food. She
wouldn't starve. Instead, she drank another glass of water, taking
it slowly. It was good that it wasn't too cold.

This time when she tried to peer up through the wooden slats there
was only pitch-black darkness. She could see nothing out there.

She listened for any sign of movement anywhere in the house.
The temptation to explore was strong – but at what risk?

She had no way of knowing if she was alone, if Irma was here,
or if John himself sat in the darkness downstairs waiting for her to
pass or fail some unspoken challenge he'd set out before her.

She opened the door.

It didn't make a sound.

The landing was in near darkness.

She assumed Kask was on the same floor. If Irma was here, she
was either above or below, given the number of doors she'd seen.
Down offered the excuse of looking for food in the kitchen if she
was challenged. Up didn't.

She was halfway down the stairs when she heard movement
below her.

Frankie held her breath, pressing herself up against the wall.

Her shoulder nudged one of the photographs of John with the latest falling star, and for one sickening second she thought it was going to fall.

The door in the narrow passage beside the stairs opened, spilling light into the hallway.

A figure emerged, backlit and featureless like something out of a Spielberg movie.

Frankie didn't dare move.

Whoever it was, she didn't want them knowing she was there.

The shadow was too large to be Irma, and wrong for Kask, she realized.

She waited.

She held her breath.

The figure disappeared through one of the other doors in the hallway. It didn't take long for the house to fall silent again.

And still Frankie didn't dare move.

She waited until she was sure whoever it was had settled down for the night and wasn't about to appear in the doorway if the staircase creaked beneath her weight.

Taking each step one at a time, testing her weight on them to be sure they wouldn't betray her, she reached the bottom.

Taking no risks, Frankie moved cautiously, not towards the kitchen as she'd initially intended, but towards the door the shadowy figure had emerged from.

Curiosity killed more than cats.

IN THE DARKNESS . . .

S he had no idea of how long it had been since the man had last come to visit her.

For ever.

She was breaking.

Her mind struggled to fix onto the code. She was failing the test. She wasn't worthy of his love. She wasn't good enough. She had never been good enough.

'*Water, please. Food. Anything. I can't think. Please.*'

She didn't know if they could hear her.

She felt the rats against her skin.

They didn't care.

She reached out into the darkness, letting one of them curl its back against her hand.

It wouldn't take much to raise it to her lips.

This was never going to end.

She cradled the rat in her hands.

She thought about what it would feel like to bite down on its spine.

And she wept.

She couldn't do it.

She would die here in this darkness.

She almost missed the sound of the door opening up above.

They hadn't forsaken her.

Her breathing was fast. Heavy. She wanted to beg. To say help me. Save me.

The footsteps moved closer. The iron lid was heaved back. She couldn't see who was up there.

'*Hello?*' *she called softly, or imagined she did, her head was so messed up.*

The man knelt and peered down into the darkness. The stark light made it impossible to see his face for shadow. She didn't know him. It wasn't the brute. It wasn't Tomas, the driver. It wasn't John. He truly had abandoned her in her need.

'*Do you have the answer?*' *came the reply, barely more than a whisper.*

'*Please. I need . . . water.*'

'*Do you have the answer?*'

'*Yes,*' *she lied. '*Yes. How much longer do I have to stay down here?*'

*The man didn't answer the question. '*John has given you to me,*' he told her. '*You are my reward. All you have to do is tell me the answer, and then your new life can begin.*'

'*We are . . . one family,*' *she said.*

'*I will be your world,*' *he promised her. '*I have to go now, but I will be back. Tell me, my love, what is your name?*'

But there was only confusion and turmoil in her head as she tried to find herself in that panicked darkness. But there was no past. And that was where her name lived. She couldn't fail this final test. Not when freedom was so close to hand.

'*I can't remember.*'

He left her, closing the iron lid on the hole. But his voice was still there. She heard him call out, full of rage . . .

SIXTY-FOUR

'Wwwhat the fuck do you think you are doing?' the guard in the doorway demanded, the business end of a Glock pointing in Frankie's face. It took her a second to register that it was her running buddy. She tried a smile, hoping to put him at his ease.

'I was looking for something to eat,' she said, sticking with the lie even though she was obviously going anywhere but the kitchen.

A moment later she heard the clatter of feet coming down the stairs.

Kask.

'Well, well, well, Ceska Volk,' Kask said as he walked past the guard. He had his own gun, a police-issue Walther P99Q in his hand. 'You have a strange idea of loyalty. Of course, when you said you would give everything for One World, I naturally assumed that included your life. You might have John fooled – he likes to see the best in people, but I don't. I'm good at what I do, Ceska. Or should I call you Francesca Varg? Did you think I didn't recognize you? Volk. Varg. You're not even trying. A wolf in Swedish is a wolf in English and a wolf in Russian. Did you think you could play games with us like your namesake toying with its food? I have news for you, woman, we aren't prey. Some of us do our due diligence. We investigate the people in our way. We learn all about them. Your name is seared into my soul, your face burned into my mind, and has been ever since you darkened my door. Oh yes, I have taken a great deal of interest in you.'

The gun didn't move.

One shot and it was all over, nothing she could do about it. No amount of fancy talking or fancier footwork would save her if Kask pulled the trigger – and it was plain as day on his twisted face, he wanted nothing more than to serve her corpse up to John and say, look, I did this for you . . . I killed the rat in our house.

She had no clue if Peter Ash was close enough to hear the gunshot – and even if he was, it would be too late for her.

She tried to think, adapt. Come up with a believable lie. But it wasn't there. It wasn't on her tongue.

'You are going to die here. You understand that, don't you? This place might not be as isolated as the forest, but it is a controlled environment. Once you set foot inside here you were doomed. They won't even find your body. That's just the reality of it. No one is coming to save you.'

Frankie shook her head. 'I walked away from that life, Maksim,' she said, deliberately using his first name, trying to connect. 'I couldn't stand it . . . the way they treated me . . . I'm good at what I do, but they had me doing shit work, wasting my life. I'm angry. They made me that way. They took everything from me. Everything. But I can still help One World. That hasn't changed, even if I'm not who I said I was. I know things. People. I have connections. I can make a difference. I can be what John needs me to be. Let me talk to The Shepherd. Let me prove my loyalty. He'll understand the value of what's inside my head. He's a smart man. There are so many things I can tell you, you say you know who I am, then you know I worked on the Anglemark case in Sweden. I was chosen by the Prime Minister himself. I'm worth more to One World alive than dead.'

Kask hesitated. The gambit was desperate, naming John, pushing Kask's insecurities by implying: do you really have the authority to kill me without your leader's nod?

He didn't pull the trigger. 'Back to your room, now!'

There was a split second when Frankie considered making a move, turning defence into attack and grabbing for the brute's arm to turn his Glock on Kask. But the space was tight, and her running buddy was in the way. There was no guarantee she'd not come out on the wrong side of the gambit. Better to retreat, and use Peter's phone to summon the cavalry.

She nodded.

Kask pushed her back along the hallway, bullying her towards the stairs with the barrel of the Walther. Her running buddy side-stepped to allow Frankie to climb first. He wasn't dumb. Neither was Kask. He stayed far enough behind her to be sure she couldn't try anything equally dumb, like trying to wrest the gun from him.

Maybe she could use him later? She'd seen the way he looked at her in the forest.

She had no more than ten seconds to the room; that wasn't a lot of thinking time.

She still didn't have confirmation Irma was here, or what, if anything, was behind that closed door.

It was all about time. Buying it. A few seconds became a few minutes, became long enough for Peter to make a difference.

But she couldn't just sit and wait to be rescued, either.

She wasn't some weak simpering Penelope Pitstop crying, 'Help! Help!' while she waited for the Ant Hill Mob to save her.

She knew Kask didn't believe her. So, what was his move? Talk to John, get the OK to pull the trigger? Would The Shepherd give him the word, or would Kask be her final challenge? Because that was what John wanted, wasn't it? To turn her into a killer. How else did you test someone's willingness to kill than to make them pull the trigger?

She walked up, shoulder to shoulder with the photographs of John's vanity.

Could that be an angle?

Maybe it wasn't a foregone conclusion after all?

She tried to rein in her racing thoughts.

But there was no Zen-like calm to be found. Peter had talked about compromising material to control people. She knew how John would look to control her, she realized. Irma. She was going to be Frankie's test, wasn't she? Was she willing and capable of taking a life for them? A bullet in the head. Ballistic evidence, maybe even filmed footage on a mobile phone. Enough to hold it over her and make her their Protector.

She'd fucked up badly.

She didn't have time to think about it. Kask shoved her into the room.

'Where's your bag?'

Her running buddy remained in the doorway.

There was no easy way past him.

'My bag?'

'Don't piss me off, Francesca. Get your fucking bag and empty it out on the bed. *Now.*'

She opened the wardrobe door. Her holdall nestled at the bottom. She hadn't unpacked.

Frankie stood slowly, holding the bag. The gun in her face made it obvious she had no choice. She unzipped the holdall. She thought about trying to stop the phone from falling out when she upended the contents onto the bed, but there was no way of hiding it.

She did as she was told.

The clothes fell in a heap. It was a pathetic collection of stuff that represented all this version of Frankie Varg had in the world.

She saw the phone half-hidden by her underwear.

'Away from the bed. Up against the wall. Go. Now.' Kask motioned her away, using the Walther like a conductor's baton. He stood over her things, poking through them with the barrel, then held up Peter's phone like he'd just discovered the unholy grail. His face remained utterly impassive as he turned around with it in his hand.

'You just lost your lifeline, Francesca.' He closed the distance between them. She didn't say a word as he pushed it up into her face. 'Want to phone a friend? No. Is that your final answer?'

Her silence was answered by the brutal impact of the Walther slamming into her temple.

Pain exploded behind her eyes.

The world turned black.

And she went down.

Hitting the floor was blessed relief.

SIXTY-FIVE

'We've got a problem,' Laura Byrne said.

He didn't doubt her for a second; the edge of panic in her voice was enough to have him moving. The clock on the display flashed up one in the morning. Peter Ash lay on a hotel-room bed less than a kilometre from Frankie. He hadn't wanted to leave Lossi Plats but couldn't exactly sleep in the car in the middle of town without raising major eyebrows.

Without knowing what was going on behind closed doors there was no chance he was storming the place like a one-man Iranian Embassy assault.

At least not without the go from Frankie.

He was still dressed. He didn't smell good, but that was the least of his worries. Grabbing his shoes, he demanded, 'What's happened?'

'We've lost the signal from your phone.'

'Shit.'

'One of two possibilities, she's telling us to move, or they've found the phone and she's compromised.'

'Either way we're getting her out.'

'Amen to that.'

There was no discussion beyond that.

If he told her what he was going to do there was zero chance she'd sanction it. So, silence saved him the luxury of ignoring her.

It wasn't like he could just walk up those steps and doorstep them. He needed back-up.

And right now he had a coincidence of wants with a certain Estonian detective, meaning he didn't have to go in there alone.

He made a second call, this one to the cavalry.

'I know where Kask is,' he said, 'Lossi Plats, right in the centre of town. Blue building facing the German ambassador's place.'

'I know it,' she said. 'I'll be there in ten minutes, just don't go in without me.'

'Ten minutes. No more. We're not losing this bastard.'

He could have walked there in that time, the hotel was so close to the square, but he wasn't leaving the car behind. The cavalry didn't charge in on foot, after all, that was the infantry. If the enemy bolted, the cavalry rode them down.

He pulled up on the street a couple of buildings away from the house One World built.

Mirjam Rebane was already in place.

She climbed out of her car. He saw the bullet-proof vest under her jacket, the grip of her police-issue Walther P99Q visible under her arm.

All Peter had was an extra T-shirt under his shirt, which wasn't going to stop any flying bullets.

'You sure about this?' Mirjam asked.

She reached back inside the car and produced another weapon for him. 'You really should start carrying,' she said.

'Not a fan. You pull the trigger, you've already lost.'

'Well, don't let Kask know that.' She looked up at the shuttered windows. 'He's in there?'

Peter nodded.

'Do I need to know how you know?'

'My partner's in there.'

'Again, do I need to know what's going on here?'

'I think she's been made.'

'There's a whole part of this I'm not following, Pete. What is your partner doing with Kask?'

'We really don't have time to stand around discussing this. Long story short, she's looking for her cousin, Irma Lutz, Annja's room-mate. She went undercover, infiltrating One World. If we're right, Irma's in that building. Or she was.'

'And Kask?'

'He hasn't left. We've had eyes on it.' He looked back towards the ambassador's building. 'All day. There's no way he slipped past Laura. Trust me.'

Mirjam nodded. She'd responded to his distress call without a moment's hesitation. But, looking around the square, he couldn't help but wonder where the back-up was. At home they'd have gone in mob-handed, a dozen armed-response officers, battering ram to the door, and stormed the barricades.

'Have you called it in?' he asked.

She nodded. 'They're on standby, two streets away.' She gestured vaguely to her right, the same side he'd entered the square from. 'Didn't want to risk spooking Kask while we waited for you to show.' He hadn't seen any SWAT trucks on the way over. 'Then let's do this,' Mirjam said.

She didn't wait for him.

She set off across the road, walking right up to the front door like she owned the place.

He saw her incline her head, leaning forwards, like she was talking into her radio: calling in her approach.

He couldn't hear what she said.

Peter followed Mirjam Rebane up the stairs as she took her badge from her pocket and rang the doorbell.

'And you're sure this is the right place?' she asked again, when there was no immediate response.

'They're in there.'

'In which case,' she leaned on the doorbell, the buzzer ringing incessantly, and didn't let go, 'better wake the bastard up.'

SIXTY-SIX

The ringing wouldn't stop.

Frankie clutched at her skull, trying to silence it.

It wouldn't end. It just demanded . . . demanded . . . demanded . . .

She lay in a foetal ball, trying to gather her wits. The entire right side of her head hurt like a bastard. The flesh was tender. The bone felt solid beneath her fingers as she tried to feel out the damage. From the pain she'd have guessed the hammer blow from the gun had split her skull in two, but everything felt solid when she pressed it, even if it was tender.

She didn't want to get hit again in a hurry, so beyond a few tentative touches she didn't dare move. If they knew she was conscious there would only be more pain. She could live without that.

The ringing was insistent. Incessant.

It wasn't concussion.

The door.

Peter.

It had to be Peter.

John wouldn't ring the doorbell, surely? He was their messiah. You didn't make someone like that bang on the door to come into their own place.

'Go and shut that fucking thing up,' Kask demanded. 'I'm going out of my mind. Shoot them if you have to.'

She waited until she heard her running buddy's footsteps heavy on the stairs.

She was alone with Kask.

Frankie opened one eye, just a fraction, enough to see the shattered remains of Peter Ash's phone a few feet from her face, the plastic and glass ground into the carpet.

If it wasn't Peter she was screwed.

She needed a way to hurt Kask.

She looked again at the shards of glass and plastic from the broken phone. There wasn't anything there that would make an effective weapon against a Walther P99Q.

Her heart sank when she heard a woman's voice.

It wasn't Peter.

No white knight. No rescue.

But there was a distraction, even if it was only a few seconds' worth of one.

Kask stood in the doorway listening to what was happening downstairs.

He wasn't watching her.

It was a lapse. A tiny, tiny mistake, but on such mistakes life and death pivoted every day.

Frankie had one chance.

She gathered herself, like a sprinter coming out of the blocks, and hurled herself at Kask, but everything about that desperate charge was fucked up; her legs didn't receive the flurry of commands from her brain.

She lurched sideways, and for one sickening heartbeat thought she'd fucked up so badly she was going to slam into the wall and miss him completely, but her leg buckled and saved her life, as her fall threw her full weight into Kask's back. There was nothing graceful about it.

She went down hard, taking him with her as he swung the gun wildly. His hand smashed into the door frame, a shriek of rage-pain tearing from his lips.

He didn't drop the Walther.

Kask tried to push her away, but her momentum was too much. He couldn't adjust his feet. He might have been physically stronger, but surprise, momentum, and the sheer awkwardness of Frankie's attack took him off balance.

The woman's voice shouted from downstairs.

She couldn't make out the words.

But there was fire in them.

Again and again the sounds rose. Demanding.

The hammering of footsteps up the stairs.

Her running buddy yelled, 'You can't go up there!'

Frankie clung onto Kask, sinking her fingers into his eyes.

He screamed.

'You fucking bitch,' Kask hissed, clawing at her hands as she sank her fingernails in deeper. He had her by the wrists, gun sacrificed.

She wouldn't let go.

She couldn't.

Letting go meant dying.

And she wasn't dying.

Not here.

Not like this.

'You're dead you fucking cunt, you're fucking dead!'

'Then you die with me,' Frankie rasped, feeling the wetness of blood or tears on her fingers as she clawed at his eyes.

She fought him, desperately trying to wrench her hands free of his iron grip, but it was vice-like, unbreakable.

And then the sudden explosion of pain as he slammed his head into her face. It was sheer black blinding agony. She couldn't see. She had no control over her hands. She tried to fight him but there was nothing. The impulses weren't reaching her muscles. She was going to die here.

And then there was no pain.

There was only darkness.

Silence. Deafening. All consuming.

There was no light at the end.

This was death.

And it was ugly.

She felt the blood on her face and his weight on her body.

She tried get out from under him, to crawl into the bedroom, as though that could somehow save her.

She wiped the blood away from her face and saw the madness of Kask staring at her, filled with hate, tears of blood streaming down his face where she had gouged the meat away. He looked like a thing out of Hell. Possessed.

He raised the Walther, the dead eye coming down level with her chest.

She couldn't get away.

There was nowhere to crawl.

He stood over her, looking down through the tracks of those damned tears.

'You die,' he said.

On her back, looking up at him, Frankie held her hands up across her face, like she couldn't bear to watch the bullet end her life. She was 13mm from the afterlife. That was the distance his trigger finger had to travel. 13mm.

Unlucky for some.

Frankie arced her back and slammed her foot up into his testicles so hard the surgeons would have needed to fish them out of his throat.

The gun fell from his grip as he tried to protect his testicles, too little, too late.

He crumpled.

Frankie kicked out, trying to kick the gun away, under the bed. But the sudden movement brought another searing stab of pain that lanced through her skull.

She raised her hand to the pain. Her fingers came away red and sticky.

Her vision swirled again, but at least this time she was already on the floor.

SIXTY-SEVEN

The man opened the door.

Peter recognized him. He was Frankie's running buddy from the compound. Up close he was thin, weedy, and he wasn't stopping Mirjam. She pushed past him like he wasn't there, ignoring the gun in his hand.

That freaked Peter out.

'You can't go up there,' Frankie's running buddy yelled at her back but she was already charging up the stairs.

Peter followed her inside. He had the borrowed Walther in his hand, the weapon aimed squarely at the ineffectual guard. 'Drop your gun,' he said, the silence between that last syllable and the gun hitting the floor shattered by the single shot ringing out up above.

For one heart-stopping second Peter thought the One Worlder had pulled the trigger, but the guy's gun was on the floor.

'On your knees, now, get down.' He didn't take his eyes off the man until he'd cuffed him to the banister at the foot of the stairs.

He couldn't let himself think about what that gunshot meant.

He took the stairs two and three at a time, charging up to the landing.

A second gunshot tore through the house.

He couldn't see what was happening up there.

'Frankie!' he yelled into the echoing silence that was worse than the thunder of gunfire for what it meant.

He took the scene in, freeze-frame.

Mirjam Rehane stood over Kask. The disgraced detective's weapon was out of reach on the carpet, blood in a pool around it. Frankie was slumped up against the side of the bed. She'd dragged the duvet down with her weight. It stained red behind her.

He didn't care if Kask was alive. His world reduced to Frankie.

'Call an ambulance,' he yelled, rushing into the room. He ran through Kask's blood. Mirjam didn't move. Shock. Her weapon hung loosely by her side.

He hunkered down beside Frankie.

'Stay with me, kiddo,' he said, seeing her try to smile as the blood bubbled around her lips. 'Fuck fuck fuck.' She was losing too much blood.

He looked up at Mirjam. 'For God's sake snap out of it. Call a fucking ambulance.'

He eased Frankie to the floor, then pulled the duvet off the bed.

He sat on the floor cradling her head in his lap.

Blood oozed into his trousers.

He brushed the hair away from Frankie's eyes.

The blood came from the side of her head. Not a bullet. Please God not a bullet, he thought, pressing a clean part of the white duvet up against the only wound he could see to stem the bleeding. Anything but that. 'Come on, Frankie, work with me here. You're a stubborn cow, be stubborn.'

He saw the flicker of a smile.

Mirjam spoke rapidly into her radio. He had no idea what she was saying, but he hoped to Christ the word ambulance was in there somewhere.

'Officer down,' he yelled, trying to make sure the dispatcher grasped the urgency.

He didn't even see Mirjam. She wasn't there. It didn't matter that they'd slept together a couple of days ago. She had no space in his head.

'Come on, Frankie, if you die on me I'll bloody kill you.'

'I'll . . . haunt . . . you . . .' she managed.

'Like fuck you will.'

'I'll go down to meet the paramedics,' Mirjam said. 'What a fucking mess.'

She left him with Kask's body. He heard her make another call as she went down the stairs. He couldn't understand a word. Where was their back-up? This was an utter shit-show. He hoped she was tearing whoever was supposed to be covering them a new arsehole. No fucking SWAT. It was ridiculous.

But she'd saved Frankie's life.

He heard the sound of sirens racing death to reach them.

'Soon,' he promised the woman in his arms.

He heard something then, only a couple of words, before Mirjam Rebane left the building.

'It's taken care of.'

Frankie moved in his arms. He couldn't understand what she was trying to say. He soothed her. 'They're nearly here, I promise. You don't need to do anything more complicated than breathing, OK? Just focus all your strength on that. Please. I really don't want to tell Akardi I've lost another partner. That would just be fucking careless.'

At least she was smiling.

At least he thought she was smiling.

IN THE DARKNESS . . .

S he was sure she heard a gunshot. There was no sound in the world like it. So brutal. So angry. It raged. Another. Two shots. What was happening?

Then she heard footsteps heavy on the stairs, running.

She had imagined the layout of the building a million times, each time it was different. She tried to imagine it again.

An outsider threatened the family.

They were under attack.

The Blind had forced their way into the sanctuary. They were going to undo everything John had achieved.

'Help me,' she cried out, her voice too weak to reach clear of the hole. She felt rather than heard the rats moving about in the darkness with her. She pressed up against the cold clay wall of the hole.

There was only silence.

Darkness.

Were they dead? The man who tossed food down to her? Was she alone now? What if no one came for her? If they forgot about her completely?

She was lost.

Irma wrapped her arms around her knees, drawing them up to her chest.

She wanted this to be over.

But more than anything she desperately didn't want to fail John in this final test.

She would not fail him.

She would prove that she was special.

She had to ignore the voices in her head and concentrate.

She felt movement around her. The rats brushing up against her skin. She didn't move.

A different kind of movement followed down into the darkness. Doors opening and closing. Sirens. It was hard to concentrate. It was so loud.

Irma rocked up against the clay wall, needing it to anchor her before she spiralled.

People came and went.

She tried to call out, but there was nothing.

Her throat was too dry to make a sound, her voice stolen by the hole.

All she could do was sit in the darkness and pray that The Shepherd still loved her.

He wouldn't forget her.

She was his special one.

That was what he'd promised her.

Always that.

She was special.

His special one.

More noise. Disassociated sounds. Voices. And then she heard the door that led down into the hole open and saw a crack of light high above.

Irma shrank back, deeper into the darkness, not wanting to be seen, trapped, wanting to be saved. To get out of the hole. But she couldn't fail. Not now. Not when she was so close.

She held her breath as the iron lid that closed the pit over her head was pulled all the way back and light streamed down into her prison.

'Irma?' the voice said. 'It's all over. I promise. You're safe. It's over.'

A man's voice, soft, gentle. English, not like The Shepherd. She didn't recognize it.

Who was Irma?

Was that her?

'Over.'

The word came out as no more than a dry whisper, barely escaping her lips, but for Irma Lutz it was all the sound in the world. It was a chorus.

She had no idea who the man was, but she believed him. The Shepherd had sent him. She had passed the test. She had done it. It was over.

A rope came down.

She tried to put the harness on, but her arms refused to obey even the simplest instructions. All she wanted to do was to lie down again and let the rats crawl over her.

'I've got you,' he promised, pulling the rope back up.

She thought that it was another test, to offer hope and snatch it away at the last moment, one last lie to try and break her.

She would not fail The Shepherd.

She didn't have to wait long for the rope to come down again. There was a loop fashioned at the end, no harness this time. 'All you have to do is put your foot in it, sweetheart, I've got you. You tell me when you are ready and I'll pull you up.'

She had to try twice before the word came out, 'Ready.'

She felt the rope grow taut in her hands, and then she began to ascend, rising slowly hand over hand, into the light.

It felt like she was being raised into heaven.

Her saviour waited there for her.

He reached for her, lifting her up and taking her into his arms. 'It's over,' he promised again, this stranger.

SIXTY-EIGHT

t was the first time he'd set foot in a church since Stefan Karius had tried to crucify him. He wasn't exactly eager to cross the threshold. He looked to his partner for reassurance.

Mirjam Rebane nodded, ready. She had the warrant. He didn't have power of arrest in Estonia. 'Ready?'

'As I'll ever be,' he said, and pushed open the door.

The Shepherd was at the front, in his pulpit, his voice amplified by huge speakers. His sermon faltered as he saw the newcomers, but he gathered his wits. 'That darkness is there in all of our souls, my brothers and sisters, but we cannot give in to it when it tries to seduce us away from reason. Together we are stronger than the devil, together we are one family,' and as he uttered those two words the entire congregation, three-hundredfold, echoed, 'We are One World,' their joyous voices drowning out The Shepherd.

He smiled beneficently down on his flock.

Peter Ash walked slowly down the aisle, side by side with Mirjam Rebane though marriage was the furthest thing from any of their minds. Heads turned as they walked by.

'John Shepherd,' Peter called out, 'you are under arrest for conspiracy to murder Annja Rosen, Danika Putin, and William Bray, the unlawful imprisonment of Irma Lutz, and a shitload of other crimes we're in the process of working out. You just won the criminal conspiracy lottery, holy man. Say goodbye to your sheep now, there's a good boy.'

'The Blind seek to bring us down, my children. They come with their lies.'

'And handcuffs,' Peter said. 'Don't forget those.'

'Do not rage against them. Pity them, for they know not what they do.'

'I don't know about Mirjam, but I know exactly what I'm doing, John. I'm making the world a better place without you.'

Mirjam climbed the few short steps to the pulpit.

John didn't fight her, he held out his hands, palms up, like a martyr.

SIXTY-NINE

'The docs tell me you'll live,' Peter Ash said. 'At least that's less paperwork for me.'

He'd thought about bringing flowers, but he didn't think Frankie was that kind of woman. Then he'd thought about grapes, and figured worst case, he liked grapes so it would give him something to eat while he sat with her. He'd eaten half of them before he walked into the room.

'So they say. With luck they might even let me out.'

'I brought you some clothes,' he said, holding up the bag with Elsa's old jogging bottoms and sweatshirt.

'Thanks, I think,' she said. 'You found Irma?'

He nodded. 'She's here. She's a mess. But she's alive and she's getting the care she needs. I don't know how long she'd been down in that hole, or how often she'd been fed. She's skin and bone. They'll transfer her to a psychiatric unit when she's fit enough. I'm not going to lie, there's no easy happy ending here. They've fucked with her pretty badly. She doesn't even know her own name. She keeps thinking this is all a test.'

'But she's in the right place. That's all that matters. They haven't got her any more. Now we just have to hope they can fix the damage that has been done.'

'How much do you know about her?'

'Not much.'

'There was stuff in that house. It's going to take Laura some serious work to sort through it all and figure out what was going on but this wasn't what I expected. She's got skills, proper computer-genius-level skills.'

'Which is why she was here.'

'And why One World targeted her,' Peter said. 'I talked to one of her professors about her. She's a proper *Rain Man* level computer genius, you know the whole "sees code in her head" bit.'

'OK, so they wanted her for her talent, that's pretty much what Shepherd said to me every time we talked, they wanted to use my unique talent.'

Peter nodded. 'They were using her to run some kind of computer fraud. It was generating a lot of money for them. A lot. We got a confession from your running buddy, Stefan Koyata. He's rolling over on Shepherd in return for immunity. You ask me, I think he's got a crush on you.'

'Shut up,' Frankie said.

'He's given us the driver—'

'Tomas,' Frankie said.

'Yep, he's put him behind the wheel of the car that killed the writer, Bray.'

'Jesus.'

'That's not even scratching the surface, this boy wants to sing. We're talking blackmail, cyber-terrorism, sex-trafficking, drugs. The Shepherd has his fingers in every pie you can imagine. He's even offered up a dark-web site where the guy is trading children. He's one sick fuck.'

'Will it stick?'

'That's down to the advocates. We do the legwork, they do the locking up. But we've got him. Mirjam and I just brought him in. She's taking him to lock-up to be processed now. He's not going to be tending to his flock for a very long time.'

'You saw the photographs on the stairs? You need to talk to every single one of them. Get their statements. That's his trophy cabinet.'

'We're on it.'

'We?'

'Mirjam, the woman who saved your life.'

'She killed Kask.'

'She saved your life.'

Frankie shook her head. 'No. She *murdered* him. He was unarmed. She walked into the room, stood over him as he begged, and executed him. Two shots. Chest and head. She wasn't leaving it to chance.'

Before he could argue, explain that he knew her, if not how well he knew her, the phone in his pocket vibrated.

It was Laura.

'Hey, Law, I'm with Frankie now. You want to say hi to our wounded warrior?'

He put her on speaker.

'We've got a problem, Pete.'

He didn't say a word.

'It's Shepherd. He's gone.'

'What do you mean gone?'

'He didn't make it to the lock-up. He's in the wind.'

'He can't just disappear. What about Mirjam? I left him in cuffs in the back of her squad car.'

'We found the car abandoned at the docks. Her passport hasn't been used to clear customs, but she's gone. The pair of them are nowhere to be found. A One World private jet left Lennart-Meri Tallinn Airport fifteen minutes ago. No registered passengers on the manifest. They're on that plane, I know they are.'

It's taken care of, that was what she had said.

Shepherd had given her a kill order and she'd carried it out. She was one of them. One World.

'She's a Protector,' Frankie said, from the bed. 'One of the cult's footsoldiers.'

'Fuck fuck fuck. OK, he's in the air. Where does he run?' Peter asked. 'Hell, maybe he's not even on that plane. The car's dumped at the docks. It's ten minutes from the ferry terminal to the airport terminal by taxi. Either could be a decoy.'

'The compound?' Frankie said. 'He ran there last time.'

Peter shook his head.

'It's crawling with state police. There isn't an inch of that forest that isn't cordoned off. No. He's run. He's left the country, it's the only choice he's got. So, he's either on that plane, he's on a boat, or he's driven out of here. No one's checking his passport on the border if he's driving. He's got a limo, right? Find that fucking limo, Law. Shit. Shit. Shit. OK. Thinking. Where can he run to?'

'He's got a refuge in every country One World preach,' Laura said.

'Not helpful.'

'Half a dozen don't have extradition treaties with the EU. Twice that are out of our jurisdiction,' Frankie said.

'Even less helpful.'

'If Rebane got him out of the country, we're not finding him,' Laura said.

'She's with him,' Frankie said. 'She's his real right hand.'

'Sometimes I wonder if you even know me, Law,' Peter said, going over to stand at the window. He gazed out over Tallinn, at the dome of the cathedral and all of the landmarks in between.

'What do you mean?'

'I mean we're just beginning. We play hunt the holy man and bring his entire church crashing down around him, wherever the fuck he's hiding. Like he's so fond of saying, it's all one world, and it isn't big enough for him escape me. We've got Irma out. We've found a treasure trove of stuff at his safe house. We've broken that compound. We've got links to every damned scheme he's running, and a gallery of people who owe him enough to risk everything to save him. We are going to find him. He can run all he likes. He can't keep on running. Eventually he has to surface somewhere. There isn't a place on this planet he can run to where we can't get to him in the end.'

'There's something else I need to tell you,' Laura said eventually.

'What?'

'You're not going to like it.'

'Tell me anyway.'

'It's about Marseilles,' which meant it was about Mitch.

'Spit it out, Law. I'm in a bad fucking mood already, so you may as well get it over with.'

'Division got a hit on the shooter.'

He didn't say anything, waiting for the other shoe to drop.

'His name is Jefferson Archer.'

'Is that supposed to mean something to me?'

'I pulled up his record, but there's nothing there. I knew the name though. I couldn't work out where from until I saw Bray's book, *Fork-Tongued Saviour*. He's in there. Bray claims Jefferson Archer is John Shepherd's bag man.'

'Say that again.'

'He's one of them. One world. What did Frankie just call them?'

'A Protector,' Frankie said. 'A hit man.'

'What the fuck was Mitch mixed up in?'

'I don't know, Pete, it feels like we're standing on the edge of a deep dark hole staring down, and I don't think we're going to like what's waiting at the bottom.'